Praise for THE LIBRARIANIST

"This engrossing fictional portrait of a retired librarian volunteering at an old folks' home unspools its main character's life—betrayals, loss, triumphs—with humor and tenderness."
—*Vanity Fair*

"Weaving accounts of wartime bravery, lost romance, and the unconventional joys of the everyday, deWitt celebrates the extraordinary moments nestled within the ordinary with wit and empathy."
—*Monocle*

"Bright and entertaining from beginning to end."
—*Minneapolis Star Tribune*

"Bob Comet, a retired librarian . . . brings to mind John Williams's *Stoner* and Thoreau's chestnut about 'lives of quiet desperation,' but it is telling that deWitt chooses to capture him at times when his life takes a turn. A quietly effective and moving character study."
—*Kirkus Reviews* (starred review)

"A poignant character study. . . . DeWitt's writing and endearing characters create a memorable world."
—*Los Angeles Times*

"Warmhearted. *The Librarianist* shares the attributes of its hero: likable, unshowy . . . reliably soothing."
—*Wall Street Journal*

"DeWitt's bemused sense of compassion for his characters recalls Anne Tyler, with whom he shares a soft spot for misfits, along with a firm conviction that even supposedly ordinary people lead extraordinary lives." —*Christian Science Monitor*

"Patrick deWitt is a twenty-first-century Mark Twain. . . . The warmth that deWitt exhibits here gives this one an emotional staying power. . . . Is it possible to change the contours of your personality late in life, with, as the woman with the prophetic space heater puts it, 'the knowledge of a long dusk coming on'? The final scene in *The Librarianist* features an answer as modest as it is revolutionary, but deWitt has spent the preceding pages making the oxymoron of a modest revolution utterly believable. The answer is: maybe a little bit. Maybe enough." —Laura Miller, *Slate*

"DeWitt imbues the people he meets with color and quirks, leaving a trail of sparks. . . . This one gradually takes hold until it won't let go." —*Publishers Weekly*

"I found the whole reading experience utterly charming. . . . The dialogue is fresh, and characters come alive immediately on the page, and there's simply an energy to deWitt's books that makes them pleasurable to spend time with, and that's all on display in *The Librarianist*." —*Chicago Tribune*

"Readers come to deWitt for his brand of slightly off-kilter storytelling blessed with exuberant characterizations, gleeful dialogue, and a proprietary blend of darkness and charm, all strung up in lights here. Gripping, random, and totally alive? Check, check, and check." —*Booklist*

THE
LIBRARIANIST

THE
LIBRARIANIST

A Novel

PATRICK deWITT

An Imprint of HarperCollins*Publishers*

THE LIBRARIANIST. Copyright © 2023 by Patrick deWitt. All rights reserved. Printed in the United States of America. No part of this book may be used or reproduced in any manner whatsoever without written permission except in the case of brief quotations embodied in critical articles and reviews. For information, address HarperCollins Publishers, 195 Broadway, New York, NY 10007.

HarperCollins books may be purchased for educational, business, or sales promotional use. For information, please email the Special Markets Department at SPsales@harpercollins.com.

Ecco® and HarperCollins® are trademarks of HarperCollins Publishers.

A hardcover edition of this book was published in 2023 by Ecco, an imprint of HarperCollins Publishers.

FIRST ECCO PAPERBACK EDITION PUBLISHED 2024

Designed by Alison Bloomer

Library of Congress Cataloging-in-Publication Data has been applied for.

ISBN 978-0-06-308513-8 (pbk.)

24 25 26 27 28 LBC 5 4 3 2 1

Dedicated to the memory of
DAVID BERMAN

1

2005–2006

THE MORNING OF THE DAY BOB COMET FIRST CAME TO THE GAMBELL-Reed Senior Center, he awoke in his mint-colored house in Portland, Oregon, in a state of disappointment at the fact of a dream interrupted. He had again been dreaming of the Hotel Elba, a long-gone coastal location he'd visited at eleven years of age in the middle 1940s. Bob was not known for his recall, and it was an ongoing curiosity to him that he could maintain so vivid a sense of place after so many years had passed. More surprising still was the emotion that accompanied the visuals; this dream always flooded his brain with the chemical announcing the onset of profound romantic love, though he'd not known that experience during his time at the hotel. He lay in his bed now, lingering over the feeling of love as it ebbed away from him.

Bob sat up and held his head at a tilt and looked at nothing. He was a retired librarian, seventy-one years of age, and not unhappy. His health was sound and he spent his days reading, cooking, eating, tidying, and walking. The walks were often miles long, and he set out with no destination in mind, choosing his routes improvisationally and according to any potentially promising sound or visual taking place down any potentially promising street. Once he'd witnessed an apartment fire downtown; the hook-and-ladder brigade had saved a baby from an uppermost window and the crowd on the sidewalk had cheered and cried and this was highly exciting for Bob. Another time, in the southeast quadrant, he'd watched a deranged man determinedly ripping out the flower beds in front of a veterinarian's clinic while dogs looked on from the windows, craning their necks and barking their sense of offense. Most days there was not so much to report or look upon, but it was always good to be in motion, and good to be out among the population, even if he only rarely interacted with any one person. He had no friends, per se; his phone did not ring, and he had no family, and if there was a knock on the door it was a solicitor; but this absence didn't bother him, and he felt no craving for company. Bob had long given up on the notion of knowing anyone, or of being known. He communicated with the world partly by walking through it, but mainly by reading about it. Bob had read novels exclusively and dedicatedly from childhood and through to the present.

On this day, Bob was fed and out the door before nine o'clock in the morning. He had dressed according to the weatherman's prediction but the weatherman was off, and so Bob had gone into the world unprepared for the cold and wet. He enjoyed being outdoors in poor weather but only if he was properly outfitted; in particular he disliked having cold hands, which he did have now, and so he entered a 7-Eleven, pouring himself a cup of coffee and lingering by the newspaper rack, warming himself while gleaning what news he could by the headlines. The cashier was a boy of twenty, friendly but distracted by a woman standing at the rear of the store facing a bank of glass doors which gave way to the refrigerated beverages. She wore a matching pink sweat suit, bright white sneakers, a mesh-back baseball hat, and a pair of dark sunglasses, and she was standing still as statuary. It was the outfit of a toddler or a teenager, but the woman had a shock of frizzy white hair coming out from under the cap, and must have been in her sixties or seventies. The cashier appeared concerned, and Bob asked in a whisper, "Everything all right?"

"I don't think it is," the cashier whispered back. "I mean, she doesn't seem to be on anything, and her clothes are clean. But she's been watching the energy drinks for forty-five minutes, and I'm worried she's going to freak out."

"Have you tried talking to her?"

"I asked if I could help her find something. No response."

"Want me to go check in with her?"

"What if she freaks out?"

"What do you mean by 'freaks out'?"

"It's things I can't even talk about in polite conversation. And the cops won't come unless there's a weapon involved. You know how many ways there are to freak out without a weapon? Literally one million ways."

All the time they were speaking they were watching the woman. Bob said, "I'm going to go check in with her."

"Okay, but if she starts freaking out, can you try to get her through the doors?" The cashier made a corralling gesture, arms out. "Once she's in the parking lot she's out of my domain."

Bob moved toward the figure in pink, humming benignly, both to announce his arrival and identify himself as a friend. "Oh, hello," he said, as if he just noticed her standing there. She didn't respond in any measurable way, her features hidden behind the cap and hair and sunglasses. "Is everything all right today, ma'am? Anything I can help you with?" Still no reaction, and Bob looked to the cashier, who touched his own shoulder in a gesture communicating his belief that Bob should give the woman a shake. Bob didn't shake her but rested his hand on her shoulder; the instant he made contact she became activated, like a robot coming to life, turning away from Bob and walking deliberately down the aisle and right out of the store. Bob watched her go. "What should I do now?" he asked the cashier.

"I don't know!" the cashier said. He was happy the woman was gone but also happy that something interesting had happened.

Bob said, "I'm going to follow her," and he left the store.

He walked behind the woman at a distance of ten paces, sipping his coffee, marking her meager progress. It took her five full minutes to travel one city block, at which point she became frozen again, this time at a bus stop, standing outside the glass shelter and looking in at the empty bench. It began to rain and the woman's sweat suit grew damp. When she started to shiver, Bob approached and draped his coat over her shoulders. But soon *he* was shivering and damp; when a police car pulled up at a red light, Bob waved to the policeman to get his attention. The policeman waved back, then drove away.

Bob moved to stand under the shelter of the bus stop, facing the woman. His coffee had gone cold in his hand and it occurred to him he hadn't paid for it. He'd decided his walk had been ruined and that he would cut his losses, forfeit the coat, and taxi home, when he noticed a laminated card hanging from a string around the woman's neck. He stepped around the shelter and, tilting her body slightly, made to inspect the card. There was a photograph of the woman, in sunglasses and cap, and beneath the photo, a text: *My name is CHIP, and I live at the GAMBELL-REED SENIOR CENTER*. Beneath the text there was an address, and beneath the address was the image of an imposing Craftsman home with medieval touches—a tower and weathervane, a wraparound porch. Bob recognized the house from his walks, and he said, "I know this place. Is this where you live? Is your name Chip?" A determination rose up in him, and he decided he would deliver Chip to the address.

He took her gently by the arm, pointing her in the direction of the center. Every ten or fifteen steps she paused and groaned, but her resistance was minor, and they made their plodding advancement against the weather. She wanted to go into every storefront they passed, and so Bob had to repeatedly correct her path; each time he did this she became tense and made further groaning noises. "Sorry, Chip," he told her. "I wish we could stop and browse but they'll be worrying about you, and we don't want them to worry, do we? No, let's keep on, we're almost there."

Soon the Gambell-Reed Senior Center was in sight. Bob had walked past the property any number of times, often asking himself what it was, exactly. It stood perched on a hill, looming over its neighbors on both sides and looking very much like the clichéd image of a haunted house. There was no signage announcing its function, but hospital shuttle buses and ambulances were commonly parked at the curb, and a wheelchair access path zigzagged up from the sidewalk and to the entrance. Bob led Chip up this path, studying the center as they made their ascent. It looked, he realized, quite a lot like the Hotel Elba; and while Bob took no stock in the unearthly, he couldn't help but wonder at the similarity between the properties, in connection with his dream of the same morning.

The front door was an imposing barrier of green-painted metals and bulletproof glass, and it was locked. Bob buzzed a doorbell-buzzer and the door buzzed back, unlocked itself with a clack, and swung slowly open. Chip walked in under her own steam, disappearing around a corner while Bob stood by, waiting for someone to come meet him at the threshold; but there was no one, and after a long, ponderous pause, the door began evenly closing. He was about to turn and go when a bellowing male voice from behind hailed him: "Hold that door!" The voice beheld so pure a conviction that Bob reacted without thinking, blocking the sweep with his right foot, which consequently was smashed by such a force of violence that his pain was only barely concealable. The door bounced back and again was swinging open. Meanwhile, the voice's owner, an abnormally large, that is, tall, broad, wide man in an abnormally large electronic wheelchair, was bearing down on Bob at a high rate of speed and with a look of steely certitude in his bloodshot eyes. As he whizzed past Bob and into the center he pinched the brim of an abnormally large beret in a salute of thanks. The same instant this man entered, there came a call from unseen voices, a calamitous, jeering greeting, a joyful commencement of an earlier communication, as though some new evidence gathered overnight had altered a prior dispute. "Pup pup pup," the man said, wagging his mitt of a hand to downplay the noise. He drove his chair deeper into the center proper.

A forty-something-year-old woman in pale green scrubs and a beige cardigan was walking up to meet Bob. She asked if there was anything she could help him with and Bob explained about his bringing Chip back. The woman nodded that she understood, but she wasn't noticeably impressed that Chip had been at large, or that she had been safely reinstalled. She introduced herself as Maria and Bob said he was Bob. When the door began closing, Maria stepped back, hand held aloft in a gesture of neutral farewell; but here Bob both surprised himself and Maria by hop-limping into the center, and afterward stood lightly panting, while Maria considered whether to call for security.

BOB LIKED MARIA INSTANTLY. SHE SEEMED SLY TO THE WORLD'S foolishness, something like a cat's attitude of critical doubtfulness, but she also beheld a cat's disposition of: surprise me. Bob could tell that she was tired, physically and emotionally; her hair still was wet from her shower, he noticed. She asked Bob what was wrong with his foot and he told her, "Your front door smashed it," and she said, "I see." She asked if he was well enough for a tour of the center and he said he was, and she led him to the airy space she called the Great Room. In the middle of the room was a long table around which sat a dozen or more senior men and women, some chatting volubly, others sitting with their heads bowed to the gentle labors of unskilled craft projects, others sleeping, chin to chest. The man in the wheelchair was nowhere in sight, but Chip was sitting at the head of the table, apart from the others, breathing through her mouth, and still with Bob's coat hanging off her shoulders. Bob pointed this out to Maria, who approached Chip from behind to retrieve the garment. This took some good bit of pulling but finally Maria managed to yank the coat free, and she crossed over to return it to Bob. He thanked her but didn't put the coat on right away, wanting Chip's body warmth to dissipate before he wore it again.

He and Maria resumed their promenade. "So, that's Chip. She's a free bird. Runs away as often as she can. Luckily, she never runs very far, or very quickly. Half the time we don't know she's gone, then there's someone at the door, like you, bringing her back home."

Bob asked how the center could house so many individuals as were present; Maria answered there were only five residents, and that the rest were shuttled to the center each morning, then shuttled back to their homes after suppertime. Most of them lived with their adult children, or relatives. Maria explained that these were people without insurance or savings, people who couldn't afford full-time care.

"Chip's one of the residents?"

"For now she is. To be honest, she needs more from us than we can give her. We're lucky to have this house at our disposal but it's poorly suited to our needs when it comes to the complicated cases. We're understaffed and underfunded and all the rest of it. Chip needs more focused care in a secured environment. The ideal from our point of view and according to what we can offer is someone more like Brighty, here. How are you, Brighty?"

Bob found himself shaking hands, or found his hand being shaken by the woman, Brighty. She stared hard at Bob but spoke to Maria. "Who's this? A new face? New blood? What's his story?"

Maria said, "This is Bob, Brighty. He was good enough to bring Chip back to us, so I thought I'd show him around."

"Okay, that all makes sense, but where does he live?"

"I don't know. Where do you live, Bob?"

"I live in a house in northeast."

"Sounds plush," Brighty told Maria.

"It's all right," said Bob.

"He's modest. I'm sure it's very plush and classy. His wife must be pleased with her—fortunate situation."

Bob said, "I have no wife."

Now Brighty looked at Bob. "Why not?"

"I don't know. I just don't. I did have one, once."

"And one was enough?"

"It must have been."

"You're a widower?"

"Divorcé," said Bob.

"And when were you granted—your freedom?"

Bob did some quick addition. "Forty-five years ago."

Brighty made to whistle, but the whistle didn't catch and so was more a puffing noise.

Maria said, "Brighty has been married five times, Bob."

"What do you think about that?" Brighty asked Bob.

"I think that's a lot of times to be married," Bob answered.

"I like a big party, is what it is," said Brighty. "And I'll take a wedding over a funeral any day of any week, if it's all the same to you." She walked off to a bank of mismatched couches lining the long wall of the Great Room, sat down, leaned her head back, and shut her eyes. "Brighty," Maria told Bob. Bob noticed Chip was no longer in her chair but had taken up a standing position next to the front door, looking at it but not looking at it. He mentioned Chip's movements to Maria, who sighed and led him to the far corner of the Great Room where a scowling woman sitting at a fold-up card table was working on a thousand-piece puzzle. She had stringy, unclean gray hair, and she wore a pair of reading glasses on top of her regular glasses. "This is Jill," said Maria. "Jill's one of our nonresident visitors. Jill, will you say hello to our new friend Bob? I won't be a minute." She excused herself to fetch Chip away from the front door. Jill, meanwhile, was staring up at Bob, who told her, "Hi." She didn't respond. When Bob asked how she was doing she raised her hands up in the style of a doctor who has just scrubbed in ahead of surgery, each finger standing alone, with space between itself and its siblings. "I can't feel my thumbs," she said.

"Just now you can't?" asked Bob.

She shook her head. "I woke up in the middle of the night thinking there was someone in the room with me. 'Hello?' I said. 'Hello?' Then I realized, you know, about my thumbs."

"You couldn't feel them."

"I couldn't and still can't." She lowered her hands onto her lap. "What do you think it means?"

"I don't know," said Bob. "Who was the person in the room?"

"Oh, no one. Probably what that was was the presence of something new that's wrong with me?" She cocked her head, as if in recognition of her own queer phrasing. She told Bob, "Don't take this the wrong way, but you don't look like a doctor."

"I'm not a doctor."

Jill drew back in her chair. "Why are you asking me questions about my health if you're not a doctor?"

Bob wasn't sure what to say to this, so he decided to reroute the conversation in the direction of the puzzle: "What will it look like when you're done?" he asked, and she took the puzzle's box top and held it up beside her grave face. She asked Bob, "Do you know what this is?"

"It's a harvest scene."

She bobbed her head, as if to say he was partly right. In an explaining tone of voice, she said, "It's about the *fall feeling*."

"What's that?"

"Don't you know?"

"I'm not sure that I do."

"The *fall feeling*," said Jill, "is the knowledge of a long dusk coming on." She looked at him with an expression of significance. Her reading glasses had a sticker attached to the left lens that read: $3.99.

She resumed her puzzle work, rooting about for useful pieces, her numb thumbs held out at odd angles, her middle and pointer fingers stained yellow by nicotine use. Bob said goodbye and walked off in search of Maria, pausing before a bulletin board choked with notices and artworks and informational papers. One flyer among the many caught his eye: a call for volunteers at the center. Maria returned to find Bob writing down the phone number for the American Volunteer Association in his pocket spiral notepad.

"What are you doing?" she asked.

"I don't know. I guess I'm interested."

"Have you volunteered before?"

"No."

She pointed that Bob should follow her out of the center and onto the porch. Once the front door clacked shut behind them, she said, "If I could be frank with you, I would encourage you to think twice before volunteering. I say this for your sake as well as mine. Because the volunteer program has been nothing but a strain on the center. Actually, I've asked the AVA to take us off their rotation because every person they've sent us has been far more problematic than helpful. Each one of them arrives here simply beaming from their own good deed, but none of them lasts out the month because the reality of the situation here is thornier than they can comprehend. You will never, for example, be thanked; but you *will* be criticized, scrutinized, and verbally abused. The men and women here are sensitive to the state of their lives; a single hint of charity and they lash out, and I can't really say that I blame them."

"Well," said Bob.

"I don't mean it as a critique against you personally," Maria told him. "You seem like a very nice man." She paused, and made the face of someone reapproaching an issue from a fresh angle. "May I assume you're retired?"

"Yes."

"What position did you hold?"

"I was a librarian."

"For how long were you a librarian?"

"From the ages of twenty-two to sixty-seven."

Maria said, "Sometimes retirees volunteer for us in hopes we'll take their malaise away."

"I don't suffer from malaise," Bob said. "And I don't care to be thanked." The cloud cover had thinned and the sky was lit in pastel pinks, purples, and orange. Bob was marking these colors when he had his idea. "I could read to them."

"Read to who?"

He pointed at the center.

"Read to them what?"

"Stories."

"What kind of stories?"

"Stories of entertainment."

Maria was nodding, then shaking her head. "Yes, but no," she said. "These aren't readers, for the most part, Bob."

"But to be read to is another thing," he told her. "Everyone likes to be told a story."

"Okay, but do they?" she asked.

They were stepping down the tall concrete stairwell set to the side of the zigzagging path. Maria restated her belief that the reading angle was a mistake; but Bob had won her over with his pluck, and she said she was willing to let him try it out. When they arrived at the sidewalk, she gave him her business card and said, "Just refer the AVA to my office number, and we'll get you placed here." Bob thanked her and shook her hand and walked off. Halfway up the block he turned back and saw that Maria was watching him. "What did you think of Jill?" she called out, and Bob made the half-and-half gesture. Now Maria smiled, and she turned and jogged up the steps, which surprised Bob; he wouldn't have thought of her as a jogger-up-the-steps.

BOB TELEPHONED THE AMERICAN VOLUNTEER ASSOCIATION THE NEXT morning and later in the week received a packet in the mail, color brochures featuring pictures of glad seniors, glad people in wheelchairs. The text was highly praiseful and petting of Bob's decision to lend a hand, but there was a hitch, which was that he had to be vetted before the AVA welcomed him officially into the fold. Saturday morning and he drove to a storefront on Broadway that specialized in such things as passport photos and notarizations and fingerprints, the last being what he was after. His prints were sent off to what he imagined was a subterranean robot cityscape, a bunker database where they kept the shit list under dense glass, to check his history for uncommon cruelties, irregular moralities. He didn't expect there to be an issue and there wasn't, but he did feel a doubt reminiscent of his experience of passing through the exit barriers at the pharmacy and wondering if the security alarm would sound even though he'd not stolen anything.

Bob had not been particularly good or bad in his life. Like many, like most, he rode the center line, not going out of his way to perform damage against the undeserving but never arcing toward helping the deserving, either. Why now, then? He himself didn't know for certain. The night before his first official visit to the center he dreamed he arrived and was greeted in the same garrulous, teasing manner as the man with the big beret had been. The scene of group acceptance was heady, but when Bob stepped into the center the next morning no one acknowledged his presence. "Hello," he said, but nobody so much as glanced at him, and he understood he was going to have to work his way toward visibility, to earn the right to be seen by these people, which he believed was fair, and correct.

Bob sought out Maria, who sat talking on the phone in her small, untidy office. She pointed Bob toward the rear of the Great Room and gave him a goodwill thumbs-up; soon he was standing at a podium before an audience of twenty souls. He briefly introduced himself and the chosen text; since this first appearance took place some days before Halloween, he'd decided to begin with a short story by Edgar Allan Poe, "The Black Cat." The reading was going well enough when on page three the cat had its eye cut out with a penknife by its owner, and a third of Bob's small audience left the room. On page four, the same unlucky cat was strung up by its neck and hung from the branch of a tree, and now the rest of the crowd stood to go. After the room emptied out a muttering janitor came in with a hand truck and began folding and stacking the chairs. Maria approached Bob with an I-told-you-so expression on her face. "I told you so," she said.

Bob walked home through the October weather. A stream of leaves funneled down the road and pulled him toward his mint-colored house, the location of his life, the place where he passed through time, passed through rooms. The house rested in the bend of a quiet cul-de-sac, and it was a comfort for him whenever he came upon it. It didn't reflect worldly success, but it was well made and comfortably furnished and well taken care of. It was a hundred-odd years old, and his mother had purchased it from the man who'd built it. This man had gone blind in his later years and affixed every interior wall with a length of thick and bristly nautical rope run through heavy brass eyelets positioned at waist level to guide him to the kitchen, to the bathroom, the bedroom, up the stairs and down, all the way to the workshop in the basement. After this person died and the property changed hands, Bob's mother did not remove the rope, less an aesthetic choice than obliviousness; and when she died and Bob inherited the house, he too left the rope in place. It was frayed here and there, and he sometimes banged his hip on the eyelets, but he enjoyed the detail for its history, enjoyed the sight of it, enjoyed the rope's prickliness as it ran through his hand.

He returned the Poe paperback to its place on the paperback shelf. He had been amassing books since preadolescence and there were filled shelves in half the rooms in the house, tidy towers of books in the halls. Connie, who had been Bob's wife, had sometimes asked him why he read quite so much as he did. She believed Bob was reading beyond the accepted level of personal pleasure and wondered if it wasn't symptomatic of a spiritual or emotional deformity. Bob thought her true question was, *Why do you read rather than live?*

As the day wore on, and Bob relived his experience at the center, he came to see it was not that he'd taken the task overseriously, but that he hadn't taken it seriously enough. He hadn't even preread the text. A cat is tortured and hung in the first pages of the story, and for some reason his appearance was unsuccessful! He telephoned Maria, explained why he'd failed, and told her he wanted to try again. Maria sighed a sigh that sounded like a no, but then she told him yes, all right, as you wish, and Bob spent the next six days preparing for his return. He put together a syllabus, a series of connected short stories and excerpts from longer works that he felt were of a piece thematically; he also wrote an introduction that illustrated his point of view. He wondered if he wasn't giving too much of his time to the project, but he couldn't stop himself, and didn't want to.

He slept poorly the night before his second reading and arrived at the center thirty minutes early, where the janitor again was muttering as he set up the chairs. Bob stood at the podium, readying himself, looking over his texts; Maria approached and asked if she might inspect Bob's books. He passed them over and she studied them one by one.

"Is Comet a Russian name?" she asked.

"No."

"But these books are all by Russians."

"That's true."

She passed the books back to Bob. "Do you read books by non-Russians?"

"Of course," he said. "I thought it could be fun for the group to try to identify the cultural through-lines and buried political opinion."

"Yes, that *could* be fun," said Maria. She obviously believed he would fail again, but wished him luck and went away. People began trickling in; there were not so many in the audience as before. Bob began with the prepared statement, which he had memorized.

"Why read at all? Why does anyone do it in the first place? Why do I? There is the element of escape, which is real enough— that's a real-enough comfort. But also we read as a way to come to grips with the randomness of our being alive. To read a book by an observant, sympathetic mind is to see the human landscape in all its odd detail, and the reader says to him or herself, *Yes, that's how it is, only I didn't know it to describe it.* There's a fraternity achieved, then: we are not alone. Sometimes an author's voice is familiar to us from the first page, first paragraph, even if the author lived in another country, in another century." Bob held up his stack of Russians. "How can you account for this familiarity? I do believe that, at our best, there is a link connecting us. A lifetime of reading has confirmed this for me. And this is the sentiment or phenomenon I want to share with you all today. I'm going to read some selections from the Russian canon. We'll be starting with Gogol—an obvious choice, but obvious for a reason. The language is a little formal, but the emotional information is, I think, relevant as ever."

Bob read "The Overcoat." He read in a clear, bright voice, and with a faith in the sideways beauty and harsh humor of the work. He knew that he could get through to these people if only they would give themselves to the words, but before he arrived at the text's halfway point they were shifting in their chairs. Soon they began to collect themselves, and then they did stand to go. By the time Bob completed the story the only people in the room were Chip and the muttering janitor, who had already begun the unhappy business of folding and stacking the chairs. As his muttering evolved to audible complaint, Bob learned the janitor blamed him for what he saw as needless busywork. Bob forbade himself from apologizing; he collected his books and made to leave, pausing to look down at Chip, who he now saw was soundly sleeping. Her sunglasses were crooked, and he corrected them. He walked past the long table in the Great Room, populated with people who had just left his reading; they were sitting side by side under softly buzzing fluorescent lighting, chatting, not chatting, doing crossword and Sudoku puzzles, cutting construction paper with safety scissors.

Bob went to say goodbye to Maria but saw through her door she was again talking on the phone. He stood around a while, then abruptly left, heading for home. He felt angry, which was not at all common for Bob; but he found himself wishing he'd never come to the center in the first place. It began to rain and he shielded the books under his coat and his face puckered against the damp. He was unlocking his front door when he heard the phone ringing. The kitchen was unlit; it was clean and orderly in the darkness of the day. He set his books on the countertop and lifted the phone off the wall and said hello.

It was Maria. "What happened?"

"Nothing happened. You were right, so I left."

"But you didn't tell me you were leaving."

"You were on the phone."

"You could have waited a minute."

"I waited several minutes."

Maria asked, "Are you pouting?"

"A little bit, yes."

"All right, well I can't say you haven't earned it, and after I get off the phone you can pout your little heart out, but can you put a plug in it for a minute? Because I have an idea. Will you listen to me?"

"I'm listening."

"I'd like to propose that you keep coming back here but without the books."

"Come back without the books."

"Leave those books at home, Bob."

"And what would I be doing there?"

"Just that: being here."

"Being there doing what?"

"Being here being around. Most of the people at the center are in a state of letting go. Some of them are unbothered by this, or unaware; but others are afraid, or confused, or angry. You're the steady, hand-on-the-tiller type, and I think your presence might be useful. I just got off the phone with a man who wants to perform sleight of hand tricks for us. Half the people at the center have some degree of dementia. The whole world's a sleight of hand trick already, and I'm not looking to give them any more examples of instability. To my way of thinking, that's where you come in." She pressed Bob to commit to visiting the following week, but he claimed he needed to think on it, affecting a coolness as he rang off. In truth, though, he was moved by Maria's assessment of his character. The functional purpose he'd known in his professional life had been put away when he retired, but now that cold piece of his person came back to life. In the morning he called Maria to agree to the schedule, and on the appointed day he arrived at the center, and without any books, as prescribed.

HE STILL WASN'T FULLY SURE WHAT HE WAS SUPPOSED TO *DO*, however.

"Just move around, circulate," Maria told him. "Ask someone what their name is, then tell them yours. It's like a cocktail party but no cocktails." She gave him a friendly little shove into the Great Room and he looped the long table, waving to anyone who made eye contact, hopeful for an invitation to linger. But nobody was inclined to speak with him, and he only continued walking. At the back of the room the woman named Jill was again at her card table, working on another puzzle. Bob was stepping up to greet her when he noticed the man in the electronic wheelchair and big beret sitting in the opposite corner beneath a wall-mounted television. This scenario struck Bob as the more promising of the two; he crossed over and pulled up a chair. The man in the big beret was watching a tennis match, men's singles; Bob took advantage of his distraction to make a thorough inspection of his features: a countenance of high, true ugliness. The ample flesh of his face was mottled with inky purple staining, so that he looked as if he'd been poisoned or gassed; he had a broad and pitted nose destroyed by burst vessels; he had no eyebrows or eyelashes, and his

eye whites were pink going red. These elements came together to form the picture of a man with unhealthy habits
and gargantuan appetites running unchecked across the
length of several decades. But there was also an animation
about him that spoke of a defiant life force; something like
joy, but mutant.

In a little while a nurse with a NANCY name tag and a gold
crucifix necklace approached pushing a cart. "Snack time,
boys," she said. The cart held four rows of rounded lumps, ten
lumps per row, half of them whiteish and furred, the other half
dark brown and resembling brains in modeled miniature. "And
who are these gentlemen?" asked the man in the big beret.

"Peanut butter balls and raisin balls."

"Which are what, exactly?"

"Peanut butter balls are peanut butter rolled into balls and
covered with coconut flakes. Raisin balls are just raisins mashed
together."

"And who fabricated them?"

"I did."

"Can I assume you wore gloves?"

Nurse Nancy looked at Bob fatiguedly, as if for a witness.
She brightened when she realized she'd not met him before. "Are
you new?" she asked.

"Yes, hello, I'm here by the AVA."

Now her face became cold, she wheeled the cart backward,
away from Bob. "I'm sorry, but the snacks are not for volunteers."

"Oh, that's all right," Bob told her. He hadn't wanted to
partake of the snacks even a little bit. But she remained wary,
as if Bob might try to lunge and snap up one of the balls when
she wasn't paying attention. The man in the big beret had put
on a pair of reading glasses and now was looking over the cart
with his head tilted back. "Is there a shortage of food in the

pantry?" he asked. "Because it seems to me these are some bullshit snacks."

"Actually, there is a shortage. And if you think it's fun to try to piece together a healthy nutritional program from what they've given me in there, then why don't you do me a favor and think again. Also, I believe I've already told you what I think about your language, have I not?"

"You did tell me, but it must have slipped my mind." He took his reading glasses off. "Brass tacks, Nance. How many can I have?"

"How many do you want?"

"How many *can I have*?"

"You *can have* two."

"Two of each?"

Nurse Nancy looked over her shoulder and back, nodded discreetly, and the man in the big beret lifted four balls from the cart, setting them one at a time in a line up his broad forearm. Nurse Nancy wheeled the cart away and the man ate his snacks, quickly and efficiently, looking into space as he chewed, swallowed, chewed, swallowed. After he was done, then he was at peace; he wiped the crumbs from his palm and held out a hand for Bob to shake. "Linus Webster." He asked Bob his name and Bob told him. "Bob Cosmic? What are you, in show business?" Bob was restating his name when Linus Webster became distracted by the television and began wagging his hand to call for quiet. A quartet of female players took to the tennis court and he was turning up the volume on the remote control, loud and louder, far louder than was necessary, or appropriate. The game commenced. The noises the players made filled up the space of the center, heartfelt declarations of physical exertion which were also, in any other context, obscene. Jill was twisted all the way around in her chair, glaring at Linus. "He's doing it again!" she called out. Bob caught

Jill's eye and waved; she stared blankly back. Over the sound
of the television, he asked, "How's your thumbs?" Jill recoiled.
"How's yours?" she demanded. Bob shook his head and explained, "Your thumbs, last time I was here, you couldn't feel
them, don't you remember?" A look of glad remembrance
crept onto her face. "Oh yeah," she said, then turned back to
the wall and resumed her puzzle work. Linus, meanwhile, had
propped his head against his wheelchair's headrest and was
basking in his audio experience when Nurse Nancy returned
to snatch up the remote from his hand and mute the television. She was breathing heavily, glaring into Linus's face. "You
should be ashamed of yourself," she said.

Linus asked, "If God didn't want us to appreciate the
grunts of others, why did He invent them in the first place?"

"Okay, hey, guess what? You just got your television privi-
leges revoked for twenty-four hours. Maybe you'd better just
go to your room, have a rest, and think about things."

"Seems to me I've thought about things enough for one
lifetime. But the resting part sounds all right." Linus winked
at Bob and drove his chair out of sight. There came the sound
of a muffled clanking from within the walls of the building;
a ramshackle elevator that delivered the residents to their
rooms on the second and third floors. Nurse Nancy said, "You
shouldn't encourage that one." She pulled up a chair and began channel surfing. She landed on a religious program and
Bob went away from the television, thinking to try his luck
once more at the long table.

He took a seat, asking those sitting nearby how they were
doing. The answers came in the shape of soft noises rather
than hard language, but the general mood, so far as Bob could
tell, was one of subdued disappointment: things were not going badly, it was true—but no one could claim they were going
very well, either. Chip sat just across the table from Bob, and

she was apparently looking directly at him, but as she was outfitted in her traditional ensemble it was impossible to say for sure. He waved; she did not wave back.

In the middle of the table sat a caddy filled with safety scissors, paste, and mismatched scraps of paper. Recalling his library days, when it sometimes fell to him to entertain groups of children, Bob took up a sheet of red construction paper, snapped it flat, and folded it onto itself, over and over, into an accordion shape. He was working with a combination of casualness and care that awakened the curiosity of certain of his neighbors; by the time he took up a pair of scissors and started cutting away at the folded paper, they all had been hooked into the mystery of what this newcomer was up to. When at last he unfolded the paper and revealed a bowed chain of hand-holding doll shapes, he saw that his ploy to engage was a success: he had surprised these men and women, he had distracted them, even impressed them. Some among the group wanted instruction, that they might make their own paper chain, and Bob gave a brief tutorial. It was not long before the group lost interest, but Bob was satisfied by this first contact.

Brighty was walking across the room with what Bob took for semiurgent purpose. "Hello, Brighty," he said; when she saw Bob, she altered her course and made for him directly. Seizing his hand, she said, "And to think I used to turn down a dance."

"Oh?" said Bob.

She formed her face into a coquettish expression and held a phantom cigarette to her lips: "'I'm going to sit this one out, thank you.'" She dropped the cigarette and shook her head at the memory of herself. "What in the world was I thinking?"

"You were following your own tastes and whims."

"Tastes and whims, he tells me!" She socked Bob in the arm and hurried off to wherever she'd been going.

Maria had told Bob he should jettison the schedule and come and go as he wished; deciding he'd had enough for the day, he bid the group at the long tables goodbye, and made for Maria's office. Her door was half-open and she was—on the phone. She made a question mark face at Bob and Bob gave her a thumbs-up. She made the OK sign and he saluted. He made walking fingers and she made the OK sign and he bowed and left the center. Stepping down the path, Bob found that he felt happy; and he understood Maria had been correct regarding her adjustments to his visits. The thought he carried with him as he made his way home was that he'd landed in a place where, in getting to know the individuals at the center, he would likely not suffer a boredom.

JILL WAS A SINCERELY NEGATIVE HUMAN BEING WITH UNWAVERINGLY bad luck and an attitude of ceaseless headlong indignation. Every day she was met with evidence of a hostile fate, and every day she endeavored to endure it, but also to combat it, but also to locate people to talk to about it. She found Bob willing to listen to a degree that was, she told him quietly, as if it were a secret she could somehow keep from him while at the same time telling him, uncommon. In this way he was precious to her, but she was never gentle with him, never thankful. Bob was like a horse run and run, and never fed or watered, only whipped. By the end of Bob's first month of bookless visits to the center he had established something like a friendship with Jill, or what passed for friendship in her world. No warmth, but a familiarity, with each party comfortable to act as him and herself. Bob couldn't say what Jill thought of him, but he found her an engaging presence, and he began to look forward to their communications whenever he moved in the direction of the Gambell-Reed Senior Center.

It was a moody day. Bob arrived at the center and found Jill at her usual station, where she sat working on another thousand-piece puzzle: a desert sky at dawn cluttered with hot-air balloons. She did not say hello to Bob, because she never said hello; but he knew she knew he was there, and he knew she would eventually speak, and that this speaking would be the naming of a complaint, and it was: she sighed a long sigh and said, "I'm so tired, Bob."

"Rough night?" he asked.

"Stupid question."

Bob took up a puzzle piece and began searching for its position in the picture. "I thought there were no stupid questions," he said.

"Where'd you hear that? On the internet?" Jill laughed ruefully to herself. Anti-internet sentiment was common from Jill. Bob had almost no experience with that overvast landscape, but somewhere along the line Jill decided he was a devotee and she was disdainful of his behaviors.

She began pumping her hands, explaining to Bob that she had at long last regained the feeling in her thumbs.

"That's good," he said.

"No, it isn't," she told him, explaining that the numbness had been replaced by a throbbing pain at the thumb joints. The reference to her thumb pain made her think of other pains, and she became expansive on the subject, soliloquizing about her history with pain: the pain of her youth, and the pain of midlife, and her present engagement with it. She spoke of pain as a perceived punishment, pain as a discipline, and lastly, about how much the pain hurt. "You understand that, right?" she said.

"Understand what?"

"It's only pain if it hurts."

This seemed self-evident. But then, as was not uncommon, Jill made Bob doubtful of his knowledge. He thought of his own aches, which in recent months had been mounting, and asked, "But what's the definition of *hurts*?"

"Do you involuntarily jolt in your seat? Are you sucking in short, sharp breaths with your eyes shut up tight? Does your vision go red in splotchy flashes, and you're worried you might fall over or faint?"

"No."

"What you're experiencing is not pain," Jill said, "it's discomfort."

"Not pain."

"Discomfort is not pain."

Jill said that her pain was near constant and impossible to get used to, to not be surprised by. She spoke of a wish to measure it, a volume or weight she might assign it, to share with doctors, with strangers, bus drivers. "People would be impressed if they knew the size of it," she said. "The way it is now, they simply can't understand. You can't." They worked on the puzzle in earnest, silent competition. With both of them going full tilt they completed the image in ninety minutes; as soon as it was done, Jill broke it up and returned the pieces to the box. Later, they were sitting under the television watching a show where four adult women screamed at each other in front of a live audience of adult women who also were screaming. There was an unknowable emotional connection between the women onstage and those in the audience; the more the women onstage screamed, then did the screaming of the audience also increase. At times the two groups were screaming with all of their vigor and volume: altogether too profound a passion for one o'clock in the afternoon, was Bob's thought. During a commercial break came a comparative silence, and Bob turned to Jill, who was staring at him. She asked Bob if she'd told him about her new heater, and he said she hadn't. "Tell me now," he said, and she did.

Her new heater, a fickle and mysterious device. It would sit in cold silence, in defiance of its own on-ness, then roar to life in the middle of the night while Jill slept, overheating and smoking—black, acrid smoke, which set off her fire alarms, which woke up her neighbors, who twice had called in the fire department, who permanently damaged Jill's carpets with their clanking, filthy boots. This was a classic Jill yarn in that the problems were multifold and collectively unwieldy. In listening to such stories as this it was easy to become lost in the mirror-maze of her misfortune; but Bob wished to be helpful, and so he always made to seek out the root of any one particular problem in hopes of uncovering a solution and improving the quality of her life in some small way. "You should unplug the heater before you go to bed," he told her.

"I did unplug it, Bob. That's what I'm saying. The heater turned itself on when it was unplugged."

Bob said, "I don't think that's true."

"Anyway it was turned off when I went to sleep," she said.

"That's not the same thing, though."

They watched a commercial for laundry detergent that featured an animate teddy bear crawling into a washing machine. Jill said, "He's going to get more than he bargained for." The screaming show resumed but Jill hit the mute button. "I'm not done talking about the heater," she said.

"Okay," said Bob.

Jill paused, as if steeling herself. "I think that the heater is not just a heater," she said finally.

"What else is it?"

"I think that the heater is what's called an oracle."

"What?" Bob said.

"The heater's behavior feels threatening to me."

"You believe the heater has a point of view?"

"I believe it's communicating bad news."

"But what is it telling you?"

"It's telling me my future."

"What's your future?"

"Well, think about it, Bob. Where is it hot?"

Bob looked into Jill's eyes for some sign of levity, but he found only the dark and swirling galaxy of herself. He understood she was confessing a difficult and fearsome truth, which on the one hand was flattering, that Bob had achieved the status of the confidant; but then, and on the other hand, the confession disturbed. Bob asked Jill if she'd kept the receipt. "It was on sale," she whispered. "No returns." At the conclusion of the screaming television show, Bob said goodbye to Jill and made for Maria's office. "Jill thinks her space heater is psychic and that it's telling her she's going to go to hell," he said. Maria looked over Bob's shoulder, then back at Bob. She said, "Okay." She waved goodbye but Bob lingered in the doorway.

"May I make an observation?" he asked.

"You may."

"I don't want to overstep."

"Spit it out, Bob."

"I think Jill would be better off as a resident."

Maria winced. "Full-time Jill?"

"I know. But maybe she'd be less Jill-ish if she felt safer."

Maria made a long exhalation. "Let me think about it," she said.

Bob took a new route home, a long and roundabout line. He was not killing time, for Bob was not a time killer; but he knew that when he entered his home, then the part of the day where something unexpected could happen would be over, and he wasn't ready for that quite yet. He was looking up and into the windows of the houses as he passed them by; he was wondering about the lives of the people inside. It was a late fall afternoon, damp in the air, damp on the pavement, but it wasn't raining. Now the lights were coming on in the windows of the houses, and smoke issuing from certain of the chimneys. Was this the long dusk that Jill had warned him about? Bob sometimes had the sense there was a well inside him, a long, bricked column of cold air with still water at the bottom.

AS A MAN OF VAST VANITY, LINUS WEBSTER SUFFERED UNDER HIS physical condition; all the more so because, as Bob discovered, there was a time in his life where his self-regard was of a piece with his outward appearance. Linus one day showed Bob a black-and-white snapshot of a bronzed and godlike young male in a skimpy swimsuit. The person in the picture was a musclebound giant, six and a half feet tall and without flaw to a point approaching the surreal. Bob didn't understand why this was happening.

"Who is that?" he asked.

"That's me."

Bob took the picture in his hand and looked at it closely. "No it's not."

Linus removed an aged identification card and gave this to Bob. There was that same impeccable skin, the ambitious bouffant of lustrous hair, and the name corresponded with his own, and now Bob understood that these two distinctly separate men were one—and he simply did not know what to say about it. Linus was staring moonily at the snapshot, and he shrugged his rounded shoulders and said, "I mated, Bob. I mated with the hostile determination of the political assassin, but also with a love for the deed, like a craftsman.

And I thought it would go on forever, that that was what life was made up of, fornicating in the buffet style with whichever beautiful partner I wanted."

"But, what happened?" Bob asked.

"I wish I had a more pronounced tale to tell you. I wish there had been chapters, eras, but no. One day, a Sunday let's say, I was Paul Newman, and when I snapped my fingers the world rushed to my side. Monday morning and I couldn't hail a cab. Elevator operators told me, take the stairs. The Fates banded together to shut me out. I still had my looks, for a time, but if one does not water the flower, the flower surely dies. When the attentions to my person dried up, then did my flesh wither, and quickly. Something had gone out inside my brain."

"Your brain felt different?"

"The rules had changed while I slept. My membership had been revoked."

"Maybe you were cursed."

"Don't laugh," he said, suddenly somber. "I think I *was* cursed. I mean, I think that's my story—my headline."

"Who cursed you?"

"Take your pick. I had no staying power in the romantic field, and this caused unrest, and not just with the women, but with their mothers, fathers, their uncles, their boyfriends, their husbands—it went on and on. Every date, and there was sure to be tenfold trouble. I sometimes asked myself if it was worth it."

"And was it?"

"Probably not. But I kept at it, all the same." He shivered. "Do you know the word *schadenfreude*?"

"Yes."

"You know what it means?"

"Yes."

"It means when people wish you poorly and are happy for your suffering."

"I know what it means, Linus. *Schaden* translates as 'harmful' or 'malicious,' *Freude* as 'joy.'"

"All right, egghead, take it easy. There's a lot of bullshitters around here, say they know things they don't. Now let me ask you this: Have you ever experienced it?"

Bob never had, at least never to any great degree. This struck him as regretful; was it not a signal he hadn't lived his life to its fuller potential? Linus agreed that, yes, it probably was. He said, "It's a powerful thing, like witnessing extreme weather. By that I mean that it's frightening but also beautiful, somehow. It follows a natural social order. I should think that schadenfreude existed before there was such a thing as German, or any language for that matter."

"Envy is one of the seven deadlies," Bob observed.

"But schadenfreude is not merely envy, Bob. It's envy plus—the revenge component. It was thrilling for me to see people come into their own as purveyors, as owners of hatred. Certain of my enemies actually said the words, put clear language to the idea that I'd been given too much, and that it wasn't fair in their eyes, and that it was their intention to level the balance."

"With violence?"

"Sometimes violence. More often it was a petty meanness or put-down of some kind. Also common was for my antagonist to tell the corrupted woman in question an ugly lie about my character. More common still: they would tell the woman an ugly *truth* about my character. It all led to the same thing, which was my return to the marketplace of carnal congress. Commerce was brisk, I had no time for remorse until after I was barred from the establishment altogether."

Linus began to regale Bob with specific details of his sexual adventures, the proclivities of certain partners, their attributes. Bob could never relate to the crude male perspective regarding the mysteries and machinations of sex. He was not an innocent, but felt that to speak of fornication as winnable sport was to demean and be demeaned at once, and there was always the question for him of, Why do this? When you could, as an alternative, not? Linus saw that his enthusiasm was not matched in Bob, and he trailed off. "I never went in for this sort of talk," Bob explained.

"A soldier speaks of combat."

"To other soldiers."

"Are you not a soldier, Bob? Have you never been to war?"

Bob said, "I've made love to one woman in my life."

Linus shut his eyes, and he became so still, as though he'd suddenly succumbed to slumber. After a while he stirred, opened his eyes to slits, and asked, softly, "What's the German word for pity, scorn, and awe happening all at the same time?"

BOB WAS SITTING IN THE KITCHEN NOOK WATCHING A NEIGHBOR ACROSS the cul-de-sac raking up the leaves in his yard. The neighbor was unshaven, his face red, a little swollen; he might have been sick from drink, but he looked happy, and Bob considered the man's experience: the scents of earth and moldering leaves, his pulse throbbing as he transferred the leaves into the garbage can. Bob thought, *It's Sunday.* This led to his wanting to perform a domestic maintenance of his own, which led to his spending the afternoon in his attic. The idea had been that he would tidy up up there, but when he arrived and was confronted with a lifetime's worth of documentation and mementos, then he lost his purpose and began simply investigating himself.

There was a wall of cardboard boxes running the length of the attic space, neatly stacked to the ceiling, as if bearing the weight of the roof. Bob had suffered a lifelong phobia of audit, which accounted for his dedication to record keeping, receipts dating back fifty years in some cases. These papers, viewed altogether, functioned somewhat like a diary—stories existed in the cumulative information. Bob's relationship with tobacco, for example: he purchased a pack of cigarettes every day for seven years up to the age of twenty-four, when he met Connie, who began at once to wage her prohibitive campaign, and so his purchases became inconsistent: a week off, then back on, a month off, back, and finally, after much needful turmoil, quitting the slender devils outright. This nicotine desire dimmed and eventually disappeared, but then, after Connie ran away with Bob's best friend, Ethan Augustine, Bob bought a carton of cigarettes, inhaling fully three packs in thirty-six hours, sitting in shell-shocked petulance lighting one cigarette off another, and was so sickened afterward that his flesh gave a greeny hue and his spit came blackish and he tossed the remaining packs into the trash and then none, not again, never another cigarette since.

Bob found a receipt for a matinee screening of *The Bridge on the River Kwai* on the day his mother died. The stub prompted the memory of his having the whistling theme song in his head as he came into her room at the hospital and found her bed empty and stripped to the mattress. He had summoned a nurse, who summoned two other nurses, who swarmed the room and hovered around Bob to worry over him. The theme song persisted in his mind, which paired with the calamity of the moment led to silent, shuddering laughter, this delivered into his fist, and which was mistaken by the nurses as grief. Bob coughed, hid his face. He was not laughing at his mother's death, but death in general, or life in general, or both in equal measure. Actually, her passing made him feel afraid, afraid of what his life would be like on his own in that house—the same house he was living in now. This was before he'd met Connie or Ethan but after he'd found his initial position at the library.

A wish came to Bob, then, which was to view the receipts from the date of his wedding, July 12, 1959. He imagined the day would be bursting with ephemera but there was only one receipt he could find. It was pencil written, a shivery, all-caps printing, and it read: *SUND x 3—VAN VAN CHOC.* Below was the figure $2.75. Further down, in an upright cursive: *Congradula-tions + good luck!!! (Your going to neeed it!!!)* Bob puzzled over the stub, trying and failing to understand what purchase it was describing, even. Soon, and a picture took shape in his mind: he and Connie and Ethan were sitting at an otherwise empty soda fountain, each of them drinking a milkshake. Ten minutes before this, across the street and within the cool marble chambers of City Hall, Connie and Bob had been married, with Ethan standing by as best man. After the ceremony's conclusion, the trio stood together on the sidewalk, shielding their eyes from the summer sun. Bob was thoroughly and completely satisfied. He was looking at his brand-new wife. "You're Connie Comet," he told her. She said, "It's true, that's who I am." When Ethan asked, "Now what?" Connie's arm came up level, and she pointed her bouquet at the soda fountain across the wide boulevard. They all three hooked arms and stepped off the curb; the street was clear but a car sped up to meet them, honking its horn as it approached. They achieved a group trot to push past the vehicle's path, but then Connie broke free from the chain and spun about, lobbing the bouquet into the open window of the car as it blew past. The driver was a white-knuckling raver, a gargoyle of the highway; he received the bouquet on his lap as if it were a ticking bomb, and it was a joyful thing to watch the sedan sliding all across the road, eventually bending into a long, screeching right-hander, up a one-way street and out of sight.

The soda jerk was an old man, paper hat perched on his speckled head, nodding as the trio set themselves down on the red leather stools. He understood what they "meant"; it was not uncommon for newlyweds to visit him postceremony, he said. Connie asked if he could tell who the groom was and the man sized up Bob and Ethan and said that obviously it was Ethan. The little group laughed at this, and Bob laughed the hardest, hoping it was not too obvious that he'd been stung by the soda jerk's mistake. The soda jerk was embarrassed; he patted Bob's arm and told him, "He just has a sheen about him, but of course you're the one, sure you are. You've got those haunted, I'll-never-be-alone-again, let's-share-everything-forever eyes." He asked the group what they wanted and they ordered—vanilla, vanilla, chocolate.

Forty-six years prior this scrap of paper was passed to a barely recognizable version of Bob, and now he was an old man in an attic, and his heart was muted as he returned the receipt to its file. He thought he should discontinue his excavation, but then the next box he came across was adorned with Connie's handwriting, and he felt he couldn't look away. SALLY ANNE it read, which was what Connie had called the Salvation Army. He opened the box and found a neatly folded stack of his own old clothing. At the top of the stack was a housecoat, a loud number in gold and red rayon, SILKLIKE RAYON as it was named on the tag; stitched to the side of these words was a small, green palm bent by a hurricane wind. He put the housecoat on, discovering that the sleeves had been folded up, two folds per sleeve, which meant that Connie had been the last to wear the garment. Connie had often worn his clothes around the house, and was always adjusting his sleeves in this way, so that it happened he would put on this shirt or that sweater, and there would be this evidence of her. Or there was her habit of using a single blond hair as a bookmark; he had seen her pluck a hair from her own head and set it in the pages of a book that she might or might not return to. And so it was that Bob would happen upon it later. When she and he were together these little touches were such sweet remembrances of her presence; but when it happened after she'd run off with Ethan Augustine, then it prompted a shock of bitterness in Bob, as if he'd been unkindly tricked. Now, after decades with no sign of her anywhere in the house, and Ethan long dead, the folded sleeves were simply bizarre. He stood looking at his own bony, homely wrists, recalling how he used to tease Connie about the sleeve-folding practice, saying she had the arms of a T. rex and that it was a wonder she could blow her own nose. Bob unrolled the robe's sleeves and resumed his survey of the box. It held several pairs of pants and button-up shirts and was a fair representation of Bob's wardrobe circa 1959–60. This box was confusing for Bob, because none of the clothes were damaged or threadbare, and it wasn't as though Connie and Bob had the money to be cavalier about their purchases—clothes were rarely bought, and only thrown out when approaching disintegration. But Connie did have strong opinions about certain articles of Bob's clothing; when she didn't appreciate or enjoy a shirt of his, she might tell him, "I don't like that shirt." If he wore it again, she would say, "Let's talk about the removal of this shirt from our lives." Recalling this, Bob formulated the theory that the box held her discards, the ones she most wished to get rid of. Why the box hadn't made it to the Salvation Army was a mystery he couldn't answer—likely it was that their marriage had collapsed before the chore could be completed.

At the bottom of the box Bob discovered a dress of Connie's. It was a summer dress with spaghetti straps, worn cotton the color of sun-bleached bone with flecks of color threaded throughout: red and blue and yellow and green. Bob remembered the dress but couldn't picture Connie wearing it—he knew it as an artifact rather than living souvenir. But he felt a pull to engage with it, and he took it out of the box and brought it down from the attic. He hung the dress from a hanger and set this on a nail on an otherwise naked wall in the kitchen, sitting in the nook to consider both the dress and the feeling the dress brought to him. He went back in his mind, and believed he could remember her wearing it in the sunshine, in the backyard. Perhaps this hadn't happened at all, but it felt a real enough, a likely memory, and he went into it, his thoughts both faraway and close by when he saw by the side of his eye that the dress was moving, undulating, on its hanger. It took Bob some few seconds to understand what was actually happening—he'd hung the dress above a heat register—but within that short span of time he experienced the hauntee's bottomless terror. After, he felt the flooding gladness of relief, and he shook his head at himself, but he didn't look away from the dancing, ballooning dress. It was Connie laughing at him the way she had laughed at him when they were in love, not unkindly, but with sympathy, with care for him and his deep and permanent Bobness. An odd-enough Sunday, he thought, running his fingers over the creases from the rolls on the sleeves of his robe. When the heater stopped pushing air the dress, as a film run in reverse, became still again.

AFTER CONNIE WENT AWAY WITH ETHAN AUGUSTINE THERE CAME into Bob's life the understanding of a perilous vastness all around him. To be hurt so graphically by the only two people he loved was such a perfect cruelty, and he couldn't comprehend it as a reality. He learned that if one's heart is truly broken he will find himself living in the densest and truest confusion. There was the initial period of weeks during which he took a leave of absence from the library and only rarely ventured out of the house; he was not eating or sleeping according to any traditional clock or calendar, and his hygiene was in arrears. He began to daydream of a means of murdering himself, weighing out the pros and cons of each style and generally fascinating at the comforting thought of long and untroubled sleep. Connie sent him a letter that he threw away without reading; Ethan sent him a letter that he burned. Six months after Connie left, Bob received the divorce papers in the mail. He sat down and read them and signed them and sent them back and took a five-hour walk without a coat on and caught a cold that furnished him with a physical wretchedness to match his mood. His fever broke on the second restless night and in the morning he peeled himself off the mattress and moved to the bathroom. Looking at his pale person in the mirror, he decided he would not die, and that it was time he resumed his fastidious habits and behaviors. "Fine, fine—fine," he said. Eleven months later he learned that Ethan had died. Bob was eating breakfast at a café up the road from his house, sitting on a barstool with a newspaper laid out on the counter and skimming through the Metro section when he happened on Ethan's name. Before he read the piece he knew something bad had happened and he stood away from his stool, as if wanting to achieve a remove from whatever information was coming toward him. He read the article standing, with his hands on his hips, looking down at the paper:

HIT-AND-RUN DRIVER KILLS PEDESTRIAN: *Ethan Augustine, 26, was struck by a motorist and killed in front of his house in Northwest Portland yesterday afternoon. Mr. Augustine had only recently moved into the neighborhood with his wife, Connie Augustine, 22 years of age. There were no witnesses to the accident. Any information should be relayed to Portland PD.*

Bob sat and folded the paper and stood. He left the café without the paper and walked home and sat on the couch in the living room and stared at the dust motes floating around and around. Later that same day he was passing through the kitchen and saw by the window that there was a man on his hands and knees in the driveway. Thinking him injured or suffering an attack, Bob hurried out to the man's side. "Are you all right?" he asked.

The man groaned as he stood, using the front bumper of Bob's Chevy to lift himself up. "Altogether I'd say that yes, I am all right, thank you. Are you Bob Comet?" He identified himself as a police detective, produced a notepad and pen, and asked that Bob should name his whereabouts at the time of Ethan Augustine's death. Bob answered that he'd been at work, and the detective took down the address and phone number of the library. He asked if he could borrow Bob's phone and Bob walked him to the kitchen and stood by, listening to the detective's conversation. After, the detective hung up the phone and told Bob, "All clear, buddy. I'll let myself out." Bob realized that when he'd first seen the detective in the driveway, the man had been checking the Chevy's front bumper for incriminating matter.

Bob waited through the remainder of that day and evening for the multitude of independent emotions inspired by the news of Ethan's death to form a whole, but it wasn't until the next morning that they coalesced and he understood he was experiencing a righteousness. He didn't believe in God or fate or karma or luck, even, but he couldn't help feeling Ethan's death was in reply to his, Ethan's, betrayal; and he couldn't pretend that he wished Ethan was still alive. Bob understood the grace of forgiveness, and he aspired to grace, but what could he do? An ugliness had been perpetrated against him and ended the way of living he thought was best; the perpetrators were punished, and he knew a foundational vindication. He became thrilled, then, energized, basking in Ethan's misfortune from the deepest places of himself. Nights, and he cleaned his home, cleaned every room and object in the house to a degree surpassing necessity and logic, as if attempting to return the property and its accoutrements to a state of newness: scrubbing the interior of his toilet's cistern, polishing the pipework beneath the kitchen sink with Brasso. At a certain point he explained to himself that he was preparing for Connie's return. Well, so what if he was? He allowed himself to daydream about it, playing the scene out in his mind. His favorite was that it would be raining, it would be night, a knock on the door, and there she would stand, drenched. "Oh, Bob." Bob would open the door for her and move to the kitchen, making a pot of coffee, but silently. The fewer words he could speak, the better, he decided. He mustn't forgive her too quickly; he should try to make it look as though he might not be able to accept her back in his life at all. These tales and behaviors were good for passing time, but waiting with such eagerness became its own sort of torture, and Connie's homecoming was taking longer than he'd thought it would. He told himself that the story only became more burnished with the passage of days; the longer Connie waited to return, the finer would their reunion be. But what wound up happening was that nothing happened. The rains arrived, but no knock on the door. Spring came, and the perennials Connie had planted stood upright in their beds, but the phone did not ring. Bob passed a long and very rotten summer sitting on the couch, but never a letter in the mailbox. He never heard from Connie again. His reaction to the knowledge that it all was actually and finally over was obscured by an alien otherness, and he hobbled along through the following months in the manner of the walking wounded. Eventually, though, he found himself returned to the path he'd been on before he'd met Connie and Ethan. He had strayed so far from that way of life; they had led him away from its isolation and study and inward thought. Now he rediscovered and resumed his progress over that familiar ground. Bob was quiet within the structure of himself, walled in by books and the stories of the lives of others. It sounded sad whenever he considered it, but actually he was happy, happier than most, so far as he could tell. Because boredom was the illness of the age, and Bob was never bored. There was work to do but he enjoyed the work. It was meaningful work and he was good at it. When the work was over there was the maintenance of his home and person and of course his reading, which was a living thing, always moving, eluding, growing, and he knew it could not end, that it was never meant to end. Ultimately it was Bob's lack of vanity and his natural enjoyment of modest accomplishment that gave him the satisfaction to see him through the decades of his lifetime. He had been in love with Connie, who had loved him, but it had been a fluke; he had loved Ethan Augustine and understood what it was to have a true comrade, but that had also been a fluke. The betrayal by and loss of these two people was hard to square, but the grief was temporary. There was something residual left over, which was an absence, the recollection of injury, but this became blurry and far-off, hiding in a corner of his mint-colored house. Sometimes he could forget what had happened for an hour, and sometimes a month. But whenever the memory was returned to him, he never reacted with bitterness, but took it up as a temporary discomfort. Days flattened fact, was the merciful truth of the matter. A bell was struck and it sang by the blow performed against it but the noise of the violence moved away and away and the bell soon was cold and mute, intact.

CHIP RAN AWAY ONE MORNING IN FEBRUARY AND STILL HADN'T BEEN found when Bob arrived at the center that afternoon. It was a cold day, getting colder and likely to snow, and Chip's coat hung on a peg by the door. Maria was pulling on her own coat as Bob walked up to meet her. She explained what had happened and asked Bob to stick around in case Chip returned or if someone called in with news of her location. The center was empty; Bob asked where everyone was, and Maria told him, "The shuttles don't run when the roads turn icy. The nurses and interns are all out looking for Chip; the residents are hiding out in their rooms. Stay by the phone, all right? And keep an eye out the window?" She hurried off and Bob sat at her desk, snooping mildly but finding nothing worth mulling over. He heard the high suffering whine of Linus's wheelchair; now he was parked in the office doorway.

"Knock knock."

"Who's there?"

"What are we doing?"

"What are we doing who?"

"What are we doing sitting around like pussies when we could be out there with the rest, looking for Chip?"

"I'm surprised to hear you care."

"I'm offended to hear you're surprised."

"I'm apologetic at your being offended."

"I'm accepting of your apology."

Bob pointed at the desk. "Maria asked me to stay in case Chip comes back or someone calls about her."

"Okay, but let's go anyway. Look at that, holy shit, it's snowing."

It was snowing, Bob now noticed: angled and heavy. Bob thought of Chip outdoors in her pink sweatsuit and was inclined to agree with Linus that they should mobilize and pitch in. When he said as much, Linus clapped, snapped, pointed, and backed his chair up, zooming away to gather his things from his room upstairs. Bob pulled on his outerwear and was standing in the half-dark Great Room waiting for Linus to return when he noticed that Jill was sitting at her card table, squinting at a puzzle. Jill, per Bob's pitch to Maria, had recently become a resident at the center. Contrary to his theory, however, this had done little to allay her naturally occurring misery; Bob thought she looked even more tragic than usual, and he invited her to come along with Linus and himself. Peering out the window, she shook her head.

"Will you be all right on your own?" asked Bob.

"So far so good."

Linus and Bob exited the center and began their cautious descent down the snow-slick zigzagging path. They were almost to the sidewalk when Jill appeared in the doorway, calling out to Bob: "Wait for me! I've changed my mind! I'm coming with you!" Bob gave her a thumbs-up and Jill ducked back into the center to fetch her things. She moved with an agility and speed that surprised Bob. Because he'd never seen her upright before, and within the context of the center, he'd assumed she was not able to walk. "I didn't know Jill could walk," Bob told Linus, who made a yikes face. When Jill came stepping down the path, Linus, smiling now, said, "Bob didn't know you could walk, Jill."

Jill stopped in her tracks. "Fuck you, Bob."

"Hey," Bob said.

"Hey nothing." She reached up her gloved hand to touch her hair. "Shoot, I forgot my hat. I'll be right back. You guys'll wait for me, right?"

"We'll wait," said Bob.

"But hurry up," said Linus.

Jill paused. "Okay, but you'll wait?"

"Yes," said Bob.

"But hurry," said Linus.

Jill retreated back up the path to the center.

Linus said, "You hurt her feelings, Bob. Her feeling."

"Actually, you did, big-mouth."

Linus looked up innocently. "How was I supposed to know not to say anything?"

"It was inferred."

"You inferred nothing."

"Decorum infers it."

Jill returned without a hat, explaining the front door was locked up tight, and she asked Bob for a key, but neither he nor Linus had one. The sky was darkening as the day pushed toward dusk, the snow continued to fall, the temperature dropping. Jill asked, "What are we going to do?"

"The answer to every problem is money," Linus stated confidently. "Now, how much have we got? I, personally, have none."

"Me neither," said Jill.

"I have money," said Bob.

"If Bob's flush, we're flush too, Jill. Now comes the question of, what are we going to spend our money *on*?"

Jill was not in the mood to engage in humors. The snow was attacking her face and collecting in a crystalline loaf atop her diminutive head. Bob pushed the loaf away, took off his watchman's cap, and pulled it down over Jill's ears. Partly he felt it the chivalrous thing to do, but also he was hopeful the gesture would play in his favor and that she would forgive him his earlier social error. She thanked him, not effusively but with sincerity, which he took as a sign there would likely be peace between them.

The trio struck out in search of Chip, with Linus in the lead, Bob and Jill pulling up the rear, walking side by side. They'd not traveled two blocks when Linus pointed at a movie theater across the street and said, "You guys want to go see a matinee?"

"We're looking for Chip, Linus," Bob said.

"But they serve pizza, beer—chocolate. And maybe that's where Chip is, did you ever think of that? Just sitting in there waiting for us." Bob made no reply to this but walked on in silence. Linus said, "This was a huge mistake." Bob said nothing. Linus swung his chair around to face Bob. "I never should have listened to you!"

"This was your idea," Bob reminded him.

"All right," said Linus, "let's not cast aspersions."

Bob agreed, anyway, that they couldn't remain outside in such weather as this for much longer; and when he proposed they retire to a café for a hot cup of coffee, Linus was enthusiastic. Jill, however, was shaking her head. "Coffee makes me go to the bathroom."

"But going to the bathroom is fun," said Linus.

Jill didn't know what to say to that.

"How about a hot chocolate?" asked Bob, and Jill said that sounded pretty nice, after all. Bob said he knew a restaurant four or five blocks away; Jill said, "If we've got that far to go, I'm going to need a puff," and she paused to tap a cigarette from her pack. Bob noticed she was smoking Camels.

Bob had smoked Camels in his day, and he felt an impulse to ask for one. He didn't, but then when Linus said, "Let's smoke one of Jill's cigarettes, Bob," he surprised himself by instantly agreeing.

They stood together as Jill handed out Camels and passed her lighter around. They each lit up, inhaling, exhaling, enjoying the lark of the day in spite of the weather. "It feels just like skipping school, doesn't it?" said Jill. She was in something like a good mood, the first Bob or Linus had witnessed, and they shared discreet looks between them in honor of the uncommon event. The snowfall seemed to decelerate as the nicotine seeped into their bodies. Linus said, "I haven't had a smoke in ten years." Bob said, "I haven't had one since 1959." Both men were transported back to the place of loving tobacco wholly; the terrible efficiency of the device was thrilling and frightening in equal measure.

As they made their progress toward the café, Jill became animated, speaking gaily of the many deaths in her family. Everyone was dead but her, she said. Her mother and father, of course; but they had not died in their dotage, but by grisly disease in the prime of their lives. They had died from what Jill called eating diseases.

"What do you mean, eating diseases?" Bob asked.

"I mean the disease ate them," she said.

"You mean like leprosy?" asked Linus.

"It was in the leprosy family. I can't remember the clinical name. Something exotic—a lot of syllables."

Jill's sisters were dead and her brothers were dead and her aunts and uncles were dead and her cousins were dead. Her husband was dead, but there was something in her tone which, said that this was not so significant a tragedy as the others. Bob imagined Jill had been trapped in a decades-long marriage with an abusive, alcoholic tyrant; but when he asked if the union had been combative, Jill shook her head. "Goodness, no. Clarke didn't have an angry drop of blood in him. But was he ever a damp one."

"A what one?" said Linus.

"A wet-seat."

"What?" said Bob.

"Unfun," she said peevishly. "But it was intentional, the unfun-ness."

"He was against it."

"Strongly, yes. He found grace in solemnity."

"That sounds admirable, actually."

"Thank you, Bob. I did admire him. I just wish he'd taken me out for a hamburger dinner every once in a while." She took a final drag off her Camel and flicked it into the street. "After Clarke passed, I thought, Now I'll finally have some fun. But, I haven't had any. Not really I haven't."

Bob said he was surprised to hear she had an interest in fun at all.

"Of course I'm interested. Can't you see I crave it?"

"I can't see that. Linus, can you see it?"

Linus said, "I can't, no. But then, and possibly you've noticed this, I don't really care about or consider anyone else's point of view other than my own."

They arrived at the café and were sheltered in a Naugahyde booth. Basking in the room's warmth, they elected to indulge in full meals. Bob wanted breakfast; Jill and Linus both followed suit, and in a little while their food was delivered to the table. Jill picked up a piece of bacon from her plate, sniffed it, and held it out, asking, "Does this bacon smell funny to either of you?" Bob said he didn't want to smell someone else's bacon, but Linus said he did, and Jill held it under his nose. "It's just a normal bacon smell," he told Jill, and so she ate it.

They finished their meal but lingered; outside, the snow

continued to fall. Bob saw a figure in pink move past the café and he hurried across the dining room to peer out the front door and see if it was Chip, and it wasn't. When he returned to the table, Jill and Linus were discussing the moon landing. Linus said, "Neil Armstrong was playing at being off the cuff, but he had memorized the words before Apollo even left the ground. He always claimed to've improvised the line, but evidence suggests it was written by an ad agency hired via NASA."

"Maybe he did make it up after all," Jill said. "Maybe he did come up with it on the fly."

"Please," said Linus. "Have you ever looked in Neil Armstrong's eyes? Talk about infinite space. You can see forever in that handsome head of his. The man couldn't compose a shopping list. We want to think of astronauts as the embodiment of the best of our collective flesh and blood when actually they're half-mannequin, and probably more than half."

In a deep voice, Jill said, "'One small step for man.'"

"It's *a* man," said Linus. "'One small step for *a* man.' Otherwise the quip doesn't even make sense. Armstrong says that there was transmission interference and that he delivered the line with the 'a' intact."

"You don't believe it?" Bob asked.

"I'm doubtful."

"I feel like you have a low opinion of astronauts generally."

"I don't like them very much, it's true."

"Well," Jill said, "I don't think Mr. Armstrong did such a bad job as all that."

"You may take solace, my taciturn comrade, in the fact that yours is the majority opinion."

Bob said, "I wonder what the second man on the moon's words were."

Linus said, "Buzz Aldrin: 'Beautiful view. Magnificent desolation.'"

"What do you think of that?"

"The first part is chilling for its banality. The second part at least achieves some general shape of a human being, though it's not a human being I'd want to, you know, go camping with."

They made their way back to the center, following their own partly filled-in footsteps and wheelchair tracks. When they arrived they found Chip still was missing, and that Maria had broken down and called 911. A muscular police officer in his early twenties was interrogating her in her office. Bob and Jill and Linus lurked near her door; Maria was in trouble, and they wished to protect her in some way. The police officer eventually stood away from Maria's desk, pausing in the open doorway as he flipped his notepad closed. "We'll do what we can, obviously," he said. "But it's a shame we're in this position in the first place, wouldn't you agree?" Maria nodded contritely, but when the police officer turned away she held up a long middle finger at the back of his head, which stirred Linus in his chair, stirred him almost to the point of mistiness; later he would admiringly describe the gesture as a "Firm, firm bird." After the police officer departed, Maria noticed that Bob and Jill and Linus had returned. "Where the hell have you been?" she asked Bob, leading him by the arm to stand apart from the others.

"We went out looking for Chip," he told her.

"In this weather? At this time of night? You can't just take out a resident without telling someone, Bob. Jill's blood pressure is so low she's practically flatlining. And there are so many things wrong with Linus I wouldn't know where to begin naming them. Either one of them is teetering—they could drop dead at any given minute."

"We can hear you," Linus called.

Maria pulled Bob a few steps farther away. "Well, what the fuck?"

"Okay, I'm sorry," he said. "Are you mad at me?"

"Can you not see that I'm mad at you?"

"You seem mad at me."

"I *am* mad at you! The whole time I was in there giving that smug shit the details on Chip, I knew I should also tell him about you three being gone as well. But I just—I couldn't do it." She touched the side of her face and she went into a kind of swoon. Her phone rang and she shooed Bob away and shut herself into her office. Brighty stepped out of the elevator and walked up to join the others. "I napped the whole goddanged day away," she said. "What'd I miss?" Linus was filling her in when Maria came out of her office and announced that Chip's son was on his way to the center.

"Chip has a son?" asked Brighty.

"Yes," Maria said, "and he sounds very angry." She returned to her office and laid her head on her desk. The group discussed the mysteries of Chip's biography. They pooled their information and found there was none; they knew not a single thing about her. "Not even her name," said Brighty.

"It's Chip Something," said Jill helpfully.

Brighty was shaking her head. "I hung that on her when she first came in. Chip, like chipper, get it?"

Jill said, "But she's not chipper at all."

"Yes, Jill, I'm aware of that. The function of the nickname is ironical." She looked to Bob and Linus. "Try to keep up, kids."

Bob asked, "Is Brighty a nickname?"

Brighty said, "Who gave you the green light to get personal?"

The Chip saga continued into the night and Bob stayed on far later than he ever had before. His presence was not helpful in any real way, but there was a vigil sense to the evening which he couldn't tear himself away from. The Great Room took on a new set of visual properties after dark; the sconce lights were set on a dimmer, and the woodwork was honey-colored, the center transformed to the stately home it once had been. Bob and Linus played cards, with Jill looking on and commenting on the plays like a cynical television announcer who believed the players couldn't hear her. "That was foolish. He's getting greedy." They were playing for factual peanuts, but something in the raking in and pushing out of these awakened the gambling impulse in Linus, who brought up the idea that Bob should bundle up and make the trek to the market for a stack of scratchers.

"You mean we'll go together?" Bob asked.

"Well, no."

"And who'll foot the bill for the scratchers?"

"I mean," said Linus.

Actually, Bob didn't mind going; he put his coat back on and left the center. Outside and the world was quiet; the snow was no longer falling but there was a full foot of it on the ground, and the moon was rising in the sky. A lone car passed in the distance and Bob was at peace as his boots punch-punched through the untouched snow. When he entered the 7-Eleven he recognized the cashier from his last visit, and the young man instantly recognized him, hopping up from his stool and pointing a two-foot meat stick like a cutlass toward the rear of the store, where Chip was standing at the glass doors, clinging to the handle for support and staring in at the refrigerated beverages. The cashier said she had arrived just as he came on shift, a full five hours prior; and whereas her presence had been alarming to him the first time around, now he was rooting for her, in the way one might root for a marathon dancer or flagpole sitter, humbled by her dedication to her arcane medium. Bob borrowed the cashier's phone and called the center. He volunteered to walk Chip back, but Maria insisted he stay put and wait for the ambulance, and he did this, standing at Chip's side and making observational comments about the weather, praising her tenacity, trying and failing to get her to drink from a bottle of water. Her legs were trembling from fatigue, and when the paramedics came they had to pry her hands from the glass door handle. She was groaning as they led her away on a gurney, her hands still gripping the air before her. After she'd gone, Bob bought several different kinds of scratchers, twenty in total, five for each of the four waiting together at the center—it didn't occur to him to get any for Maria. "How've you been?" he asked the cashier, who made the half-and-half gesture. Bob admitted he'd forgotten to pay for his coffee all those months earlier, and volunteered to pay now; the cashier raised his meat stick up above Bob's head, then gently tapped it over his right and left shoulder. "On behalf of the 7-Eleven corporation and all of her subsidies, I absolve you of your debt." Bob thanked him and returned to the night. By the time he got back to the center the Great Room was dark, save the light bleeding in from Maria's office, where she sat opposite a man in a worn canvas coat and blue jeans. The man was turned away, so Bob couldn't see his face, but Maria's face was drawn, and her body language read of remorse, apology, shame. Linus hissed from the rear of the Great Room and Bob moved to sit beside him.

"What are you doing in the dark?"

"Spying, what does it look like?"

"Where is everybody?"

"Gone to bed."

"Where's Chip?"

"They took her to the hospital."

"Is she okay?"

"As okay as she ever was."

"And that's the son?"

"Yeah."

"Is he mad?"

"He's mad. Did you get the scratchers?" Linus had laid out two quarters in readiness; he wanted to scratch all the scratchers elbow to elbow with Bob. Bob counted out ten per each of them; Linus tidied his stack and took up his coin. "Ready?" he asked, and Bob said he was, and they began.

There had been evidence of an odd-shaped fate running through the day, and both Linus and Bob were taken by an unspoken potentiality. But neither of them won anything, not a solitary dollar, and they sat for a time in silence, feeling the feeling that was failure. Linus said, "When we gamble, we're asking the universe what we're worth, and the universe, terrifyingly, tells us." He patted his hand on the table, pinched his big beret. "Good night, amigo," he said.

"Good night," said Bob.

Linus wheeled away and Bob sat alone in the dark, looking into Maria's office. Chip's son was standing now, pulling on his gloves and hat, shaking his head at Maria, who stared wanly, saying nothing. Bob considered Chip's son as he left the center. He was in his middle forties, working-class, and his handsome face was tight and he was muttering to himself, still angry, and who could blame him. But Bob felt sorrier for Maria than Chip's son, or Chip, even. He watched as she rose up and pulled on her coat. When she left her office, Bob scraped his chair to let her know he was there; she startled and squinted. "Bob? What are you doing?" It was past midnight. Bob told her he needed a ride home. "Well, why not?" Maria said, aloud, to herself.

It was odd being in Maria's car; the cramped vehicle was filled with fast-food trash and smashed coffee cups. The roads were empty and Bob said, "Left here. Left again. Right here." The car slipped around corners and slid past stop signs and Maria was quietly laughing; she was dead on her feet, she said.

The car pulled up in front of Bob's house; Maria said, "What a nice little place." Bob felt her disappointment and frustration regarding the Chip situation, and he wanted her to know how much everyone at the center liked and appreciated her. Maria in turn intuited that something bulkily sincere was moving in her direction and she told Bob she was too tired to field anything of the sort. "One kind word and I'll burst into tears, Bob, I'm serious." Bob said that he understood and thanked her for the ride and exited the car and walked up the snow-covered path to the house. There was the sound of his footsteps and of Maria's car driving away. There was the sound of his keys jingling, and the soft sound of his breathing. The house was completely silent. He went upstairs and drew a bath and bathed and put on his pajamas and lay down to sleep but couldn't sleep. He put on his robe and came downstairs and sat on the couch to read but couldn't do that, either. He moved to sit in the kitchen nook and look out the picture window. All was still, the snow glittering in the moonlight, untouched save for Maria's car tracks and his own footsteps. Bob was thinking of the events of the day. Nobody had congratulated him on finding Chip, and he wondered if anybody ever would. *No one will ever thank you*, he remembered Maria telling him. It occurred to Bob that he would never have come to the center in the first place if it weren't for Chip; and how curious a thing it was that their story had looped back onto itself at the 7-Eleven. Bob thought of Chip's son, and the look of anger on his face, but also how handsome he was, and of the unlikeliness that Chip should sire such a specimen. He had looked familiar, Bob realized, like some famous bygone film actor, or politician. Or was it a face from the past, a library regular? It nagged at Bob, and he made to locate the answer. The furnace groaned in the basement and now the heat came on and Connie's dress, which Bob had never put away, started its undulations, and something in this visual delivered Bob the answer to his question; and when the answer arrived, then did Bob shoot away from himself for one airborne moment, as if his tether had been cut. Chip's son looked like Ethan. Bob covered his shut mouth with his hand. He worked out a problem of arithmetic in his mind. The data was sound and he crossed the kitchen to seek out Maria's business card and found it pinned to the cork board beside the phone on the wall. The clock on the oven said it was almost two o'clock in the morning but Bob couldn't not call, and he punched in the number and waited. It rang four times and went to voicemail. He called again and Maria picked up but didn't speak. Bob said, "What's Chip's real name?" Maria wasn't fully awake; she thought she'd entered another chamber of the multivenue persecution nightmare she'd been having relating to Chip's disappearance. In a crouching voice she said, "Connie Augustine," then hung up the phone.

2

1942-1960

BOB CAME TO READING IN HIS YOUTH. IT WAS THE OLD STORY OF AN isolated child finding solace in the school library while his peers shrieked their joys and agonies up from the playground. Books led Bob to libraries which led to librarians which led to his becoming one. His first librarian was Miss Middleton. She was gentle to the level of docility, and she enjoyed Bob, and so was kind to him. From time to time she would silently cross the room and set a peeled orange on the table beside him, a cup of water. She did not smile, exactly, but she did give Bob the occasional softish sideways grin, which he took as proof of her fondness for him, and it was proof.

He read adventure stories exclusively and with the pure and thorough commitment of the narcotics addict up until the onset of adolescence, at which point he discovered the dependable literary themes of loss, death, heartbreak, and abject alienation. It was in his senior year of high school that Bob began to think of becoming a librarian, a consideration borne by a friendship or kinship with a man named Sandy Anderson, a middle-aged autodidact and closeted homosexual who happened to be the librarian at Bob's alma mater. Sandy came to know Bob and soon understood the depth of his literary interests; he started sharing obscurer works with Bob, who was glad for the guidance and pleased that he had been singled out as the one granted access to Sandy's private syllabus.

One day Bob asked, "How did you become a librarian?"

Sandy went back in his mind. "It seems to me I went to school for it, but that might just be a nightmare I once had." He had a seen-it-all attitude and treated everything under the sun or moon as a joke; sincere declaration of any type was mocked without mercy. At the start of Bob's interest in what Sandy called librarianism, he refused to answer the earnest young man's questions directly. "It's a nice idea, Bob, but as with so many specialty careers, librarianism doesn't hold up in our society's real time."

"What do you mean?"

"It's a job whose usefulness has gone away. The language-based life of the mind was a needed thing in the syrup-slow era of our elders, but who has time for it now? There aren't any metalsmiths anymore, and soon there'll be no authors, publishers, booksellers—the entire industry will topple into the sea, like Atlantis; and the librarianists will be buried most deeply in the silt."

But Bob would not be deterred, and Sandy said he couldn't deny the sickness of enduring desire in Bob's eyes. At last he brought in a stack of pamphlets, information about schools where he might attain the needed degree. Bob received these with a Christmas morning fervor while Sandy looked on, shaking his head. "You're breaking my heart. You're supposed to be out there getting girls you don't love pregnant."

"These are just the thing."

"You should be in a gang, Bob. You should be getting into knife fights."

Bob brought the pamphlets home to his mother. She touched the top pamphlet with the tip of her index finger and made a questioning face. Bob told her, "I'm going to be a librarian."

"Are you?" she asked.

"Yes."

"Can I ask why?"

"I don't know. Why not?"

His mother frowned. "I think you're too young to start asking yourself *that question*, don't you?" Bob shrugged and she said, "What I mean is, once you start asking yourself *that question*, it's not so easy to stop. And then, before you know how it's even come to pass, you've given it all away." She looked into Bob's face as though she were looking around a corner. "Isn't there something else you'd rather do with your life?"

"Like what?" Bob asked. Here and he had located a respectable position, suited to his interests and strengths, and it didn't feel like a compromise in any way. What more did his mother expect from him? Sandy Anderson's apparent dislike of the field was personal and related to his ongoing life-disappointment; but Bob could never understand his mother's lack of enthusiasm at his career choice.

He graduated high school with an A average and not a close friend, on campus or off. And why? There is such a thing as charisma, which is the ability to inveigle the devotion of others to benefit your personal cause; the inverse of charisma is horribleness, which is the phenomenon of fouling the mood of a room by simply being. Bob was neither one of these, and neither was he set at a midpoint between the extremes. He was to the side, out of the race completely. From an early age he had a gift for invisibility; he was not tormented by his peers because his peers did not see him, his school teachers prone to forgetting and reforgetting his name. He would have been a highly successful bank robber; he could have stood in a hundred line-ups and walked free from every one. Of course, he'd had instances of minor camaraderie, even romance, through his school years; but none of these achieved any definition or meaning to Bob. The truth was that people made him tired.

After high school he went straight into Portland State to study library sciences, not bothering even to pause for summer break. The course was meant to be three years but Bob managed it in under two. He had a particular life fixed in his mind, like a set on a stage waiting for the play to begin; and while he could not ever be mistaken for ambitious, he was steadfastly driven, that the life he'd pictured and hoped for should commence.

The school years were unremarkable, but Bob was contented. His earliest class began at ten o'clock and the house was empty as he roused himself to meet his day. The schoolwork itself was boring, and often impressively boring. One of Bob's instructors explained that very little of what Bob was being taught would ever be put to use; and indeed, he found that almost none of it ever came up again. This same instructor also told Bob that the reason the degree took as long as it did was to scare off loafers who saw the role of librarian as a soft career; which it both was and wasn't, he would learn.

Bob graduated with top honors, which afforded him nothing that he could see. He had decided he would not take part in the graduation ceremony but both his mother and Sandy Anderson insisted, and so he was fitted for cap and gown, and then came the day, the event, which took place on a too-tall stage in an outdoor amphitheater on a muggy summer evening in the southwest hills. Bob's mother and Sandy looked on from the crowd; they'd never met but took to one another at once, leaning in and sharing humorous confidences. After the ceremony Bob's mother insisted Sandy come along to the celebratory dinner; as Sandy climbed into the front seat of the Chevy, Bob was visited by a premonition of catastrophe.

They went to a seafood restaurant, though Bob didn't like

seafood. Sandy and Bob's mother drank four martinis each and became chummy in their teasing asides about Bob's solitude and self-seriousness. "All this time I've been living with a librarian and I didn't even know it," his mother said. "If only someone would've told me when he was born, then it all would have made sense to me. Years of him sitting silently in his bedroom." When Bob's mother went to the restroom, Sandy slipped Bob a letter. He said it was a graduation gift, but that Bob mustn't open it until he was alone.

At midmeal the mood was high, but by the time the dessert course arrived, a gin-born sullenness took hold of Bob's mother and Sandy both. Bob's mother was sitting lowly in the booth with her arms crossed; Sandy began making barbed, catty asides to himself, and his typically wry, kind-but-tired eyes became blotted and blurred, as though his thoughts were wicked. The bill came and Bob volunteered to pay it and to his surprise no one made to debate the gesture. Bob lifted his inert mother up from the booth and walked her through the restaurant and across the parking lot to the Chevy. After installing her in the backseat, he got behind the wheel and started the car. Sandy was standing in the headlights, trying and failing to connect the flame of his lighter with the end of his cigarette. Bob rolled down the window and asked him what he was doing and he answered, "I know a place, perfect for us."

"I have to get her home."

"Leave her to sleep it off. I don't think it'll be the first time she woke up alone in a car. And we've got so much to celebrate." Gesturing toward downtown, he asked, "You want me to get us a cab? I'll get us a cab. Should I get us a cab?" Bob backed the car up and the headlights jumped away from Sandy. Halfway home Bob's mother woke up suddenly and completely and asked, "Why didn't you tell me?"

"Tell you what?"

She sat looking out at the world as they drove along beside it. "Did you think I'd be upset? Give me some credit for having lived a bit, Bob. I mean, look: you can keep the details to yourself, but I say it takes all kinds to make a world, and good luck to the both of you." The idea that Bob would have any manner of romance with Sandy was so far away from his mind that he didn't know what his mother was actually saying until the next morning. He corrected her over breakfast, but her hangover was severe, and she obviously didn't believe what he was saying. In the time between her meeting Sandy and her death, fifteen months later, she occasionally asked how he was. "He's welcome to come by, you know. Why don't you invite him to dinner sometime? We had such a laugh at your graduation." The letter Sandy had given Bob was a passive-aggressive, constantly evasive declaration of what he named a *devotion of special friendship* but which Bob, for all his inexperience, could see was something carnal, amorous. Bob had no negative impressions of homosexuality, but he didn't feel the same way Sandy Anderson did, and was at a loss in terms of what his reply should be. Months went by, and no word between them. Bob felt badly about the schism, and he missed his friend; he wondered what he was reading. After he landed his first library position, clerking under the dread thumb of Miss Ogilvie in the northwest branch of the Portland public library, he thought to tell Sandy the news, and Sandy received it with sincere enthusiasm. He invited Bob to his apartment for dinner and Bob happily accepted.

Sandy answered the door in a cooking smock, a cigarette dangling from his lip. "The quiche is cooling," he said. He led Bob to his den, put on a Martin Denny record, and promptly made a pass. Bob drew away, wiping his mouth and describing his disinclination; Sandy looked surprised, almost incredulous. "You're telling me you're not a fairy?" he said.

"Yes, I'm not."

Sandy sat down. "Are you just saying that because you don't trust me? Because, Bob? I'm a fairy to the tips of my toes."

"Yes, I understand. But no, that's not why I'm saying it."

"Huh," Sandy said. "All along and I was sure you were."

Bob wanted to say he was sorry, but that didn't feel correct, or fair, or true, so he said, "I'm sorry for the misunderstanding."

Sandy shrugged, his face reflecting a thorough disenchantment. He said, "What a lot of time I gave you."

Bob was hurt to learn that Sandy's lengthy attentions were rooted in something other than fellowship. Sandy saw this hurt and said, "I'm sorry, Bob. I know I'm being an asshole about it. But you have to understand I had a whole story going. I thought this was the beginning of something, and it's not, and that's okay, but I'm going to need a minute to recover." They sat to eat the quiche and Sandy told Bob what it would be like to work under Miss Ogilvie. "Ogilvie the Ogre. People call her a bitch and in their defense I believe she is a bitch. But she's also the librarianist *par excellence*. The northwest branch is the tightest of tight ships, which endears her to the top brass, which is why she gets all the new stock and periodicals, new carpeting installed every five years, fresh paint, amenity updates, and all the rest of it. Actually, Bob, you may have lucked into something good here, because the Ogre's not getting any younger—not that anyone is. But she'll be gone before too long, and whoever gets her recommendation will likely inherit the kingdom. A word to the wise. Are you listening to me?"

"Yes."

"Any intelligent young person's inclination would be to go against her. It's the correct thing to do in that her ideas are old and awful and in all honesty she probably should be cast aside; but it's the wrong way to go about it if you want to make a difference in the long term. Don't battle a battler, is what I'm telling you. When she's put out to pasture, or when she receives her last reward, then you can slip right into her hobnail boots and revamp the entire apparatus."

As the evening wound down, Sandy became maudlin in the looking-back manner. "All my life, all I ever wanted was to be alone in a room filled with books. But then something awful happened, Bob, which was that they gave it to me."

"But that's the same thing I want," said Bob.

"Well hang on to your hat, funny face, because it looks like they're going to give it to you, too." Later, when he walked Bob to the door, Bob held out his hand to shake and Sandy looked at the hand and said, "Oh my God." Bob never contacted Sandy again, and neither did Sandy contact Bob, which was fine, actually, though Bob would always think of him with a fondness of almost-admiration. Bob had liked him for his meanness, drollness, intellect, and antiworldness; but he was relieved by his own relative simplicity, if that was what it was.

DURING BOB'S TWENTY-THIRD YEAR HIS MOTHER ABRUPTLY AND unexpectedly died, leaving him the mint-colored house, which she owned free and clear, the Chevy, which was two years old, and an inheritance of almost twenty thousand dollars. He was not very much burdened by her passing but made lonely by his not understanding who his mother had been in life, and why she'd had a child in the first place. She was not in any way a bad person, but disappointed, and so by extension disappointing, at least to Bob she was.

One does not anticipate premature death by disease, but his mother wasn't surprised by the news. She asked Bob into the living room one morning to speak about what she called a few things, but it was only one thing, which was that she had cancer in her brain and would soon be dead, and this proved accurate: she retired in February and was gone by June. The last time Bob saw his mother alive was at her bedside in the hospital. She'd lost nearly half her body weight and had the attitude of someone distracted by an imminent voyage. But there was a gravity to her diminished stature that she wore well, Bob thought. Her illness was impressive, and she held in her eye a curious glimmer that hinted at the understanding of a mystery. A nurse stuck her head in the room and told Bob, "Five minutes." The way she'd spoken these words, slow and throaty, and the way her eyes met Bob's, he felt she was telling him it was likely time for a final goodbye. And perhaps Bob's mother was thinking along these lines when she said, "We've never discussed your father." Bob had wanted to know about his father in the past, especially when he was a young boy; but each time he had brought it up his mother had shied away. Now, as an adult, and in the context of the hospital room, he thought he didn't want to know at all. "You don't have to talk about it if you don't want to," he told her.

"No, I don't mind it," she said.

"Okay, but if it's a bad story then I'd rather not hear about it."

"It's not bad. Or I've never felt that it was." She went quiet for long enough that Bob thought she'd forgotten what she was talking about, but then she began. "It was right in the middle of the Depression, and I was sharing an apartment with two girlfriends, and every Friday we went out somewhere, any-where, and tried to figure out a way to have fun with about a dollar between the three of us. This night we went to a saloon that served a shot with a short beer for a nickel. So, okay, we had a few, and everything was fine until one of the gals got sick to her stomach, so that the other gal had to run her home, and now I'm all alone, and I noticed a fellow looking at me from over in the corner, there—stealing glances when he thought I wasn't paying attention. But I was paying attention. He was kind of usual-looking, but he had a nice enough suit of clothes on, respectable—but sad. Well, he did look that way, Bob."

"Sad."

"Yes. Like something was the matter in his life. For all I know he was always like that, but I had a hunch he was only blue that night, or that week, and I found myself wondering what the problem was, and if there wasn't maybe something I could do to cheer him up. So what I did, I got up and took my last ten cents and ordered us a shot and chaser apiece, then went over with the drinks on a tray and I set them down on the table and told him, 'Hello, I'm buying you a drink. Because buster, you look sadder than an old bandage floating in a cold bathtub!'" Bob's mother was grinning at her memory of this. "Oh, I got him laughing. He had a nice laugh. And you know, sometimes that's all it takes to make a person funny—to have someone laugh at what you're saying. But I hit a streak, the way you sometimes do, and it got so that he was slapping the table, and this was how your father and I made friends. Well, he bought the next couple rounds, then he says he'd like to see me home." Bob's mother paused to cover and uncover her eyes. "Next morning, and we were not at our best, but there weren't any sour grapes there, you know what I mean? I was never any grand romancer, but this young lady lived somewhat, and I can tell you that the next morning sometimes is damned awkward, and even awful. Because there are nasty, unhappy men walking around out there, Bob, and they like to trick you into thinking they're one way, then when it's too late they show you who they really are. But this guy? He was still the same in the morning as he was in the night—he was himself, and he was, just, good. So, we talked through the morning, and I made him a little breakfast, and we shared a cigarette and there was the question of, what was going to happen? But then the spell of us sort of blinked off, and he stood up and said he should be going—he had to go, he said. And probably it was wishful thinking on my part but it seemed like maybe he wanted to stay longer, for us to spend more time together."

"What was his name?"

"I don't remember."

"Do I look like him?"

"No, not really."

"Why didn't you see him again?"

"I don't know, Bob. Maybe he was married, or engaged. Maybe he had kids. Who knows?" She shrugged. "But, I wanted you to understand that the story of your father and me is a small story, but that doesn't mean it's an unhappy one. I can't pretend to've loved the man, or even to've known him, but I liked him, okay? And he liked me too. And that's not so bad a thing, when you consider all the hell people put each other through." Bob's seventy-five-pound mother lay there saying these things to him, her hand folded in a bony clutch, the hospital sheet yanked up to her chin. The nurse returned and told Bob it was time to let his mother rest, and he left.

There were no decisions to be made in terms of the funeral ceremony because every detail had been addressed by Bob's mother. There were ten or eleven people in attendance; Bob recognized certain of them, women his mother had worked with, some with their husbands, none of whom introduced themselves. It occurred to Bob that these individuals were likely looking at him not as the son of the deceased but as the burden she had shouldered in her lifetime—the infamous bastard child in the flesh. A priest gave a reading of familiar, possibly overfamiliar Bible texts; it was like listening to a recitation of the Pledge of Allegiance, where the words formed shapes on the air, but the meaning of the words was absent. Bob's mother's vessel was witness to this from the comfort of the coffin, which was open just enough that one could view the top of her hair and a small, shadowy segment of the side of her face. Bob had noticed this coffin arrangement when he entered the room but had no reaction to it at first. But soon and he began to dislike it, mildly, then less mildly. There was a funeral matron standing at the head of the pews; when the coffin situation became problematic for Bob, he left his seat and walked up to meet her. "Hello," he said.

"Well hello to you," she replied.

Bob explained that he was the son of the deceased and the funeral matron gave his arm a squeeze of sympathy with her white-gloved hand. She asked if he was satisfied with the arrangements and he said he was, but that he was curious about the coffin. Why was it set up like that?

"Like what, sir?"

"Open just a little bit."

The matron modulated her voice to near a whisper. "The coffin is as requested by the department."

Bob was alarmed. "Which department do you mean?"

The woman's eyes suddenly widened and a blush drew up her throat. "Excuse me, my goodness! Not department. *Departed.*" She exhaled, collecting herself. "The casket is displayed as per your mother's preference."

"She asked for it to be like that?" said Bob.

"That's right, sir. It's not uncommon, actually. Both the fully open and fully shut casket can feel extreme, when you think of yourself, you know, in there."

Bob said, "I guess she just wanted to be a peeker."

"Yes, sir, I believe she did."

"Okay, well, thank you."

Bob returned to his seat to find someone was sitting in it. He was a well-fed professional man of sixty years preceded by the reek of eye-stinging cologne. Bob paused to stand over him; the man looked up with a wracked expression that told Bob: go away from me. Bob took a seat in front of the man and resumed his study of the funeral.

Two attendants in matching white button-up shirts came forward to seal the coffin. One was young with a new shirt while the other was not-young with a less-new shirt; Bob thought they looked alike and wondered if the attendants were connected by blood. They wheeled the coffin out of doors and into the adjoining cemetery, with the mourners trailing behind in a shuffling bunch, up a winding footpath and to the top of a grassy hill. A green canvas tent with four rows of folding chairs had been set up; Bob took a seat at the rear of the pack, and the cologne-reeking man sat beside him. The attendants transferred the buffed coffin onto a metal pallet positioned above the open grave. The senior attendant spoke in the junior attendant's ear before walking away down the hill and in the direction of the church. The junior attendant stood by awhile, looking skyward, then spun about and commenced lowering Bob's mother into the ground by means of a winch. But the winch's mechanism was rusted or obstructed and so was squeaking, and then squealing, and finally shrilly squealing so that the sound defined the moment, and the mourners all were wincing by it, and some were covering their ears. Bob's mother was half underground when the squealing ceased, because the winch had stuck fast on its track. The junior attendant began to harass and jerk the winch in hopes it would become unstuck. This caused the coffin to undergo a similar jerking motion, and all in the small audience were transfixed with the troubling and unwanted thought of the corpse being jostled about. Both Bob and the cologne-reeking man had stood, leaning forward in readiness to cross over to the junior attendant when the senior attendant returned from wherever he'd been, walking as fast as a man can walk without being said to run, and his face was tight and stern as he rested his hand upon the junior attendant's to still it. The senior attendant again spoke into the junior attendant's ear, and now the junior attendant went away down the hill. The senior attendant turned to face the mourners and said, in a voice that surprised Bob for its melodious delicacy, "Please bear with us, ladies and gentlemen. I apologize for the disruption and delay. It is the familiar tale of man versus machine. I assure you that man will win out the day, but I ask for your patience, and I thank you for your understanding." The senior attendant now busied himself inspecting the winch mechanism, while the cologne-reeking man and Bob sat back down.

The mourners all were silent; they sat looking at the casket, or not looking at it, each entertaining his or her thoughts. A gust of wind whipped up from down the rolling cemetery hills and the canvas tent above their heads became full. The wind dropped and the canvas became slack; but seconds later it returned, and in greater force, so that the tent now was lifted completely off the ground, as though an invisible hand had reached down and plucked it clean away. Bob craned his neck to follow the tent's course of flight, watching as it traveled upright through the air and landing in this same position, the poles behaving as legs, like a drunken horse struggling to maintain its own verticality. The tent tripped and collapsed and lay flat and Bob looked around for someone to make a surprised face at; in doing so he noticed the cologne-reeking man was softly crying. He was staring woebegonely at the casket, and he didn't register Bob's interest in him or even that the tent had been blown away. The senior attendant, meanwhile, jumped into action, rushing over to collect the fallen tent, with Bob following after to offer his assistance. Together they stood the tent upright and began walking it back, a pole in each hand, to shelter or rather reshelter the now-squinting, wind-tousled mourners. As Bob was setting his poles back into the holes in the ground he saw that the cologne-reeking man had stopped crying and now sat with a vacant look on his face, a hanky in his fist that rested in such a way as to resemble a melted-away ice-cream cone. Returning to his seat, Bob recognized the gold-embroidered initials sewn into the corner of the hanky, and realized that this man was George Baker-Bailey, his mother's longtime employer, he of the Christmas hams and late-night telephone calls. He radiated wealth and heft, self-importance, or perhaps just importance, and he must have sensed Bob's interest because he had turned to meet him as Bob sat down. Holding out a hand, Bob said, "Dad?" and the man shrank in his seat in response to his disgust at the word. "I'm only kidding. Hi, I'm Bob."

While the senior attendant lapped the tent to shore up the poles, the junior attendant had returned with a ball-peen hammer in his hand. He approached the winch by wide strides, paused to square his feet, and began bashing indiscriminately away; and before the senior attendant could get to him the winch became unstuck, the coffin loosed, dropping the remaining feet in a free fall, and a column of dust shot up from the grave. The junior attendant turned to the mourners, his audience, and he was breathing heavily, and his face told his truth, which was that he was doing his best. There was defiance in his eyes but also a measure of apology. It was clear he suffered both from poor luck and authentic stupidity. The senior attendant stepped forward and took the hammer away from the junior attendant, and now he too faced the small crowd. Bob had a fleeting wish that these two men might join hands, raise them up above their heads, and bow.

MR. BAKER-BAILEY WANTED TO DINE WITH BOB. BOB DIDN'T WANT TO do this but Mr. Baker-Bailey left no room in the conversation to allow for Bob's wishes, and so it was that they met at a steakhouse downtown. When Bob entered the restaurant he discovered Mr. Baker-Bailey had already finished his first drink and was fitting the second into his hand. A waiter stood by the table, hugging a tray flat against his chest and leaning in to receive Mr. Baker-Bailey's instruction: "I want you to pay attention so that I'm never without a fresh drink. I don't want to have to ask, you understand? Because I buried a saint today, and it's your job to keep me in bourbon until I can't speak to say stop." The waiter was turning to go as Bob took his seat; Mr. Baker-Bailey hooked the waiter's arm and told him, "Not so fast, we're ready to order." He told the waiter they would have two rare T-bone steaks, two baked potatoes, and two sides of rice pilaf. The waiter made a note of the order and went away. In explanation of his behavior, Mr. Baker-Bailey told Bob, "T-bones are the specialty of the house. It's reliable." Now he relaxed in his seat, looking out the windows at the citizens passing by on the sidewalk. His breathing was slow and measured and Bob suspected the man was preparing to address the life and death of his mother, which was what he was doing. He asked Bob, "What a day, huh?"

"Yes," Bob said.

"Were you happy with the ceremony?"

"I think so."

"You *think* so? I should hope you knew one way or the other, for what it cost, good God." Mr. Baker-Bailey squinted at the glass of water in Bob's hand. "Where's your drink?"

"Water's fine."

"Are you kidding me? You don't drink water on a day like today." He raised his hand and began snapping his fingers in the air.

Bob said, "It's all right. I don't want a drink."

Mr. Baker-Bailey's hand came down slowly to rest on the table. "Why don't you drink?"

"I do drink, only I don't want one now."

"Why not?"

"I just don't want to feel that way."

It took a moment for Mr. Baker-Bailey to accept this; it seemed he thought Bob was being a poor sport. But eventually he shrugged it off and said, "Well, I'll tell you what, that priest was top shelf. He didn't come cheap, but I figure he was worth it. It was as important as hell to your mother that she get that particular priest, and I made a promise, so there you go. It costs what it costs, no point grousing about it now, is there? Did you know that she and I worked together for more than twenty years?"

"Yes."

"Twenty years! That's a long time, after all." He paused, and said, "It's funny, isn't it, that it took you and me this long to meet?"

"I guess it is," said Bob. "Though, actually, I did see you once before this."

"Oh yeah? And when was that?"

"I was eleven years old and you were slow dancing with my mother in our living room."

A little flash of panic came over Mr. Baker-Bailey, and he finished his bourbon in a long swallow. Looking at the ice cubes in his glass, he began to rattle them around, then raised up his head and called across the restaurant, "What did I tell you?" The waiter came hurrying over with a fresh drink and took away the empty. Mr. Baker-Bailey glared at the waiter's back in retreat. He told Bob, "I'm upset. Do you know what I mean by that?"

"You're upset," said Bob. He was starting to wonder how he might get away without causing a fuss or disruption.

Mr. Baker-Bailey took another long drink. "So what's your line these days?"

"I'm just starting out as a librarian."

"That's good, good. That's a functional position." He held his finger in the air, as if checking wind direction. "Somebody wants a book but they don't know if they want to buy it. Well, here you go, pal, take it home and read the hell out of it. And free of charge to boot. I support the practice. I mean, you're never going to get rich, but I guess that's not the point, is it?"

"I guess it's not."

"You must have got the book thing from your mother, huh?"

"I must have," said Bob, though he'd not known his mother to read anything other than magazines and newspapers.

Mr. Baker-Bailey went back to his sidewalk people-watching, speaking to Bob but not looking at him, performing his grief for him: "Your mother? She was my good right hand and then some. And the two of us together? There was nothing we couldn't do, not a problem we couldn't solve. Because I *knew* her. I *knew* that woman. I knew her better than my own wife!" He chuckled to himself. "Christ, she was just a kid when she started out. We were both kids, really. Young and dumb and full of beans and baloney, baloney and beans." He finished his drink and another appeared, along with the two identical meals. Mr. Baker-Bailey was heartened by the arrival of the food, glad as he commenced sawing at his steak; but soon and something turned inside him, some unpleasant notion spoiling his mood. "Anyway," he said, "I figure she made out all right by me." Bob said nothing; Mr. Baker-Bailey added, "By which I mean I think she could have done worse." Bob looked at Mr. Baker-Bailey, and something in the look prompted Mr. Baker-Bailey to ask, "Who do you think bought her that house?"

"I thought she bought it."

"Fine, but where'd she get the money to do that?"

"I thought she earned it."

Mr. Baker-Bailey sat watching Bob. There was a blockage in his nasal passage and a miniature whistle occurred each time he exhaled. "You got something you want to get off your chest?" he said. "Because I'm here, and I'm all ears."

Bob thought about it, then shook his head. "I can't say anything to you."

"Why not?"

"I don't have the words."

"Why not?"

"I don't know. Just that there are no words for you."

Mr. Baker-Bailey blinked at Bob, then returned to his meal. It was disturbing to watch him eat because his head was the same color as the steak. He was pushing red meat into his red mouth, and his head was red, and it was like witnessing an animal consuming itself. "Good steak," he said, mouth filled.

"Okay," said Bob.

"Why aren't you eating?"

"I am sickened."

"Eat your steak, you'll feel better."

But Bob couldn't eat, and didn't try to. When Mr. Baker-Bailey was done he snapped for the waiter to take the plates away. After, he lit a cigarette, peering up at the smoke as it rose up over their heads. "You know what though?" he asked—and here his composure fell away, and he began crying, and not the modest weeping of the funeral but a hard, loud bawling. All in the restaurant, diners and staff, stopped to stare and wonder; Bob folded his napkin on the table and stood to leave, passing the waiter on his way to the door. The waiter had been walking over to deliver another bourbon, but now he stood by watching the crying man and wondering whether he should bring the drink or not bring it. Bob felt a sympathy for the waiter's position; the point could be argued both for and against bringing a crying man another drink, and the impasse was almost certainly unprecedented to the waiter's experience.

NEVER HAS THERE BEEN A LIBRARIAN LESS INCLINED, LESS SUITABLE to represent the limitless glory of the language arts than Miss Ogilvie. She cared not at all for literacy or the perpetuation of any one school or author, and Bob never once saw her take up a book for pleasure. Her function, as she saw it, was to maintain the sacred nonnoise of the library environment. "What these people do with the silence is beyond my purview," Miss Ogilvie told Bob. "But silence they shall have." The human voice, when presented above the level of whisper, invigorated her with what could be named a plain hate; as such, her branch was the quietest in the city of Portland and likely the state of Oregon.

For all her strictness of standards, Miss Ogilvie was not beyond reason, and she took things on a case-by-case basis. The homeless population, at least the saner individuals of that group, were for the most part spared the rod. If you kept your mouth shut and your odors were not so flamboyant and you read or believably pretended to read a book or magazine, then yes, you were welcome to come in from the rain of an afternoon. Students of the high school and college age were filled with life, or over-filled with it, Miss Ogilvie believed; they had an inclination to noise-make, but for all their spirit were easily put down. Young children were the real problem, the pinpoint of Miss Ogilvie's ire, and she saved up all her best and finest venom for them. She spoke of a world without children in the same way others spoke of a world without hunger or disease. Put them all on an island, was her thought, an island far away and surrounded by icy, deadly swells and rocks so sharp and jagged even seabirds could never light upon them. Here the children might make all the noise they wanted or needed to; and here they would be no bother to those who'd had enough noise and chatter to last out their days.

Across Bob's first year in service, Miss Ogilvie slowly and by degrees took him into her complex confidences. She spoke to Bob of the days of her apprenticeship when she had been allowed, even encouraged, to strike problematic children. During the Second World War, and with so many fathers gone away, there was a laxity of discipline in the home. With no threat of the strap lingering in the minds of the youth, then did they give in to their animal selves. The women of America came together to discuss the issue; a growing faction warmed to the idea of corrective force. "Violence was for men only," Miss Ogilvie said. "They assumed it as a burden, thinking we were lucky to be apart from the fray. Little did they know there were some among us, and not a small number, either, who had long wished to take part."

"You were for it," Bob said.

"Oh yes. And I assumed a role of leadership that was quite a surprise to myself and my colleagues both. It was a case of my not knowing I felt so strongly about something when all at once I was shouting my demands from the podium at the union hall." She sat up straight. "Do you know what I like most in life, Bob? Practicality. A child is unruly. The child is struck. The child is no longer unruly. Mathematics of the heart. Oh, it was a fine tool. But they've taken so many of our tools away from us, and now our youngsters grow ever more blunt, ever more pointless, ever more coarse. The thing I don't understand is, why should it come down to us to teach them manners? Why should it come down to me?"

Miss Ogilvie and Bob had no common ground aesthetically or intellectually but Bob, always mindful of Sandy Anderson's advice, was supportive of her quest for soundlessness, and did not attempt to bend her will toward a more moderate environment. She was wrongheaded, perhaps a little bit insane; she was also two years past the traditional point of retirement. Soon enough and she would be gone; in the meantime, Bob was learning his craft.

The work itself was not ever difficult, at least not for Bob. He felt uncomplicated love for such things as paper, and pencils, and pencils writing on paper, and erasers and scissors and staples, paper clips, the scent of books, and the words on the pages of the books. Sometimes he thought of the women and men who'd composed these documents sitting at their desks and aiming for the elusive bull's-eye and almost always missing but sometimes not, and Bob was certain that a room filled with printed matter was a room that needed nothing. His colleagues weren't unfriendly, but vague in the face, and with not much to say. Some among them complained of the tedium of the profession, and Bob always expressed his sympathies, but really he had no comprehension of the sentiment. He understood that the people who knew boredom in the role of librarian were simply in the wrong profession. He didn't judge them for it but felt a relief at not being like them.

As the newcomer, and lowest on the pole, he was given the morning shift, which was considered undesirable owing to its hours, but for Bob it achieved a lifestyle ideal. Every morning his alarm sounded at 5:00 a.m., and he came downstairs in his pajamas to light the fire he'd assembled the night before. As the fire took shape, Bob went back upstairs to shower and dress for the day. He owned two suits and alternated one to the other, going casual each third day: tieless, white button-down shirt under a dark V-neck, black slacks, black socks, black penny loafers. Dressed, his naked face stinging with aftershave, Bob returned to the living room to find the fire crackling and throwing its shifting light across the floor and walls. He ate his breakfast, then prepared and packed his lunch. If it was a particularly cold morning he would start the Chevy and leave it idling in the driveway while he washed the dishes.

As a child and teenager, Bob had been afraid of becoming an adult, this in response to an idea his mother had unwittingly instilled in him, which was that life and work both were states of unhappiness and compromise. But Bob's mother had never understood the pleasures of efficiency, the potential for grace in the achievement of creature comforts. She cooked but hated cooking. She cleaned and felt cheated. Bob didn't feel this way; the actions he performed each morning were needed, and each one fit into the next. He drove over empty, rain-wet streets and across the river to work. The parking lot was empty, the library silent as he crossed the carpeted front room and to his desk, where he turned on his green-shaded lamp and smoked a cigarette and read the library's newspaper. After, he set up for the day, turned on all the lights, unlocked the doors, and then came the workday proper. At the commencement of his career he was uncomfortable in his dealings with the public but his shyness passed when he recognized they were not addressing him as a human being but using him as a tool, a mechanism of the library machinery.

Miss Ogilvie saw in Bob a librarian in his element, and she left him to his own devices. When she told him she was taking him off the mornings and putting him on afternoon shift, he asked if he couldn't stay on as he had been. She asked him why and he explained his preference, his affection for the quiet mornings, and Miss Ogilvie stared, surprised that she should still be able, after all this time, to feel any manner of connection with another person. Her path was ever more rigid, crueler than Bob's; but she liked that he was the way he was, and she understood it, even if it didn't mirror precisely her personal experience.

Here was where Bob Comet had landed, then, and he was not displeased that this should be the case. The northwest branch of the public library was where Bob Comet became himself. It was also where he met Connie and Ethan. Connie came first but she didn't appear as Connie until after Ethan, so really, Ethan came first.

CONNIE CAME FIRST BUT WAS OBSCURED BY HER FATHER, SOMETHING of a legend around the neighborhood in that he did wear a self-made cape and was given to bursts of critical public oration. His mind was teeming with unfriendly thoughts and special threats and he felt these were of a rare and high quality and that it was for the greater good that they be heard. But the era of the soapbox-in-the-square had passed; for want of a forum he gave voice to his points of view in the streets, in parks, often at bus stops, but most commonly on the buses themselves, where people were held captive. The content of the speeches was various but typically of a nature hostile toward mankind's contemporary behaviors, with close attention paid to the Catholic Church.

The bus drivers did not like Connie's father's performances very much, and some did eject him, but many, owing to complacency or fear, let him go on and on. There was one driver who encouraged him via the overhead address system, saying things like "Could you repeat that, sir?" and "Do you have any documentation to support the argument?" and "He seems to really mean that, folks," and "Let's give a round of applause to the lively little fellow in sandals."

There was a figure behind this obstinate individual, and

that was Connie. Bob didn't notice her for a time, as she was hidden away beneath a cape of her own, hers featuring a generous hood, obscuring not only her face but also her gender. She never spoke or made any sudden movements; she trailed after her father or sat in a chair by the library entrance to wait for him, sometimes for the better part of an hour, her posture straight, her hands folded on her lap, gaze focused on the ground.

Connie's father was on his better behavior in the library. He was always curt, but he was quietly curt. When Bob engaged him, Connie's father did not try to hide his contempt, but neither did he rail against Bob, as he surely would have had they met on the sidewalk. Connie's father's area of focus in terms of his reading was American history, from the country's conception and up to the current year of 1958. It had become something of a game among the younger library employees to try to uncover the mysteries of the man; one morning at the checkout counter, Bob asked, "No interest in European history, sir?" Connie's father sighed at the energy he would need to expend in answering the question. He said, "Europe is in the past, is deceased, and so is not my concern. America is imperiled, and will almost certainly follow Europe's path, but we've not yet fallen, and we're here now, and must do what we can with the time remaining."

"I didn't know Europe was doing so bad as that," Bob said.

"Try opening your eyes. Try opening a newspaper."

"I'll do that, sir. Have a nice day."

Connie's father turned away, and there in his place stood Connie, watching Bob from under her hood and with a sly look that told him she knew her father was a foolish person, that she knew Bob knew this, and that she was gratified they were in agreement on this point. From this moment forward, and whenever Connie came to the library, she and Bob engaged in a study of one another, but modestly, and with not a word between them. Many weeks passed, throughout which Connie's father behaved himself; but there was always the sense, for Bob and Connie both, of the situation's tenuousness, that Connie's father would at some point lose control of himself. His undoing could have come on any day of any season and for any reason, but it came in the summer, and was encouraged by the presence of two priests.

It was not uncommon to see a priest, or more often a pair of priests, making use of the library. There was a seminary some miles away in Forest Park and so Bob came into regular contact with their ilk. They were unimportant-question-askers and very-small small-talkers, remarkable for their sameness and, according to Bob's experience, uniformly desirous to make contact with the world outside of their own. Not one among them could ever simply check out his books and depart; he had to contemplate this or that author, ask for recommendations, review the day's weather or the weather of the day preceding. Their reading favored current fiction of a page-turning sort: cozy mysteries, tales of wartime adventure, espionage—just so long as the narrative moved at a nice clip and was devoid of art and sex and vice. Bob had no particular care for or opinion of the priests. When they spoke to him, he picked up a labored modesty that was the result, he supposed, of their belief that they were representing God on Earth. As a nonbeliever, Bob found this weary-making but endeavored to think of the priests as eccentric rather than boorish.

The two who came in the day Connie's father was barred from the library were well known to Bob. There was the full-faced, florid priest, a squat fellow of thirtyish years, and his senior, a priest of the classical Irish mold: tall and rangy, bushy eyebrows and thick white hair combed back. They walked among the stacks, the white-haired priest pointing out this book or that, while the florid priest listened with an attentiveness that did look embellished, sycophantic. Bob was pondering their dynamic when he noticed Connie's father, a wolfish grin on his face, edging closer to the pair. Connie stood behind her father; Bob couldn't see her expression behind the hood but her physicality read as worried, bothered: she held her hands together at her chest and crept forward, forward, then halted. She knew something had to happen, and that it would not be pleasant, and that there was nothing to do but wait for it, to watch it, and now it began: the white-haired priest was reading a book's back jacket when Connie's father moved in and snatched it from his hand. "Excuse me," the priest said, "I was looking at that book."

"Yes, and getting your dirty handprints all over it!" said Connie's father. "You should be ashamed to come in here with hands as dirty as yours."

The priest was surprised by the outburst, so much so that he couldn't find his language; he turned to his colleague with a look of incredulity, an invitation to become involved on his behalf. The florid priest took up the challenge, asking Connie's father, "Look here, what is this? What are you after, eh?"

Connie's father turned. "And you!" he said. "Walking around with filth all across your face. How dare you speak to the likes of me with your face in such a state!" He batted a hand across the florid priest's nose. It was not a blow of true violence; it did not injure the man, but he was startled by the physical contact and drew back in a flinch, raising a hand to shield his face against any further molestation. Connie's father was pleased by the effect his behaviors had upon these two, and he considered them bettered. "What is it, don't you have running water up at that buffoon's academy you live in? Or are the pair of you simply too lazy to maintain the most basic levels of hygiene?"

Miss Ogilvie and Bob were standing side by side at the Information desk, and so had witnessed the episode together.

Bob was moving to intervene when Miss Ogilvie clamped a hand on his forearm. She walked around the desk and toward Connie's father with an eerie, sideways glint in her eye, as one in a trance. Touching her long finger to Connie's father's shoulder, she asked, "May I see your library card, please?" Connie's father turned away from the priests to consider the person of Miss Ogilvie. They had been sizing each other up for months, each of them knowing this reckoning had to come, and here it was, and they stood staring at one another for what Bob felt was an awful length of time. The emotional information moving between the pair was unknown; clearly, though, there was some manner of psychic showdown taking place. In the end it was Miss Ogilvie crowned the victor: Bob watched as Connie's father's hand began to move, as if without its owner's consent, to seek out and pass over his library card. Miss Ogilvie received this, held it up, and with a glorious slowness, ripped it in half. Tucking the two pieces into the pocket of her cardigan, she told Connie's father, "You have irrevocably lost your rights to access the public library system in Oregon, effective immediately. If you ever set foot in this or any other branch in the state you will be arrested at once and prosecuted as a malicious trespasser. Now I'll ask you to walk this way, please." She gestured to the exit and stepped in that direction. Connie's father did not follow immediately after but stood by, blinking and making to collect his wits. He had been temporarily dazzled by Miss Ogilvie's awesome powers of negative confidence but now, recognizing his time of triumph had passed, some of his own negativity returned: looking back to the priests, he leaned toward them and spit at their feet. With that, he left the library, and Connie followed quietly after. After they'd gone, Bob came forward with a rag to wipe up the spit; Miss Ogilvie took the rag from Bob, got down on her knees, and cleaned the floor herself, bony backside bobbing in the air. Bob looked to the priests, to gauge their reaction at this unexpected visual, but the florid priest was gently touching his nose to check for tenderness while the white-haired priest made a discreet inspection of the state of his hands.

A week after this event, Connie came to the library alone. She was decked out in her usual garb but with the hood of the cape worn down. Her hair was middle length, blondish and flat, and she had not a trace of makeup on her face; but it seemed to Bob she was enjoying visibility, being a young woman in the world, in contrast to whatever genderless figure her father wished her to be when they were together. She set a tall stack of books on the counter and stood by, watching Bob. "Returning?" he asked, and she nodded. He was wondering if she was allowed to speak in public, or at all, when she shifted and said in a raspy voice, "I can't tell if you recognize me or not."

"I do," he said. "The cape gives it away."

"Oh, right," she said, looking down. "Well, I'm returning my father's books to you. But, I also have a list of books I'm meant to check out. Is that going to be a problem?"

"Why would it be?"

"Because of what happened. The books are for him, not me."

Bob said, "It's not for me to ask who the books are for; and you don't have to say. If you have a valid library card and no outstanding fines, you can check out whatever books you wish."

"And what if I don't have a library card?"

"Then we'll get you one."

"And what if I don't have any identification?"

"You don't have any on you, you mean?"

"I mean I don't have any at all. Personal identification is one of the things father is against."

Bob wouldn't have considered commenting on this were it

not for the young woman's obvious amusement in discussing her father's behaviors, which prompted him to say, "He strikes me as the kind of man who is against many things."

"Oh, yes, and more all the time," she said, and began naming them off one by one. "Television, obviously, and film—moving images. But also radio—fictitious writing of any sort. Privately owned automobiles. All unnatural scent or flavor. All music. Exercise for exercise's sake. Sunglasses. Calendars, watches. Escalators, elevators. Police, government, doctors, medicine."

"What is he for?"

"Gender segregation. Sterilization of criminals. Public transportation. The death penalty. Disease. Gardening."

"Gardening he supports."

"He himself doesn't garden, but he supports the action; it's one of the very few things he encourages me to indulge in."

"You like gardening?"

"Gardening is very important to me."

"Decorative gardening or gardening for the table?"

"Both." She liked that he'd asked that particular question. She watched him without shyness, and Bob felt exposed but he affected, as best he could, an unruffled ease.

"How can someone be in favor of disease?" he asked.

"He believes it achieves God's will."

"That's not very friendly."

"No, but friendliness isn't in his wheelhouse. I mean, it's not so simple as his believing that someone dying of cancer deserves it. There are many, he says, who the Lord calls back because He wants them close by."

Bob and Connie were smiling at each other. "How does your father expect you to check out books without identification?"

"He believes I'll fail; but he was game for me to try."

"So this was your idea?"

"Oh, yes. His history books give him something to do. He's away for hours each day, reading himself blind. For me these are precious and necessary hours, and I honestly don't know what I'll do if I lose them, and so here I am." She paused. "I don't mean to put you on the spot. I understand you may not want to involve yourself. I wouldn't have bothered to try for a card at all but I thought I saw some sympathy coming from your side these last few months."

Bob understood by this that his presence was a requisite piece of the young woman's plan, and he was so delighted to have been in her thoughts he would have given her the keys to his car if she'd wanted to borrow it. "Of course, you can have a card," he said.

"Really?" said Connie. "You're sure that would be all right?"

"Why not? I'd ask you to keep my part in it to yourself."

"Oh, yes."

"And, I'd advise you to leave the cape at home next time. Even with the hood down, Miss Ogilvie might make the connection."

"Is that the woman, who went after my father?"

"Yes."

"She's formidable. My father thinks she's inhabited by Satan."

"That's a popular theory," said Bob. "I myself don't believe it." He brought out the necessary forms for receiving a library card, filling them out on her behalf, which allowed him both to spend more time with her and ask her all manner of personal questions. This was how he learned her name: Connie Coleman.

"What is your age, Connie Coleman?"

"Twenty years of age."

"I'm twenty-four."

"Okay."

He handed over the temporary card and watched her flipping it over. Bob wondered if her life was small in the way his was small. Knowing that he was crossing a boundary, he said, "I can't tell if you believe any of this stuff your father believes." Connie tucked her card away into the folds of her cape. "Well," she said, "I live in an abnormal environment. So I must be at least a little bit abnormal myself, right?"

"Right," said Bob.

"And while the partial truth is that I don't believe, the fuller truth is that I believe just enough that I'm uncomfortable talking about my not believing." Bob held up his hand, as if to say he understood, and wouldn't follow the line of questioning any further. "My aspiration is to become a completely normal human being," Connie said. "That's my aspiration as well," said Bob. Thinking this was the conclusion of their conversation, and wanting to end on a note of charity, he told her, "I'm sorry about what happened with your father."

"Oh, yeah," said Connie lightly.

"What I mean is—I'm sorry that it happened the way it happened."

"Well, thanks," she said. "But, that's the way it always happens."

Bob wished her a good-day and stepped tentatively away, watching as she looked over the list of titles her father had written out for her. Looking up, she stood puzzling over her position in the library. Bob returned to her and volunteered to assist in collecting the books, which she agreed would be helpful. "It's a funny little list," she said in warning. "I'm just the man," he told her, and together they walked up and down the aisles. He soon found each of the books her father wanted, then checked them out for Connie. After, he walked her to the exit, and they stood together a little longer, awkward in their parting. Connie told Bob, "I'm not sorry my father was kicked out of here. Because it's nice to get out and speak to people without having him around. Honestly, it's nicer than I can say. Thank you very much."

"You're welcome."

"I'll see you again sometime, maybe."

Bob pointed at the Information counter. "That's where I like to stand." After Connie was gone Bob walked to the restroom and locked himself in a stall to stand and relive his meeting with this new person, this young woman. He was confused and giddy and scared. At one point he wondered if he was charming. Was he? He had never been before. Or was it that he'd simply never had the chance to indulge?

By this time, Bob had established the beginnings of a friendship with Ethan Augustine. Male comradeship, like romantic love, had eluded Bob through the length of his life, when suddenly here was Ethan, and he was charming and good or goodish, and he liked Bob, and Bob didn't quite understand why, but he went along with it if only to see where it might go. The night of the day Bob had first spoken with Connie, he met Ethan for a drink at the bar down the block from the library, and set about explaining his experience in detail. By telling the story, it sounded flimsy to Bob, as if nothing much had happened at all. But why could he not stop thinking of Connie even briefly? And was he such a fool to think the connection was shared? "Maybe it was all in my head," said Bob. Ethan, who understood as well as anyone that romantic emotion was often to the side of language, said, "But maybe it was in hers too." Bob was doubtful, but he began watching his days afterward, watching the door of the library and wondering when this person would come again. When he next saw her she was cape-less, in a wine-colored sweater and tweed skirt, black tights and flats, and he understood when their eyes met that he was very seriously sickened by an ancient and terrorific affliction.

IT WAS ON ONE OF BOB'S FAVORED QUIET LIBRARY MORNINGS THAT he first met Ethan. Bob pulled into the lot and discovered a battered and hubcapless 1951 Mercury parked at a skewed angle in his spot. He sat idling in his Chevy, and he understood for the hundredth time that it was other people who made for problems in this life. He parked and approached the Mercury. There was a body slumped facedown across the front seat, and for one instant Bob thought it was a corpse. But when he rapped on the window the body stretched itself, and groaned, and this was Ethan. Sitting, he looked up at Bob, smiling already, easy in the skin of himself, handsome in his dishevelment. "Hi," he said, rolling down the window. "How you doing?"

"You can't park here," Bob told him.

"Can't I?" Ethan looked around at the empty lot. "Why not?"

Bob pointed at the sign in front of the car: PARKING FOR LIBRARY STAFF ONLY. Ethan read the sign. He said, "I've parked in your special space."

Bob couldn't say for certain whether or not this person was making fun of him. "Just, move it along, all right?" he said, and Ethan began the ritual of starting his car: pumping the gas and jiggling the steering wheel back and forth. He reached to turn the key in the ignition, then froze. "I just remembered something."

"What?"

"I can't move the car. Or I could, but I can't go home, and so I'd really rather not move it, because there's nowhere else for me to be right now." Ethan pointed. "What if I parked in one of these other, less special spots?"

"Why can't you go home?"

"Well, there's a whole long story there, but in a nutshell it's that it could be bad for my health."

"Why?"

"I'd have to tell you the whole long story to answer that question."

Bob looked at the library and back. "Couldn't you tell me a shortened version?"

"Yes, I could do that," said Ethan, and he sat up straight to tell it.

He lived in an apartment above the pharmacy across the street from the library. The night before he'd returned home after seeing a movie, and in prowling up the block in search of a parking spot noticed that the light in his apartment was on, though he distinctly remembered turning it off. He sat idling awhile, and soon saw an individual he now described to Bob as "a man I know who wants to kill me" stepping around inside his bedroom. Thinking to wait it out, Ethan moved his car off the street and into the library lot, behind a shrubbery bisecting the library property from the sidewalk. From this vantage point, Ethan explained, he could see into his apartment but was himself hidden away. He had spent the night on stakeout, then, succumbing to sleep only as the sun was coming up.

Bob asked, "How do you know he's still in there?"

"That white pickup truck's his," Ethan said.

"Why don't you call the police?"

"That's a fair question, but a complicated one, and the answer, unfortunately, is that the man who wants to kill me is himself a policeman." Ethan lit a cigarette and sat there as if considering the experience of smoking. It was here that Bob had his first sense of liking Ethan. It came over him strongly and was confusing in that he didn't understand what had happened to inspire it. At any rate, his initial annoyance at the distraction from his perfected morning was gone. "Okay," said Bob. "Next question. Why does the man want to kill you?"

"Well, now, there's a story there, also."

"A long story?"

"No, it's quite a brief story." He ashed his cigarette out the window. "Can I ask your name?"

"Bob."

"Nice to meet you, Bob. I'm Ethan."

"Hi, Ethan."

"Hi. Now, the truth of the matter in terms of this man's wanting to kill me is that there is a wife involved."

"The man's wife."

"The man's wife and not mine, that's right, Bob. It's a dusty old tale and they've written a thousand lousy songs about it but what are you going to do? The wife and I achieved a familiarity. And my understanding had been that she and I would keep this off the books. So maybe it's that I made a mistake in supporting the understanding, or she made one in betraying it. Either way, here I sit."

They both had been gazing up at the window of the apartment as Ethan explained his position, and so they both saw the figure of a man passing by, a blur of ruddy flesh, a significant, heavily browed face looking quickly out and around, then disappearing. "Did you see?" asked Ethan excitedly.

"I saw. Big fellow, isn't he?"

"He isn't small," Ethan said.

"Is he not wearing a shirt?"

"He took it off around four a.m."

Bob shifted his weight. "Why would he take off his shirt?"

Ethan made the I-don't-know gesture with his hands, and his expression read of world-weariness. Bob invited Ethan in for a cup of coffee. "I don't want to get you into trouble," Ethan answered, but he was grinning as he spoke, already moving to open the door of his car.

They entered the library and Bob made a pot of coffee while Ethan poked around. He didn't appear to consider any of the events of the morning odd or worrisome. Bob went about his setting-up routine and Ethan followed behind. He instantly understood what Bob might enjoy about this process. "It's nice here, isn't it?" he said. "All quiet like this?"

Bob felt a little shy, as though a secret vice had been uncovered, but said, "I like it."

"And I suppose you're a fiend for books?"

"I suppose I am."

"I keep meaning to get to books but life distracts me."

"See, for me it's just the opposite," Bob said. He thought it a good quip but its quality was not remarked on. "And what do you do?" he asked Ethan.

"Not very much. My father used to ask me, 'How are you going to make your living answer, Ethan?' And I would say, 'I don't know, Dad.' And I wasn't lying, either—I didn't know, and I still don't know."

"Do you have any job at all?"

"I *have had* any number of jobs, Bob, thank you for your concern. But none of them held my interest for very long. I'm at the sweet spot of my unemployment just now."

"What's the sweet spot?"

"It just started, and I don't have to think of it ending for months."

"And what do you do with your time?"

"Goof around, have fun adventures." He shrugged. "I'm twenty-four, and I'm not very worried about it."

"I'm twenty-four too," said Bob.

"You don't seem twenty-four."

"I don't feel twenty-four," Bob said.

Ethan pointed out that he might be stuck there awhile, and he asked for a book recommendation to pass the time. Bob, sharing a joke with himself, gave him *Crime and Punishment*.

"What's it about?" asked Ethan.

"Just those two things."

Ethan shrugged and sighed and settled in at an empty table and opened to the first page. Bob unlocked the front doors at eight thirty. It was raining all through the morning hours, and foot traffic was sparse. Ethan sat with his Dostoyevsky, occasionally peering out the window to see if the white truck still was there, and it was. At lunch they split Bob's sandwich. Bob asked Ethan what he thought of the book and Ethan said, "I wasn't interested at the start, now I can't stop reading. But why does everybody have two names?" After the sandwich, they sat smoking in the break room. Ethan said, "I've been thinking. What if you went over and knocked on my door?"

"Why would I do that?"

"To gather an impression of the scene."

"Is your impression of the scene not as clear as mine?"

"Yes, all right, but you could speak with this guy, maybe get an idea of how long he's planning on hanging around, you know?"

Bob was surprised to be giving the idea any consideration at all, but there was some aspect to the story of Ethan's morning, in addition to the way he had approached the situation, that prompted in Bob a similarly casual attitude. He was having fun, and this was uncommon enough that he felt a compulsion to carry on. But now, with Bob pulling on his coat, Ethan was having second thoughts. "I wouldn't want him to kill you," he said.

"He doesn't want to kill *me*," said Bob, suddenly defending the plan.

"So far as we know. But what if his mechanism has gone haywire and now he wants to kill for killing's sake?"

Bob said he thought that was unlikely. If the man wished to kill generally, would he hide himself away in an empty apartment? Ethan accepted this as true-sounding and he wished Bob luck and health, a speedy return. Bob crossed the street and climbed the stairs and knocked on the door of the apartment and the door swung open and there stood a man around forty years of age, his hair a shining, molded pompadour, his eyes glassy, and his face set in the expression of someone amused by his own exclusive sickness. He'd put his shirt on but it was untucked and unbuttoned, exposing a great belly, bald, blotchy-red, rotund but firm, as if filled with air. Bob's impression of the man was that he was crazy and scary and that he would be hard to hurt. He bid him a good morning and asked if Ethan was at home; the man answered in a high, antic voice: "No, he's not around right now!"

"Do you know where he is?" said Bob.

"I don't know, no!"

"Are you expecting him anytime soon?"

The man became solemn. "Well," he said, "the way I see it, at some point he'll *have* to come back, isn't that right?"

"Yes, I guess it is," said Bob, peering over the man's shoulder to survey Ethan's apartment. He was seeking out any sign of vandalism or defacement when he noticed a stubby, snub-nosed black handgun resting atop Ethan's coffee table. Bob told himself he mustn't stare at the gun, but then he found he couldn't not. The man followed Bob's sight line and now also was staring at the gun. A look of grim amusement crept across his face and he started nodding, as if at the shared understanding of the weapon's presence. "I'd invite you in to wait," he said, "but I don't think that I should do that!"

"Of course, yes, I understand," said Bob, backing into the hallway. "Why don't I try again another day?"

"Why don't you?" the man said, then shut the door, and Bob went down the stairs and returned to the library. Ethan was back at his table, reading with an intense look on his face. As Bob walked up, Ethan dog-eared his page and looked up questioningly.

"Yeah," said Bob, "you're definitely not going to want to go home for a while."

Ethan winced. "He's angry?"

"He seems pretty happy, actually. I mean, you know, he's insane." Bob lowered his voice. "I think there was a pistol on the coffee table?"

"You think there was one or there was one?"

"It looked like a pistol."

"Nothing looks like a pistol but a pistol."

"I guess I meant it could have been a toy."

"Who brings a toy pistol to the apartment of the man you're planning on killing?"

"I don't know. No one, I guess."

"I don't think anyone would," said Ethan, agreeing. "Let's assume, then, that it was a pistol and it was real and it's his intention to use it to kill me."

"Let's assume that," said Bob. And then, brightening: "He put his shirt on. Unbuttoned and untucked, but still—moving in the right direction." This news gave way to a long silence. Bob said, "Maybe it's time to find a new apartment."

Ethan shook his head. "Out of the question, Bob. I love that apartment. No, I'll wait him out; after he's gone, I'll just need to keep on my toes for another week or so. Our friend's bitterness will last forever, but his rage has to pass. He'll tell himself and his beer buddies he set out to kill me but couldn't find me. Then he'll get drunk and screw his wife for the full forty-five seconds—really teach her who's boss. By lunchtime of that next day he'll be lost to the cycle of his miserable life and I'll become one more unhappy memory in his rearview mirror."

This was said so casually that Bob thought it must surely be a case of false bravado; but in time he learned Ethan almost never felt things like fear, embarrassment, worry, regret. Bob returned to work and Ethan to his book. It was after three o'clock in the afternoon when Ethan saw that the white truck had gone. "And he turned off the lights, how thoughtful." He stood up stretched and asked, "Can I borrow this book?"

"It's a library," said Bob, "so yes, you can."

But Ethan didn't have a library card, and so, as with Connie, Bob filled out the paperwork and passed over the temporary card. Ethan thanked Bob for his help and turned to leave. Bob asked, "What if it's a trick and he's waiting in there still?"

"I don't care anymore," said Ethan. "I'm going home. If I'm slain, tell the world I died for love, or some close cousin of it."

Bob watched Ethan move the Mercury from the library lot and across the street, parking in the same place the white truck had been. He slipped up the stairwell, and as there was no clap of gunfire, Bob decided Ethan was not murdered. The next afternoon Ethan returned the Dostoyevsky, having finished the book after reading long into the night and through the morning. He said he wanted another book that made him feel just the same way, and did Bob have any recommendations that he would care to share and Bob answered that as a matter of fact and as it happened, he did.

CONNIE'S FATHER WAS SURPRISED AT HER SUCCESS AT KEEPING HIM in books, but also paranoid the whole operation might fold under scrutiny; he began digesting texts at a mad pace, and so it was ever more common that Bob should see Connie's knowing face coming in the door at the library. She established a routine of first gathering her father's books, then lingering at the Information desk opposite Bob, perched lightly on the edge of a stool. She had many questions for Bob, and she asked them, and she found his answers encouraging: he owned a house, he lived alone, he was satisfied in his work and didn't engage in any of the off-putting pastimes of the young American male. She thought it odd he had only one friend; and then she learned the friendship was quite new. What had he done with his free time before? And why did he smile so strangely at the words, *free time*? When she accused him of staidness, he made to defend himself by telling her the story of the Hotel Elba, which in brief was that Bob had run away from home at the age of eleven, stowed away on a train and then a bus, traveling clear to the ocean, where he managed to insinuate himself as a guest at the seaside hotel. He stayed several days, one among a cast of human curiosities who seemed in his memory to have existed inside of some enigmatical play. Connie could only just believe that the event had truly taken place, but she liked that Bob had run away, and was moved at the thought of Bob-as-child, entering an unknowable world in search of a superior experience to the one he knew at home.

Bob had his own set of questions for Connie, and she was forthcoming and undramatic in a way that made his asking enjoyable. Connie's life had not always been so particular; by which it is meant that her father had not always been so unsound. She had attended public school, for example, from kindergarten and through to graduation from high school. It was not until Connie's mother died during Connie's seventeenth year that her father veered from the traditional devout suburbanite and into the realm of the zealot. Weeks of polite inquiry gave way to thornier territory, and Bob one day asked, "What exactly is the matter with your father?" Connie didn't mind the question particularly, but it was not so simple to answer as it dealt in myriad phases, multilayered narrative, and a goodly amount of conjecture. In short, she said, life was what was the matter with him. But the fuller answer came over many visits and conversations.

Her father was disillusioned not by what had but by what had not happened to him; and as with so many unhappy people, he was defined by his failure. He'd known the call of the church from his childhood and when he came of age had approached the priesthood by running leap. The church did not feel he had a place in their ranks, however; he was discouraged in his efforts, and then sharply discouraged. When Connie's father demanded to know precisely what the issue was it was explained to him by a parish representative that the men and women of the community didn't like being around him, didn't like *him*, and so it ran contrary to common sense that the church would train and prepare him for a position that would inevitably put him in close contact with said community. "Your faith is evident," the representative told him. "It's your social talents, or lack of them, that we take issue with." Connie's father received this assessment as a blunt trauma from which he could never recover. Even after he achieved a distance from the church, after he'd married and sired a daughter, there still existed in his mind a fixation, a powerful need for any stripe of revenge that did not diminish with the passage of time.

Connie's mother proved a steadying presence, and talented at diffusing her husband's less-healthy inclinations; she allowed him his letters to the editor but drew the line at physical confrontations and one-man demonstrations. Connie spoke of her mother appreciatively, but without love. "That she would choose to give her life to a man like my father tells me she entered into adulthood looking to make compromises, so I never did respect her, but she was comparatively down-to-earth, and her influence over my own life was helpful. Looking back I guess I have a lot to thank her for. Because my childhood experience wasn't half as risky as my home life is now. After she died, my father was let off his leash."

Connie's mother possessed a modest legacy that had long kept their home intact; once she was gone it was revealed by way of the will that the legacy was not so modest after all, which would have been good news were it not for the sting of betrayal that accompanied it. Connie's father had no inkling that he was a member of the upper-middle rather than the lower-middle class, and he was scandalized that such a thing should have been kept from him. This bad feeling joined forces with his other bad feelings and became one big bad feeling. Free to do as he wished, now, and with all the money he could need for the upkeep of his lifestyle, Connie's father gave in to his long-suppressed and stranger inclinations.

His demands of his daughter came one at a time, and almost sheepishly. He would bring up this or that concern as though it were only half a thought: "I've been wondering if we shouldn't make some changes to the clothes you wear, Connie." Once an individual concern was addressed and the change enacted he behaved as if it had always been so and was the norm—and to stray from the norm was sinful, unthinkable. Over the next eighteen months he became an unbending and tyrannical maniac for whom to leave the house was to enter the field of battle. Which was all fine for him, Bob supposed, but why was Connie made to come along on these campaigns? "Well, that's a toughy, Bob. I think the short answer is that he believes he's earning his ticket to Glory, and he's after my being saved along with him. I don't doubt it's hard to read, but my father, in his way, is very devoted to me." She paused. "You understand he's never hit me or anything, right?" This was helpful for Bob to hear; because he had not understood this, and the thought had nagged him. Connie, sensing his further curiosity, told him, "And he's not one of these perverts, either."

"Good, great," said Bob.

She was two years out of high school with no plan or desire to continue her education. As it had been with Bob, she'd made no significant friendships in school, but whereas he had been an unknown in his peer group, Connie had had a more involved and confrontational experience. She came under the category of Other, as her language and behaviors were considered obscure by those around her. Certain of the bolder boys made romantic overtures in her direction but they were met with unblinking ambivalence and cryptic dismissals; these same boys came together to discuss Connie Coleman's *spookiness*. She was made uncomfortable by the young men, and young men in general. They were so totally without empathetic sensation that Connie thought they should not be granted access to walk among the population, much less given permission to operate automobiles on our streets and highways. Her female peers, she said, explained her away by saying she was a snob and a witch both. "And at the same time," she told Bob. "Imagine that." The word *snob* was not an accurate descriptor, according to Bob's understanding of her personality; but he was not surprised by its employment. Connie could never be demure, and confidence of her sort, in the era of the mid-to-late 1950s, was unwelcome. He believed her ostracism was borne of a kind of envy summoned by Connie's self-knowledge. Bob saw no evidence supporting the theory of her being a witch.

Time passed at the Information desk with Bob and Connie coming to learn the details of one another's lives. Bob felt the burgeoning relationship was going very well, and it was, but the next level felt far-off for him. Connie had offered any number of hints she would like to visit Bob's house, hints that became declarations: "I'd like to see this famous house sometime."

"Oh, sure, of course," Bob would answer, then excuse himself to blot the sweat from his forehead in the restroom. Connie saw that Bob was out of his depth and that she would need to give a nudge; at last she dinged the counter bell and said, "If you don't invite me to your house right this second, I'm walking out the door forever, Bob Comet. How's that for Information?" Bob touched the brass dome of the bell to quiet it and said that yes, she was officially invited, and on the following Sunday she played at being ill so to excuse herself from her traditional bus-riding rounds with her father. After he'd left for the day, she dressed, picked an assortment of flowers from her garden, and took a taxi across the river to Bob's house. She knocked on his front door, bouquet in hand; when Bob answered, he was also holding a bouquet of flowers. They exchanged bouquets and moved to the kitchen, where Connie sought out a vase and filled it with water, mingling the flowers together. She set the vase on the table in the nook, then broke off to look about the house. Bob followed behind her, naming things: here was where he read; here was where he also read; here was his childhood bedroom; here was his workshop. Connie walked with her hands clasped at the small of her back, like a museumgoer. She was impressed by the rope handrailing and agreed it had been best to keep it in place. They stood side by side in Bob's room and Connie said, "I suppose you think I'm going to jump right into bed with you for some wild afternoon lovemaking, is that right?" Bob turned so red that Connie thought he was choking. He'd not thought to prepare anything to eat but had made a pot of coffee, though she wanted tea. "I'll buy tea for next time," he said—his stab at flirtation, to reference a future meeting, as though it was understood they'd be spending time together again. They took their coffees into the backyard and sat on a mossy bench among the overgrown tangle of weeds and grasses and bushes. Connie surveyed the area with a stony face. "This garden is a disgrace. Did your mother keep it up when she was alive?"

"No, she couldn't have been less interested."

"And you take after her in that way?"

"I think any similarity between my mother and myself is coincidence." The truth was that Bob had never once even considered the possibility of engaging in the act of gardening. His mind went upward then, and into the trees. Connie wore a red cable-knit sweater and gave off the just-detectable scent of rosewater. It had been raining, and the damp hung on the air, water trickling away somewhere. Connie said, "You don't know how lucky you are to have all this space to yourself, without anyone to pester you."

"I do know," said Bob. "You could always move out of your father's, though, couldn't you?"

"I mean, I could, sure."

"Why don't you?"

She considered the question. "I used to fantasize about being a professional woman. The idea of a salary, and what I might buy with the money. I was going to have a purple car."

"What kind of car?"

"Just purple. And I'd drive it to and from my job, maybe stop at the dry cleaners on the way home. I'd have an apartment somewhere, and nights I'd drink a bottle of beer at the table in the kitchenette and I'd have a record player playing. This was how it was going to look when I got away from my father. But I didn't understand what a job really was, I don't think. I'd only been daydreaming about the paycheck, rather than the time and effort required to earn it. At a certain point I figured out it was going to be forty years behind a desk typing up some slob's memos for him, you know what I mean?"

"Yes," Bob said, thinking, naturally, of his mother.

"When I was a child," Connie continued, "I'd considered my mother and father as two entities in the same caste. But then I saw that she was aging in a way that he wasn't. He says he works for God. Fine, but he doesn't scrub God's toilet, while my mother scrubbed his, and now I do. She worked; I work; he doesn't. But whereas my mother worked herself literally to death, my work will be finite." She took a sip of coffee, then told Bob her special secret: "Mother, once, not too long before she died, explained that my father's health is screwy."

"Screwy how?"

"His heart in particular is very screwy, and it's a thin-ice situation. In other words, I've come around to the idea that this subservience to my father *is* my career. I might have to work another year, or five years, but sooner or later, and not too much later, he's going to go. My father owns his house and has money from my mother and I'm going to get it all after he dies. Then I'll be able to do whatever I want to do, and without my father looming in every doorway like a ruiner."

"What are the things you want to do?"

"Tiny little things, Bob. I like being in my room. I take walks and I work in the garden. I like to sew, cook. But also I want to do all the things he won't let me do. Books, movies, television, travel, you know?"

Bob asked, as casually as he could, whether or not she had designs toward a family. She poked Bob's side. "Kids?" she said. "I'm not so sure about that."

"Don't you like kids?"

"I don't know any kids."

"Maybe you don't like the idea of them."

"No, to be honest, I don't. It's a steep investment for a woman, with unreliable returns." She glanced down at her watch.

"Am I boring you?"

"Shut up," said Connie, but kindly.

"You have to go?"

"In a little bit I do. But I want to keep talking. Will you tell me about the library? Now that we're away from there I want to know more about it."

Bob said, "It's a library."

"But why are you there?"

"I want to be there. I like it there."

"What do you like about it?"

"I like the way I feel when I'm there. It's a place that makes sense to me. I like that anyone can come in and get the books they want for free. The people bring the books home and take care of them, then bring them back so that other people can do the same." Bob explained about his happinesses on the quiet mornings, of his arrival at the library, the dense soundlessness of the carpeted mezzanine, and the occasional empty illuminated bus shushing by over the damp pavement.

She said, "You like being alone."

"Being alone is normal."

"Is it?"

"It's normal for me."

"Don't you like people?"

"I don't know any people."

"Clever," she said, pointing.

"I like the *idea* of people," Bob said. Then, "Do you like them?"

"I do, actually." She thought about it. "I like them on the bus, when they look out the window all lonely. I like when they count their change in their palms as the bus is pulling up. I think most people are doing the best that they can." She shrugged, and said she'd have to leave soon, and she looked at Bob, and Bob wanted to kiss her but he didn't know how to do it. After a while of waiting, she stood up and went back into the house and he followed her. She walked to the front door and took her coat off the peg and put it on.

"Look," said Bob, "why don't you let me drive you home?"

"That's impossible. But, you can drop me down the street from the house, how about that?"

"I'll take it," said Bob, reaching for his coat. Soon Connie stood on the landing, watching Bob's back while he locked up the front door. "You're a little bit of a weirdo, aren't you Bob?" she asked, and Bob, turning, said, "I think the truth is that we're both weirdos, Connie."

As with the house, she gave Bob's vehicle a thorough going-over, opening and closing the glove box, turning the radio off and on, adjusting the volume. She rolled the window down and closed her eyes as the breeze touched her face. "It's nice, being in a car," she said. They crossed the river, passed the library, closed up for the day. They were a mile from Connie's house when she became rigid in her seat. "This is far enough."

"Why don't you let me take you all the way?" Bob asked, but Connie grew stern and told him, "Stop this car, Bob Comet." When he did not immediately slow down, she yanked at the steering wheel so that Bob had to pull over. The car sat idling at the curb; Bob was grinning and Connie could see that he had some mischief coming up in him. But she was unamused, and she said, "You want to see me again, is that right?"

"You bet it's right."

"Okay."

"It's really right."

"Okay. That's good. I like that. But you've got to understand about my father. It's not some small concern and he's not, you know, grumpy. He's a delusional fanatic whose relationship with reality has been severed. And if it comes to his attention that I'm in any sort of romantic entanglement he is going to go berserk, okay? Berserk is the word."

Bob said, "Has it occurred to you that he might like me?"

"He's not going to like you."

"Maybe he won't like me at first but then time will pass and he'll come to see I'm a good guy and like me against his better judgment."

"He's going to loathe you. He's going to pray for the death of you."

"Maybe he'll weaken with time."

"No. Bob? Listen to me. Listen to the words as I say them. Understand them. Are you listening?"

Bob looked at her mouth. "Yes."

"He's not going to change so long as you have any interest in me. He's going to bar you totally from his and my areas and I wouldn't put it past him to engage in something extreme, along the lines of violence."

"Okay," said Bob. "Well, what are we going to do about that?"

"We're going to not introduce the two of you, is what we're going to do." Connie kissed Bob's cheek and exited the car. Looking in at him from the sidewalk, she said, "I don't know what more to say to you. But this is the shape of our problem. There are ways around it but not through it, and I'll thank you to pay attention to what I tell you, right?"

"Right."

"Thank you for the ride."

"You're welcome. When will I see you again?"

"Just as soon as it's possible, obviously. I'll let you know, okay?" Bob watched her walk away. After she was out of sight, he held up his finger and said, as if to a jury, "The young woman herself admits that the entanglement is of a romantic nature."

MOST WEEKDAY AFTERNOONS, BOB AND ETHAN MET AT THE FINER Diner for lunch. The diner was oddly situated: when you entered you were faced with a horseshoe-shaped bank of stools screwed into the green-and-red-checked linoleum flooring. There were no other seats besides these, and no booths; in the center of the horseshoe was a sort of anti-stage, a sunken area where the waitress, Sally, performed her duties. The first time Ethan and Bob entered they were met with the scent of burned coffee and wet rags, an assemblage of gray-faced men looking up from their plates of beige foods, beasts at a trough. "Finer than what?" Ethan asked. None of these men answered; but Sally turned away from the cash register to look Ethan full in the face. Resting her hands on her hips, she told him, "Well, honey, I guess I'll have to show you."

Sally was a fascinating character in certain waitressy ways. She was of the seen-it-all variety of working human, and possessed a lusty attractiveness, this partly due to her silhouette but also the unmistakable vulgar glimmer dancing in her eyes. From the instant she first saw Ethan she gave him her every attention, which generally took the form of innuendo-heavy observational wisecracks. After Ethan ordered a patty melt, she began addressing him as Patty, not because she didn't know his name—she had asked him that off the bat—but because she wished to establish a unique connection, and a pet name worked in favor of this. Each time Bob and Ethan entered, Sally would call out "Patty!" from wherever she stood in the room, and the lonely, unrich diner men, with their ulcers and pep pills and skull-throbbing toothaches, would turn to mark Ethan's response. These men longed for nicknames from Sally, but Sally was beyond their grasp, just as Ethan was beyond hers. Five years earlier and she probably could have conquered him, if briefly; but now there was not a chance. She didn't love Ethan, she knew almost nothing of his life or personality, but craved his attention as a representative of youth and virility, and in homage to what her social currency once had been. Her own youth was only just cooling off, she seemed to be saying to him; and when she called him Patty, then she must have felt some reverberation from those sleeker, wilder days. Ethan feigned obliviousness at the attention Sally paid him, behaving neutrally, never in an unfriendly fashion, but never reciprocating the advances even slightly, which would have sent the wrong signal. "Cruel to be kind?" Bob asked, and Ethan touched a finger to the tip of his flawless nose.

A day came where the diner was all but empty and Bob decided he would talk to Ethan about Connie, and sex, and the idea of sex with Connie, and the fact that he'd not had sex before. He'd come close, once in the eleventh grade, and then again in college, but he felt no true connection with either girl, and so close had been close enough. He'd begun to think of himself as one who could and would live without experiencing carnal relations, when here was Connie, and while he couldn't say for certain, she did seem to want something more of Bob than was the norm according to his circumscribed experience. She'd visited Bob's house three times by this point, but they'd never shared a proper kiss, even. Intercourse was as sheer an event as murder, to Bob's mind; how could he do such a thing with Connie? After they placed their orders, Bob stated his position and named his concerns. Ethan said nothing until after Bob had finished, when he asked, "Has it occurred to you she might want you to do it?"

"It's occurred to me," said Bob. "I guess it feels far-fetched."

Ethan spoke of a need for action in terms that were not crude for the sake of crudeness but which did not account for Bob's sense of reverence. "I don't know this girl, obviously," Ethan was saying, "but in my experience, I've never met a young person, male or female, who didn't enjoy fucking a partner of their choosing." Bob felt a flash of anger at the use of vulgarity in such proximity to Connie and said, for the first time, "Now, look, I'm in love with this girl." Ethan was startled by Bob's declaration; his expression cycled from an amusement to a sudden kindness, then into a sheepishness or shyness. He said, "Well, that's something else, then, Bob. I really wouldn't know much about things like that. So maybe it's true that I'm out of my depth, but my understanding is that love and fucking go together pretty well. This young lady is flesh and blood and bone, and while it's possible she doesn't ever wish to be made love to in her lifetime, it does appear to me that you're doing her a disservice by putting her on whatever pedestal you're putting her on. Here, let's ask Sally. Hey, Sally?"

Sally was setting their plates on the counter. "Yes?"

"What we're after is some worldly advice, do you mind?"

"Could not mind less."

"Thanks. Well, Sally, it's news to me, but I've just discovered that my buddy here is head over heels in love."

"Is that right? Well, hell, congratulations. That's a great thing." Sally was petting Bob's hand, and her smile was genuine.

Ethan said, "But, wait, there's a problem. So enamored is he that he believes his paramour is too good for the act of love."

"Ah, one of those," said Sally, and she shook her head, as if she'd seen the detail coming. "Oh, brother."

"But what do we say to him?" Ethan asked.

Sally told Bob, "I'll say it only once, and you can take it or leave it. Understand, though, I'm speaking to you honestly and with all good wishes for you and your little sweetie, all right?"

"All right," said Bob.

"You listening to me?"

"Yes."

Sally looked hard into Bob's eyes. "Even the unsoiled and snow-white dove wants to get nailed to the wall every now and then."

"See?" said Ethan.

"Am I right or am I right?" Sally asked.

"You're right. She's right."

It can't be said that Bob gave very much consideration to the advice he'd received from Sally and Ethan that day; but perhaps it wasn't mere coincidence that Connie and Bob consummated their alliance on their very next date. Her father had been experiencing a shortness of breath and had gone into the hospital overnight for observation and so Connie was free, for the first time since Bob had met her, for twenty-four hours. They had not explicitly discussed her spending the night, but she arrived at Bob's house with a suspiciously large shoulder bag, which Bob noticed and was noticed noticing. They ate spaghetti and split a bottle of wine and afterward walked about the neighborhood. Bob pointed at a fire hydrant. "Tripped and smashed my head against that one time. Eight years old. Blood all over the place." The streetlights clicked on as they climbed the steps to the house; once inside, Connie simply continued climbing steps, up to Bob's bedroom. He followed behind and after some grappling they lay down to succumb to friendly tradition. It was not a lengthy exercise. Afterward Bob lay there thinking his happy, foolish thoughts. He was a fornicator now, and everything suddenly was good. Bob explained about his never having done it before, and Connie was plainly moved to have been his first. When she did not make the same claim as Bob, however, then he had to wonder why. A coldness came over him; knowing he should not ask, he did ask if Connie was a virgin and discovered she'd made love to three other men prior to Bob. She called the men *guys*. The word was sharp and wounding to Bob; when he asked what she meant in using it, she said,

"What do you mean, what do I mean?"

"I mean, I'm assuming these were kids from your school, or what?"

"No, Bob, I told you, the boys at school were so awful. I couldn't think of them in that way at all."

"Then who were they?"

"Just some guys."

Bob's entire body stiffened in the bed. His eyes were shut up tight and Connie, lying on her side, chin resting in her palm, watched him. "I'm not going to talk about it if you're going to make it into a big deal."

"I'm not. It's not. It feels like it is but I know it's not."

"It's not for me," said Connie.

"Right," said Bob. "I understand." He knew it wasn't in his personal interest, but he couldn't help himself and had to ask for details of the events. Nothing graphic, he clarified, just the soft pencil sketch; Connie agreed to give him what he thought he wanted. "Guy number one," she said, "a carpenter replacing the tread on the stairwell to the basement. He was in his early forties, sleepy, friendly, big belly, divorced. That my father would leave us alone together should give you an idea of the man's looks and status. This was not Gary Cooper, okay?"

"Okay."

"Are you okay?"

"I'm okay."

"Weeks before I'd made up my mind to get the whole business over with, and that the next time I had the chance, I'd take it. Well, here it was. So I put on some lipstick and brought the guy a piece of toast, which I watched him eat, and after, I asked, 'How was the toast?' 'Very good,' he said. I asked him if he was attracted to me and he put on his glasses and squinted. 'Sure,' he said. I asked him if he wanted to come to my room and he looked at his watch." Connie winked luxuriously. "He was sweet, actually. I mean, he wasn't a pig or anything, and he was physically clean, which was nice. But the act itself was pretty sad. After, he stood at the foot of my bed, staring at the walls of my room. He had this huge, fleshy back with love handles, but a tiny little ruby-red ass, like a ten-year-old boy who'd just been spanked. And there he was, looking at my diploma, my drawings of ponies and fairies, and he said, 'I shouldn't have done this.' He got dressed and I put on my robe and walked him to the door. We shook hands, and he said, a second time, 'I shouldn't have done this.' I never saw him again. Not that I was hoping to. And that was guy number one.

"Guy number two was the manager at the supermarket. He'd been chatty with me since the tenth grade. After I came of age and graduated, he started flirting in a sort of reckless way.

And I had the feeling he knew I'd done it, right, with the carpenter. Not knew-knew, but knew on the caveman level, and that was interesting to me. I noticed he was wearing a ring and said 'I can see you're married,' and he told me, 'But barely, barely.' That made me laugh. And I figured, I already did it the once, what's the difference? I guess I was hoping it would be more fulfilling than the first time in terms of, you know, the physical sensations. But it was exactly the same as with the carpenter."

Bob said, "And where did this happen?"

"With the supermarket guy?"

"Yes."

"At the supermarket."

"Where in the supermarket?"

"Romeo had a cot in his office. I call him Romeo because that was his name—that was the name on his name tag. And it looked like he was living in that office of his, so maybe he was telling the truth about being barely married."

Bob said, "What about the third guy."

"The third guy was a cop."

Bob held up his hand. He had heard enough and wished to hear no more. And he had no defense besides immaturity but he behaved with petulance that night, seized by jealousy, an emotion he'd hardly known before, but that now possessed him entirely. Connie placated him for a time, as much as she cared to, but soon she'd had enough of it and fell asleep. When Bob finally slept himself, his dreams were cuckold narratives, and he woke up with his upper body falling fully out of the bed. Connie still was sleeping; as Bob watched her face, he recognized the smallness of his behaviors and took hold of his emotions, waking Connie up to apologize to her. She welcomed him back with congratulations and assurances of her uncommon affections for him in particular, and again they succumbed to friendly tradition and again it was expedient but Bob told her he would soon become an expert love-maker and Connie said that she was certain it was so and that she was supportive of every manner of self-improvement.

Days later, and Bob and Connie were riding a bus together. They had no destination but were riding to ride, Connie attempting to show Bob what it was she liked about public transportation. In this she failed, or perhaps the failure was Bob's, but he never managed to achieve even a minor affection for the bus-riding act, which isn't to say he wasn't enjoying himself at this particular moment. By now they were immersed in their affinity for one another and their future was open before them. It was a time of sterling certitude and grand plans, a kingdom coming into focus through the lens of a telescope, and they were riding in silence across the southwest quadrant of the city, holding hands and gazing out the window in the dreamy way lovers sometimes did and do. Bob noticed an Italian eatery called Three Guys Pizza; he pointed and told Connie, "Look, there's your favorite restaurant." Connie read the sign and turned to Bob and was about to give voice to her response when the man across the aisle, a ruddy duffer in a tweed cap and London Fog trench coat, leaned over and asked Connie, "Excuse me miss, did I hear correctly that you're a fan of the pizzeria we just passed?" Bob said, "Oh, she's a very passionate fan of that pizzeria, sir. You should hear all the things she has to say about Three Guys." The duffer was impressed; he shook his head smartly to the side and issued a brief, sharp outbreath. Dinging the bell, he stood to exit. "I live nearby, you see," he explained. "And I love a good recommendation. Citizen to citizen, like in the animal kingdom—birds telling other birds what's coming their way, from one treetop to the next." The man flung up his tall collar, cinched his belt, and was away. Bob turned to Connie to communicate his surprise at the unexpected poetry of the moment. She still was watching Bob, not in a friendly or unfriendly way, but levelly. She had been holding on to her response during the duffer's interruption; now she passed it off for Bob to hold: "It's four guys including you, sweetheart. Four guys and counting."

ONE NIGHT, AFTER STAYING TOO LATE AT HIS APARTMENT, AND AFTER having drunk two too many fruit jars of wine, Bob laid himself out on Ethan's itchy green couch and made to pass his night there. He'd been asleep some hours when there came a knock at the door. Ethan crossed the room in his underwear to answer; he led a heavily perfumed female figure through the darkness and back into his bedroom. According to the noises made by the visitor, their communications were successful on a scale Bob could not fathom; which is to say that he truly did not understand what was going on in that room. He stared at the ceiling and waited for the noises to end. He smoked a cigarette, then lit a second off the first. When the duo at last achieved finale and completion, the noiselessness was so sudden and total, it was to Bob a noise in itself, and there came from somewhere deep in the building a round of applause, neighbors of Ethan's who were likely used to such sounds emanating from the apartment. In the morning Bob had a headache fashioned by the wine but also confusion, envy. He brewed a pot of coffee and sat at the kitchen table, waiting for Ethan and the woman to emerge from the bedroom, but then Ethan entered by the front door, alone, and with a pink box of pastries under his arm. "Good morning!" he said.

"Morning," said Bob. "Where's your screaming, agreeing friend?"

"She went home hours ago." Ethan poured himself a cup of coffee and sat at the table, waiting for the interrogation that he knew had to come. "So," Bob began. With this one word he was saying many things. He was saying, *So this is your life.* He was saying, *So that's the way lovemaking sounds for you.* He was saying, *I don't recognize those sounds in regards to my own lovemaking.* He was saying, *Is it all as nice for you as it seems?*

"Yeah," Ethan answered.

"But, who is she?"

"A woman I know."

"Where'd you meet her?"

"On the street."

"What?"

Ethan opened up the pink pastry box and perused its contents. "It was during a carless time of mine, and I was sitting at a bus stop on Broadway when she pulled up in a new Pontiac to ask me directions to the Rose Garden. She had Oregon plates and frankly, I didn't think she needed directions in the first place. 'All right,' I told her, 'you've got so much free time on your hands, why don't you give me a ride home?' That appeared to be what she was thinking about, anyway. And I hadn't meant it meanly, but she took offense, or pretended to take offense. Then my bus came and I got on. I forgot about her, but when I got off at my stop, there was the Pontiac again. 'Excuse me, young man,' she said." Ethan selected a pastry and took a bite, catching the crumbs with his free hand.

"And then what happened?"

"She said she supposed she was going my way after all. I got in her car and she drove me home."

"Then what?"

Ethan raised and lowered and raised and lowered his eyebrows.

Bob said, "Right off the bat?"

"Yep."

"Was this in the daytime?"

"Yep."

"And when was that?"

"End of last winter."

"How often do you see her?"

"Every couple weeks she shows up. There's no schedule; it's all down to her. I don't even have her phone number." Ethan pushed the pink box toward Bob but Bob couldn't focus on anything other than the discussion at hand.

"But who *is* she?" he asked again.

"I really can't tell you, Bob. I mean, that's a part of the whole deal. I know her first name is Pearl, and I know she's rich, and that she's married, though she acts like she's not—takes her ring off before coming up. Okay, fine. She wants to pretend about certain things and I'm comfortable with that. She told me once, 'The first time you ask me for money, Ethan, you'll never see me again.' Can you top that? She's always chasing after the upper hand, and I let her think she's got it, but she never will—not really she won't."

"Why not?"

"Because I truly don't care if she never comes back."

"But you welcome her when she does."

"*Welcome her* is a bit much. I don't turn her away, though, it's true."

"I think she probably felt welcome last night," Bob observed.

Ethan bowed in his seat. He took another bite of his pastry. "As time goes by, I think of my visits with Pearl, and the Pearls of the world, as practice. Because someday, buddy, I'm going to fall in love too, just like you. And when I do, that woman will be doted on to within an inch of her life." When Bob said the scenario felt a little dark or heartless to him, Ethan said he was giving the whole thing too much credence. "Really, it's just a small courtesy she and I are doing for one another, like holding the elevator open for a stranger." He patted the pink box. "These sticky buns are excellent, Bob."

Bob sat there smoking his cigarette and drinking his coffee and watching his friend and considering the vast differences of their respective experience. He hadn't yet introduced Connie to Ethan, but it was only now that he admitted to himself he'd been intentionally keeping them apart. It wasn't that he believed Connie would, against her own free will and faithfulness, swoon over Ethan for his profile and charisma; and neither did Bob think Ethan would utilize his tools to woo Connie away from him. His fear, or fearful belief, was that Connie and Ethan would both, upon meeting each other, come to learn and understand that they were true mates, truer than Connie and Bob could ever be. It felt paranoiac, but also commonsensible, true enough in its potential. For the first time in his life, Bob had love and friendship both, and all he had to do to maintain this was nothing at all. Thirty minutes later he sat out front of Ethan's apartment in the idling Chevy, and the danger of it was clear and vivid: he mustn't ever let them meet, he told himself. He would not let them meet.

THE SITUATION WITH CONNIE'S FATHER EVOLVED. CONNIE ARRIVED AT
the library an hour after Bob came on shift, her face swollen
and raw from crying. "Good morning, I've made an error."
The night before she had approached her father with news of
her relationship with Bob and it had not been well received.

Bob said, "Wasn't the plan to not tell him?"

"It was, but then I did, because I'm an idiot." She touched
her face. "Am I a mess or am I a mess?"

"You're a little bit of a mess."

She sighed. "I was trying to eat my cereal but he wouldn't
stop shouting, so I left."

"I thought you said you told him last night?"

"Yes, he was shouting then too. Finally he went to sleep
and I thought the shouting was over but when he woke up
it started all over again. And I'm not sure what to say other
than he's insane, and that I really am an idiot, and I don't
know what we're going to do." She retired to the restroom
to cry awhile longer. After, she and Bob sat together in the
break room to discuss what they might do about the situation.
Bob understood they were at a crossroads of some kind, and a
rare boldness possessed him and he put forth the idea that she
shouldn't go home at all, but stay at his house instead.

"What does that mean, 'stay'? Stay for how long?"

"For however long you want. For forever."

"What about the will?"

"What about it?"

"He says if I see you anymore he's going to cut off my inheritance. The money, the house, everything."

"Do you think he means it?"

"I don't know."

"Well, even if he does mean it, we don't really need anything from your father at all, do we? I have a house. I have money."

Connie looked confused, almost annoyed. "I'm sorry, what are you telling me?" she asked. "Are you proposing?"

"Do you want me to?"

"I guess I do."

"You guess you do."

"I do."

"Okay, I'm proposing."

"Okay, propose."

"Will you marry me?"

"You're supposed to get down on a knee to propose."

Bob got down on both knees. "Will you marry me?"

Miss Ogilvie had walked in at the point preceding Bob's question; before Connie could answer, she said, "Personal business elsewhere, Bob, thank you." She exited the room and Bob came up from his knees and led Connie outside. She said nothing about the question of marriage but agreed that Bob should pick her up that night, and that she would stay with him at least until the situation calmed or became clearer, and they worked over the details while waiting for Connie's bus.

At 11:55 p.m., Bob parked the Chevy across the street from Connie's father's house and cut the engine. The streetlight angled across the hood of the car, bisecting his torso; he held his wristwatch under the light to follow the sweep of the second hand. The street was quiet other than the ticking of the car. Midnight occurred and Bob stared at Connie's second-story bedroom window. His heart thrilled when he saw that it was slowly opening; but then it became stuck in its casing, and Connie shut the window to try again. Suddenly the window shot up with a loud *bang* which set off the barking of area dogs. When the barking died away, Connie's hand emerged from her darkened bedroom, and two suitcases came to rest on the roof above the porch. Bob exited the Chevy and slunk across the street and up the front yard to stand at the predetermined point of contact. Connie crept along, cases in hand; she tossed these to Bob, then knelt down and hop-dropped off the roof. Her skirt shot up and Bob noticed, for he couldn't not, that she wasn't wearing any underwear—a curious detail, but there was no time to consider it just then, as Connie landed on the grass, performing an impressive and unanticipateable paratrooper's forward somersault. Bob helped her stand and took up her suitcases and together they hurried across the street to the Chevy. As Connie sat, she realized she wasn't wearing underwear. "I'm not wearing any underwear!" she said, and Bob replied that yes, he had noticed, and so Connie suffered a short period of mortification. She explained she'd only just woken up and had dressed herself so quickly that she'd forgotten about her *bottoms*, as she called them. She said she was sorry for the visual, if the visual had been bothersome, and Bob told her it hadn't been and could never be, and besides that it was dark, and he was having a fun, funny time. He was a young librarian living through an adventure of love and his scandalized sweetheart was falling through the sky without underwear on and the Chevy's glasspacks were burbling reasonably in the summer night in Oregon. Bob drove across the river; the windows were down and the water gave off a coolness that poured into the car. Connie's hair was twirling up and up; she had what could be described as an amorous expression on her face.

"I will marry you, Monsieur Bob."

NINE DAYS LATER, CONNIE'S FATHER DROPPED DEAD WHILE WATERING the lawn out front of his house. Connie had left Bob's number with a neighbor-confidante, and now the neighbor rang up to share the news on a lazy Sunday afternoon. Bob lay on the sofa looking down the hall at Connie standing in the kitchen and talking on the phone; she wore a white apron and held a long wooden spoon in her hand and she was nodding, and the spoon was also nodding, in the style of a conductor's baton keeping time. "All right. Yes. Fine. Thank you." She set the phone in its cradle. "My father's dead," she called, then returned to the stove to stir the soup. Bob moved to the kitchen and came up behind her to hold her about the waist, but she was behaving frostily and so he steered back to the sofa. A voice told Bob he should let her be; after dinner, after she'd thought of it, she calmly told Bob that, while her father was not a bad man, he *was* a foolish one, foolish and bad-minded, and she'd decided she didn't want anything to do with his remains because he'd have enjoyed her discomfort in the face of them, and she refused to give him that final satisfaction. Bob said, "Remains." Connie explained, "I'm supposed to go to the coroner and funeral parlor, sign off on the arrangements. Well, I won't do it." She was recalling all the little indignities she and her mother had suffered under her father's vanity over the years and these memories were sitting poorly with her. Her anger was a healthy response, and Bob, unfond of the man himself, understood it, but he didn't like to see her graciousness marred in this way; also, he thought she might regret her behavior later. When Bob proposed that he take care of the arrangements, Connie told him, "You don't want to do that," and this was true, he didn't, but he said he thought he should do it anyway, unless she felt so strongly about it that she was prohibiting him from taking part. "I've never prohibited in my life, and I'm not about to start now," she said.

Bob was tasked with identifying the body at the coroner's ahead of its transportation to the funeral parlor, and he took the morning off work so that he could attend to this. The coroner was a friendly, unhealthy man; he led Bob to a broad white-tiled room with a single window casting a beam of sunlight over a gurney, upon which lay a body draped by a sheet. As they crossed over to meet the figure, the coroner explained to Bob that he had performed an autopsy on the corpse earlier that same morning. This was not the norm for a death by natural causes but had been done according to the express demand of the deceased. "The funeral parlor had a letter written by Mr. Coleman on file, which they passed off to me yesterday, in keeping with Mr. Coleman's orders. It was a little confusing to follow, but the gist was that the gentleman was phobic of murder by poison, and wanted someone to check him out postfact."

"Who did he think was going to poison him?" asked Bob.

"Well, the Vatican, is the short answer. The longer answer points to a group of priests living in the Forest Park area who Mr. Coleman believed had it in for him. The letter paints a clear picture of mental instability but I went ahead with the procedure, to be a sport."

"And was he poisoned?"

"He was not. His heart was faulty, and no sign of foul play whatsoever. One thing I will say that was unusual: this man had the lungs and liver of a nineteen-year-old boy. All shiny and clean like they'd never been used." When Bob explained about Connie's father's beliefs, the coroner said, "Yes, you could see he'd never taken a drink or a smoke. I suppose they tell themselves the lack is worth it. Personally, I'm happy as a clam to lose the fifteen years." Connie's father's letter had prompted a curiosity in the coroner, who asked Bob round-aboutly, almost apologetically, what the situation of the man's death had been. Bob spoke of Connie's father's unhappiness about the pending marriage of his daughter.

"And you're the groom-to-be?"

"That's right."

The coroner made the noise of understanding. "The so-called broken heart is the heart stilled by romantic disappointment or some other great loss—death of a child, say. And while the phenomenon does from time to time occur, death by sorrow is highly uncommon. What is far more common is death by bitterness, outrage—pique. It sounds to me that this man died from pique." As he spoke he began rolling back the sheet to expose Connie's father's corpse. There was a staged effect to this which brought to Bob's mind the magician's elegance of gesture: voilà.

"Is this your man?"

"That's him."

The coroner watched Bob making his survey of the deceased, the light of curiosity still glowing in his eyes. Bob gamely explained his dislike of Connie's father, naming all of his shortcomings and awfulnesses. Bob was becoming impassioned in his critique when he caught himself and smiled at the coroner, who was listening with evident interest and enjoyment. Bob said, "You must hear all sorts of sordid family gossip in your line."

"All sorts, yes. I'm not really supposed to say it, but the truth is that it's a fascinating position." He went about covering Connie's father back up. In a wistful voice he said, "Really, though, you should have seen this man's liver and lungs. They were right off the assembly line, new in the box."

When Bob got home the radio was on but Connie wasn't in the house. He found her in the backyard, digging up weeds. She'd outfitted herself in some old clothes of Bob's, and she told him, "Just you wait. I'm going to make this garbage dump into something special." Bob sat on the patchy grass, watching her as she worked and waiting for her to ask after his visit to the coroner's. When she didn't ask, Bob told her he'd be glad to discuss his experience if she wished him to; but, she said she didn't care to hear of it. She thanked Bob for his assistance, and Bob told her, "You're welcome." There was no funeral service and the whereabouts of the ashes remained a mystery. Six weeks after Bob had viewed the corpse a lawyer sent a letter to Connie explaining she would receive nothing from her father's estate. But she'd already known and accepted this, and so the letter held no weight of consequence with her. Bob watched as she deposited the letter, with comical care, into the trash can under the kitchen sink. Her face read of unaffected amusement, and he loved her very dearly.

THE PROBLEM WITH KEEPING ETHAN AND CONNIE SEPARATED WAS
that they both came to the library regularly. First there
were the close calls, with Connie leaving just before Ethan's
arrival, or vice versa. Then there was the unhappy instant
of the both of them being in the library simultaneously,
only each wasn't aware of the other's presence, and Bob
said nothing about it, and so they somehow avoided com-
mingling. But then one day at the Information desk, early
in the evening and to Bob's ripe horror, Connie and Ethan
came into the library together, and Ethan was guiding her
by her elbow, and they were laughing. They approached
and stood before Bob, presenting themselves; Ethan did
not let go of Connie's arm; Connie's face was flushed with
pleasure. Bob instructed himself to play along, to mimic
their mischievous gladness, but the unpleasant surprise he
knew was so thorough that the best he could do was offer
up a blank look. "What happened?" he asked.

"Do you want to tell him?" Ethan asked Connie.

"I'll tell him."

"Tell him if you want to tell him," Ethan said.

"Let me tell him." Connie spoke to Bob while looking at Ethan:
"Well," she said. "I was riding the bus and minding nobody's

business but my own when I realized the man across the aisle was staring at me. And everyone likes to be stared at from time to time, but after a while I'd had enough of it and asked him, you know, to please stop. And he did stop—for about three and a half seconds. But then he's back to staring and I'm starting to get a little worried, because for all I know I'm dealing with an active pervert, and so I'm looking around for another seat to sit in but there aren't any, and finally I take out my book and start reading, or pretending to read, because this way he can see that I'm busy and not interested, right? So a minute goes by, and now I'm really reading, and I've pretty much forgotten about the pervert peeper across the aisle when he reaches over and he *taps his finger* on the open page of my book. And when I look up he's all leaned over, his face serious, and he says to me—"

"You're not telling it right," said Ethan.

"I'm not? Sure I am."

Ethan told Bob, "She's not telling it right."

"Why don't you tell it, then," Connie said.

"Okay, I will." Ethan took a minute to locate himself. "Well, look Bob," he said, "I *was* staring at her. And I'm sorry. But when I got on the bus I noticed her sitting there all upright and prim, and how could I not stare. And I was staring for the normal boy-girl reasons but there was also another reason underneath the normal ones, which was that there was something funny about this person, some sort of question hanging in the air around her. Had I met her before, or seen her somewhere else? There was just this . . . *thing* about her, but I couldn't place it. Then she reaches into her bag and pulls out a book, and I see that it's a library book. And not just any library book but *Crime and Punishment*. And not just any copy of *Crime and Punishment*, but the very same one I had checked out, with the title smudged and the stain on the spine. And the minute I saw that, then the mystery was solved because I knew absolutely who she was."

"And he leaned over and he said to me—"

"Let me tell it. It's my punch line. I leaned over and said to her, 'You're Connie, and I'm Ethan, and I think we need to have a discussion, because we're both in love with the same man, and I can't go on sharing him like this.'"

The pair resumed laughing, and here Bob wished to vanish, or for Ethan to vanish, or Connie, or all three of them. He also wished Ethan and Connie would stop enjoying each other, and he strongly wished Ethan would take his hand off her elbow. Connie's laughter trailed away, and now she was watching Bob with a crooked, curious expression. "What's the matter, honey?" she asked, and Bob answered that he was fine, just that it had been a long day.

Ethan and Connie decided they should all three go out to dinner, and they waited together on the sidewalk outside while Bob began the process of shutting the library down. He stole glances out the window as he righted the chairs and turned off the lights; Connie was laughing again, and she and Ethan were standing close to one another. Bob locked the door and walked down the path toward the sidewalk. Connie was facing away from him but Ethan looked up as Bob approached. When he saw Bob, his smile faded and his face softened into a look of concern, or kindness, as if he suddenly understood that Bob was in pain, and why. Bob felt an ache of shame but wished to keep it private.

It was a cold walk on hard concrete. Connie was positioned in between Bob and Ethan, and she did not take Bob's arm as was usual, but walked alone and independent of him. When he felt he couldn't stand it, he took her hand in his, but she quickly removed it and put it in her pocket. By the time they arrived at the restaurant, Ethan wasn't behaving as before. He was quieter, almost formal as he asked about their wedding plans, and whether or not they would honeymoon, and would they have children, and how many? It made for poor conversation, and Connie tried to lead Ethan back to himself by asking teasing questions: How long had he been a masher on buses? And what was his success rate? Was there honor among mashers? If he got on a bus to mash, for example, and found another masher already onboard, did he then exit the bus to give his mashing peer room to work without competition? When this line failed to get a rise, Connie made to engage Ethan in some banter against Bob, but Ethan would only praise Bob's influence, declarations of admiration that Bob felt were rooted in pity.

Altogether the meal was, for Bob, a spectacle of emotional discomfort. At its conclusion Ethan snatched the bill out of the surprised waiter's hand and made a play at casual largesse by paying for the dinner, though he was broke, and Bob knew he was broke. After Ethan had hurried off and gone, the silence he left behind was a wretched creature, and Bob couldn't tell where his insecurity ended and the factual dreadfulness began. He and Connie walked back to the library, and the Chevy; all the way home, they spoke hardly a word to one another. Entering the house, Connie said she was sorry his friend hadn't liked her. When Bob asked her what she meant she said, "First he's as friendly as a puppy, right? Then at dinner he hardly says a thing to me other than to grunt, and God forbid he should look me in the eye."

"He felt shy, maybe."

"Not before dinner he wasn't. And on the bus he was the least shy man I've ever met in my life. Anyway, why would he become shy around me? Didn't you say he's some kind of playboy?"

"What does that have to do with anything?"

"I just mean that I'm plain."

"No, you're not. But what does the way you look have to do with Ethan?"

"Nothing. I don't know. I'm sorry."

"Why are you sorry?"

"Bob, stop." She busied herself taking off her coat and hanging it on the peg in the hall. She stood watching the wall. "I want your friend to like me, okay? It's important to me that he and I get along." Bob didn't take his coat off. He walked upstairs and lay down on top of the comforter, listening to Connie making the usual house-at-night noises downstairs: water on and off, back door open and shut, lights clicking off. Bob hadn't named his concern, but by the way he was behaving it must have been obvious he had again been overtaken by a jealousy. He felt he was making himself unattractive, but no matter how he approached it he couldn't think of a way to force the jealousy to cease. As he lay there squirming in his unhappiness, he became aware that Connie's house-at-night noises were growing more pronounced—she was banging and clattering things around in the kitchen with more force than was necessary. Bob listened with care and interest—yes, she was definitely expressing an anger. Bob thought she had considered the source of his concern, translated it, and now knew a sense of insult, which rather than bringing Bob to a place of remorse or sorrow made him soothed and hopeful. Was it not likely, after all, that Connie's anger meant she didn't recognize Bob's fear as plausible, or even possible? As the banging and clattering grew louder, so did Bob's relief grow. When Connie came upstairs she was stomping her feet and cursing under her breath and Bob was more or less thrilled. She took an angry shower and got into her pajamas angrily, punching her feet through the leg holes; she sat down hard on the edge of the bed and glared at Bob, who calmly explained that he loved her so much it had made him a little bit crazy that night, and that he was very sorry if he had insulted her, or insulted their life. It was a process for them to arrive at a place where Connie forgave him, but after, late in the night, Bob took her hand in his, and she didn't pull away from him. In the morning Bob issued a warning to himself. He hadn't understood the fallibility of their pact; now he saw that it was not a permanent structure but something that had to be cared for and tended to. He was afraid of what he'd done and by the way he'd behaved and he told himself that the only way forward was to believe in what he and Connie had made and to protect it.

There followed a period of four or five weeks where Bob heard no word from Ethan; and neither did Bob contact him. Bob was glad for them to take the break, but also bothered by it, because it seemed to confirm his fears. Twice through the course of the month Connie asked after Ethan, and both times she was playing toward a casualness, but Bob disliked that she was considering him at all. He told himself he was willing to forgo the friendship with Ethan if it meant he didn't have to feel so badly as before; but really, it was more complicated than that. At some points during this lull he missed Ethan terribly, and he thought of the pair of them walking up the sidewalk at night, and they'd had three of four drinks each and were talking volubly, oblivious to all but the thoughts and considerations they passed back and forth, huddling against the cold. For the rest of his life, whenever Bob thought of his former alliance with Ethan, this was the scenario that came to mind: the two of them hurrying along, talking over one another and laughing, cigarette smoke pooling in their wake. Where were they going in such a rush as that? And what were they discussing with such enthusiasm?

From the start of their friendship Bob had wondered who Ethan was when they were apart, but it happened only once that he caught a glimpse of Ethan in his element. It was a foggy morning and Bob was reading the newspaper at the Information desk when a car pulled up across the street, a rattling junker filled with young men and women, loud and jeering, 7:15 a.m. Ethan sat in the backseat, crammed in with the rest; he made to exit the car but as he stepped on the sidewalk the hands of his friends reached up and pulled him back in. This happened twice more before he finally broke free, the collar of his T-shirt stretched out, his hair yanked up in a shock, and he stood facing his fellows, bowing grandly as balled trash rained down on his skull and shoulders. When the car puttered away Ethan disappeared up the steps and to his apartment. Bob returned to his paper but the text was elusive to him, and he could think only of Ethan's gloriously shambling homecoming.

Forty-five minutes later Ethan walked into the library. He'd showered and changed and combed his hair, and he offered a calm good morning greeting before making a sober appraisal of the latest books Bob had recommended to him. He didn't mention anything about his late night; Bob understood by this that Ethan thought of him as a serious person, someone he might learn from or better himself by, but one who might not need to hear all the details of his social life. This was not unflattering, but there was also some part of Bob that wished he could have been in that rattling car, coming home when most are waking up, after a full night spent in what had to have been the most thorough and joyful kind of sin. What did Ethan see in Bob, then? Was Bob exotic in his plainness? Was he merely a straight man for Ethan? How had it happened that these two people should become friends? Connie believed it was important that someone as isolated as Bob not abandon his one friendship, which was logical, sound; but he did nothing to bridge the gap and had accepted that the era of his having a male companion had passed. Finally, though, Ethan came to see Bob at the library. He wore a tailored suit and overcoat, his hair was cut short, he was tanned, and he had a puzzled expression on his face. At his side there stood an attractive, elegant young woman whom he introduced as his fiancée, and that her name was Eileen.

EILEEN WAS NOT CHARMING BUT HAD CONTEMPLATED CHARM AND could perform a version of it that was convincing so long as you didn't inspect it very closely. She was not shy, was not capable of shyness, and she did not seem to be in possession of a sense of humor; at any rate she was not funny on purpose. Ethan stood by watching as his fiancée communicated with his friend, and the puzzled expression that had read on his face when he'd entered the library remained. He wasn't unhappy; he had the look of a man unsure of his location. Eileen was saying to Bob, "We came here to invite you out to dinner tonight."

"You and Connie both," Ethan added.

"That's why we came here," Eileen said.

Bob explained that he and Connie had plans for dining in with their neighbors that night, but invited Ethan and Eileen to join the group, and he named a time, and that they needn't bring anything other than themselves. After the couple left the library, Bob telephoned Connie to tell her the news.

"Well," said Connie, "what's this fiancée like? I suppose she's very beautiful."

"Yes," Bob said.

"And in the personality department?"

"She doesn't give a lot of clues about that."

"Still waters, maybe."

"Maybe not," Bob said. Connie was evidently happy at this attack on Eileen's personality, and Bob began to dread the thought of the dinner and he moved slowly toward it with a foot-dragging petulance. When he arrived at home, Connie was upstairs getting ready for the evening. She was humming a jazzy tune, and when she came downstairs Bob saw that she was wearing makeup, a fancier-than-normal dress, and heeled shoes. Before he could catch himself, he asked, "Why are you all dressed up?" Connie stood up straight to let her disappointment shine, then said, "Bob, if you think I'm not going to make myself look nice to meet your best friend and his fiancée, then I don't know what to tell you other than that you should consider going and fucking yourself." Which was fair enough, after all; and the words had the effect of a splash of cold water on Bob's face. He apologized and Connie accepted the apology and together they set the dining room table.

Ethan and Eileen arrived thirty minutes early. Bob was getting dressed upstairs when he heard the doorbell; he came down to find Connie and Eileen standing face-to-face and making their greetings while Ethan lurked to the side, wearing another tailored suit, and staring blankly at Bob. He made a *drink* gesture, and Bob made a *follow me* gesture, and they moved to the kitchen, where Bob poured them each a tumbler of whiskey. Ethan bolted his, and said, "Thanks, I needed that." He held out his glass for a refill, which Bob gave him, and which he again drank down. "Thanks, I needed that."

"What's the matter?" asked Bob.

"Nothing. No, something. It's hard to say. I'll admit to a degree of disorientation, but that's as far as I'll go right now. Let's talk about something else, maybe."

"All right," said Bob. "Why are you so tan and how many suits do you have now?"

"I've been in Acapulco and I've got seven suits."

"Why were you in Acapulco and why do you have seven suits?"

"I was working as a waiter in a resort there; Eileen's family has a tailor."

"Why did Eileen's family's tailor make you seven suits?"

"It was my idea that I should have *a* suit, for the wedding. But Eileen said that every man should have seven, and I went along with that, because why wouldn't I."

"Who's paying the tailor?"

"The father, I think."

"What does he do?"

"Something with boats."

"Shipping?"

"Anyway there are ships. Maybe it's that he builds them. I can't get to the bottom of it because it's hard to talk to Eileen's father because he's such a hateable little pigman."

"And what does he think of you?"

"Not so much, buddy. But he says he's not that worried about me because he's met my type before and that we always come to a bad end." Ethan shrugged, as if to say that time would tell. Bob corked the whiskey bottle and he and Ethan went in search of Connie and Eileen and found them seated at the dining room table, and they were drinking red wine and Eileen was saying, "Ethan was our waiter at the resort. And he was not very good at recalling our orders or bringing us what we wanted in a timely style, but he *was* good at seducing me, which he did without any sort of shame whatever, and in broad daylight, isn't that right, Ethan?"

"Yes, that's right," Ethan answered.

"Wait," Connie said. "I've missed a detail or two. How is it that Ethan was working in a resort in Acapulco?"

Ethan raised a finger. "One day in the market I was approached by a headhunter working for a hospitality firm with ties all over Mexico, and who offered me a job as a waiter in a resort down there. It's seasonal work, and the deal is, they bring down a fresh crop of young men for three-month stretches. We're assigned ten tables each, three meals a day, and a lot of the customers stay for weeks at a time, so you wind up getting to know people fairly well." Ethan made his hand into a gun and shot Eileen. "I never really did get the hang of the job, it's true. All the bowing and hurrying. You'd think a lukewarm egg was the end of the actual world."

Connie asked Eileen, "Were your parents impressed by this news of your plans to marry a waiter?"

"Oh, no, it's been a terrific scandal," said Eileen. "Mother slapped me right across my face! I did mention that, didn't I, Ethan? About Mother slapping me across my face?"

"You mentioned it, yes," said Ethan.

"And Daddy kicked over the cocktail caddy in protest, then walked across broken glass and there were little bloody footprints all over the veranda. Did I tell you about the cocktail caddy, Ethan? And the little bloody footprints all over the veranda?" Ethan was filling Eileen's not-empty wineglass. He placed the glass in her hand and she drank without awareness she was drinking. "Mother did admit," Eileen continued, "that if she were younger it would have been her running through the cane with Ethan. I think that's sweet, really, don't you, Ethan? She recognizes your value as a male specimen. Oh, but Daddy can't hear Ethan's name without spitting. Mother says he's after disowning me but it's too late, because I'm of age, and I've already received the bulk of my legacy."

"And have you mapped out your plans?" said Connie.

"So much as they can be. Marriage first. We want to get that over with right away."

"Will you have a large wedding?"

"Oh, yes. My extended family is sizable and they all want to get a good look at the cad I've given my person to. After the wedding, we'll get out of that hovel of Ethan's—which is where we've been staying, if you can believe it—and find a house in the area. Decoration and renovation while we honeymoon, and when we come home, then we'll start our family. I want five children." Ethan was again topping off her glass. "Yes, it's quite full, Ethan, thank you." She held her hair back and bent her head to sip at the wine without lifting the glass, which she could not have done without causing a spill. "We'll have to find some sort of career for this layabout," she said, "but so far we can't name what that might be. Have you thought any more about what that might be, Ethan?"

"I haven't," said Ethan.

Eileen asked, "Don't you think you should think about it?"

"I think I probably should," Ethan said, sensibly. He turned to Bob. "I'm hungry."

"You're early. We're waiting on the neighbors."

It was only recently that Bob and Connie had established a rapport with the colorfully named Chance and Chicky Bitsch. They were genus *Suburbiana*: jolly drinkers and avid bridge players and bowlers; they chain-smoked Pall Malls and entertained nightly or nearly nightly. Chicky was the bartender and ashtray-emptier while Chance posted up at the stove, speaking through a veil of cigarette smoke, one eye clamped shut as he prepared his signature dish, a pepper-heavy boulder stew. Chance was a veteran of the Second World War, and while he rarely discussed his combat experience, Bob and Connie got the impression he'd seen extravagant grisliness there and now was devoted only to his comforts and leisure. Chicky was devoted to Chance and was not displeased by her earthly position, but still and she suffered regrets, a feeling of missed opportunity that comes to so many taking part in the matrimonial custom. When the Bitsches finally arrived they were fifteen minutes late, ice-clinking drinks and cigarettes in hand, apologizing for their tardiness, asking what they had missed, wondering if they should ever be forgiven for their rudeness and further-more whether or not they deserved forgiveness. They were introduced to Ethan and then Eileen, who instantly asked after the origin of their surname. Chance, sitting, said, "My grandfather's name was Heinrich Bitschofberger. He immi-grated to the States by way of Dresden in advance of the First World War. Arriving in San Francisco, a helpful customs clerk pruned the name down for him. The clerk's identity has been lost to time, sadly. I know my father would have liked to speak with him. He, the clerk, told my grandfather that Bitsch was a 'good, strong, American name.'"

"You believe the clerk was being intentionally comical?" Eileen asked.

"I believe he believed he was being, yes."

"Have you considered changing your name back to the original?"

"I've considered it. But when it comes down to actually performing the deed a defiance rises up in me and I elect to stay put."

"And why?"

Chance sat a while, wondering how to put it. Looking at his wife, he said finally, "We are the Bitsches."

Chicky explained that their being late was due to her im-mersion in an article she'd been reading in *Time* magazine, an exposé of the raucous and scandalizing goings-on at an

East Coast liberal arts college that stoked and enflamed her sense of missing out. "These kids have it all sussed out," she said. "They're screwing in bushes."

"Screwing in bushes is not a new thing," said Chance. "Remember the Garden of Eden?"

"You never screwed me in bushes."

"I didn't know you wanted me to."

"It's not the sort of thing a lady should have to ask for. Anyway, it was a very interesting article. These art students are some lucky bunch, I'll say."

"Do you suffer the artistic impulse?" Eileen asked.

"Not at all. It was more the social aspect of the school I found intriguing. The article made it sound like a perfectly civilized four-year orgy. But here I've never been with another man besides Chance."

"I think we're all about the same, though, no?" said Chance.

"I feel doubt about that," Chicky admitted.

"Has it ever occurred to you that I'm the best there is?"

"That hadn't occurred to me, no." Chicky turned to Connie. "Understand, please, my fondness for the man. I adore him, yes?"

"Of course," said Connie. They were nodding at each other and Bob became uneasy because it seemed that they were drawing unflattering parallels.

Chance asked Connie, "Bob ever screw you in bushes, honey?"

"He never did, no."

"Some men, these men of ours," Chicky said.

Eileen said, "Ethan screwed me in bushes in Acapulco."

"Okay, wow," said Chicky, rolling up imaginary sleeves. "Now we're getting somewhere."

Connie said, "I thought you'd said it was in the cane."

"It was in the cane as well as in bushes."

Chicky slowly raised her glass in salute. "Best of god-damned luck to the both of you, and a long life to boot." Now she saw her glass was empty, and reached for Chance's, which also was empty. "I guess we should switch to wine, Chancey, what do you think?"

Chance was frowning; he told Bob, "She wants me to screw her in bushes, all she's got to do is ask. But I'm not a mind reader."

Dinner arrived and was consumed. Everyone praised the meal other than Eileen, who had made a long and thorough investigation of her plate before eating only half of what she'd been served. Chance and Chicky volunteered to clear the table, stacking and shuttling the dishes from the dining room and into the kitchen. Bob heard the soft squeak of the screen door opening and closing. Connie, meanwhile, sat watching Eileen. "I hope you were satisfied with your supper?" she asked. Eileen said, "It was very interesting, thank you. I've heard of meat loaf's existence, but this was my first experience with it in person." Connie took the blow, rallied, and announced that the dessert course would come next. She made for the kitchen to plate it and Ethan jumped up to help, leaving Bob alone with Eileen, who held her wineglass to her cheek, looking vaguely away. As though replying to something Bob had said, she told him, "It *is* a shame, that he's not wealthy into the bargain."

"Oh?" said Bob.

"Yes. If he was rich he would be, absolutely, the perfect man." She took a long drink of wine. "I keep telling my mother 'But Mother, once he's married, he *will* be rich.' 'Not like we are,' she says. '*Exactly* like we are,' I say. 'And by the same money.' But no, she insists it isn't the same."

"No, I suppose it's not." In looking at Eileen, Bob felt he

could say anything in the world to her, that he could admit to some enormous sin and that it would have no effect whatever. "It must be nice, wealthiness," he said.

"Oh, I like it very much. Of course it has its own problems, like anything."

"Yes," said Bob. "And what are the problems?"

"Well, to fight for something, if and when you win it, it becomes more yours than if you're simply given it. This ranges from little things to much larger."

"And so," Bob said, "when one doesn't have to fight, then what?"

"To not have to fight may lead to—complacency." She spoke the word as if it represented a state of depravity.

"Have you ever succumbed to complacency?"

"I've not known it in the first hand," she said. "But it would be a bald lie to claim never to've seen it in others."

Connie and Ethan returned and distributed the dessert portions, cherry pie with a thick wedge of Neapolitan ice cream.

"Oh, I love cherry pie," said Eileen. "Is it homemade?"

Connie performed a small collapse. "It was homemade by the woman in the supermarket, and God bless her crampy little hands." Ethan laughed hard at this; Eileen made a face of not seeing what was funny.

Ethan and Connie had returned to the same state as that first day they'd met, when they'd entered the library together, happy with themselves and each other. Bob watched as Ethan reached out to touch Connie's forearm. He was only making a punctuative gesture, but it continued for such a duration, and Bob believed that this contact pleased Connie, so that he felt a quick queasiness. No sooner had Ethan and Connie finished their desserts than they began stacking dishes and gathering the cutlery, and again they went away to the kitchen, this time to do the washing up together. Eileen watched them leaving with a glazed expression; she'd drunk too much, too quickly. Reaching up to draw a lock of hair away from her face she toppled her wineglass, afterward contemplating the liquid as it soaked into the lace tablecloth. Bob sat there thinking of what it would be like to be married to this person, and decided it would be partly but not thoroughly terrible. It would be lonely. He didn't understand Ethan's decision to marry her, and he didn't understand why she was in his home. Connie's laughter sounded from the kitchen, and Eileen and Bob were looking in the direction of the noise. Again the screen door opened and shut and Chicky came in correcting her dress and picking pieces of grass from her hair. "Well, he screwed me in bushes," she announced as she sat down. Chance entered the dining room smoking a cigar.

"How was it?" Bob asked.

Chicky made the half-and-half gesture; Chance said, "What are you talking about? It was great." The chatter and laughter from the kitchen continued and Bob wondered how it was possible the dishes weren't done yet. Eileen's face had gone pale and she told Bob, "I'm going to lie down for a little while, if you don't mind." She moved to the living room; Bob heard the couch groan. He went into his head for a time and when he returned he decided he was ready for his guests to leave his house. He called out to Ethan that Eileen was ill.

"What did he say?" Bob heard Connie ask.

"That Eileen is ill."

"Eileen is not well?"

"She has suffered a spell."

"Has she toppled and fell?"

"Shall we give her a pill?"

Their laughter was a raspy cackling and Chicky sat watching Bob with a look imparting, he thought, condolence. He forced his face into a smile, to show he was not bothered, that there was nothing to be bothered by; but Chicky's eyes were cold and staring. Connie still was laughing and Bob was no longer smiling and Eileen started retching, then loudly throwing up wine and meat loaf on the carpet in the living room, and everyone came into the room to watch, and after she was done then the dinner party also was done.

THE ENGAGEMENT WITH EILEEN DIDN'T LAST OUT THE MONTH. BOB found out from Ethan, who called him at work and told him, "I'm at the hospital."

"Has someone been hurt?" Bob asked.

"I've been hurt. I'm still hurt, actually. Will you come visit me? There's no one fun to talk to here." Bob took a long lunch break, stopping for a bouquet of flowers on the way. When he arrived at the hospital he found Ethan abed, bored-looking but apparently healthy. When he made to sit up, though, he winced in what Bob took for significant pain. Bob pulled up a chair and asked what had happened. "The whole thing started," Ethan said, "with Eileen's mother, Georgie."

Georgie, Ethan told Bob, was Eileen but twenty-five years older, and hardened by a life of lovelessness and languor. She could drink a bottle of champagne at brunch with never so much as a slur, she smoked two packs of cigarettes a day, and her pastime was viciousness, directed at her daughter in the morning hours and her husband after the sun set. Georgie endeavored to get Ethan off on his own and she succeeded without very much trouble at all, for she wore her age and vices well, and Ethan had not met a woman before who thought so little of telling him precisely what she wanted him to do. Georgie was a force, and she had style, and for a time these two were simpatico. "The other waiters got wind of my position and explained my good fortune to me. All I had to do was keep the husband in the dark and at season's end I'd have a hundred-dollar tip and fond memories to boot. Fine, but there was Eileen, looking up at me as I poured her coffee, and I just had to engage with her. Georgie got wind of the budding friendship and made to head us off at the pass but it was too late, we'd already broke bread. Broken bread. The bread was in pieces."

"So, the story you're telling me," Bob said, "is that you made love to your fiancée's mother."

"No, Georgie wasn't my fiancée's mother at the time of our entanglement. If we have to name a crime here, I guess you could say that I became engaged to the daughter of a woman I'd had an affair with."

"So there was never any overlap?"

"That's not a very friendly question, Bob. But yes, all right, preceding the engagement there was overlap, and yes, it became messy and complex. There was a lot of running around and ducking into closets, things like that. Each woman wore a strong perfume but not the same brand; I've never taken so many showers in my life. I managed to keep my relationship with Georgie hidden from Eileen and Eileen's father but there were some very close shaves, and the stress level was high, and between the romantic cloak-and-dagger and the work schedule I wasn't sleeping hardly at all. Around the same time Georgie and I started falling apart, Eileen and I became engaged. She told her folks and they packed up and dragged her to the airport. And that would have been that but for the fact of their living in Portland. Eileen's folks had me fired, you see, and I was sent home, and so we all four were on the same flight back. When we landed, Eileen came away with me and we stayed in my apartment for however many weeks it took for me to figure out, you know, I could never marry this person."

Bob said, "I didn't understand the quickness of the engagement."

"I was confused by that also."

"So it was her idea?"

"If you want to get technical, it was my idea. But really, I had only meant it as that—an idea."

"Something to discuss."

"Something to bat around."

"Something to chew on."

"Put a pin in it, consider it later. But then she agreed with such—aggression. Anyway, yesterday was the day where I finally told her we'd have to call it all off."

"And how did that go?"

"Bad, badly. Yelling and tears, cursing, the breaking of cups and plates, leaving, returning—she kept returning. Her point, and it was a fair point, was that she had already debased herself by agreeing to marry a waiter, ruining her standing. And then this same waiter breaks off the engagement? It's a double ruining." He shifted in his bed and again there was the look of pain.

Bob said, "I still don't understand why you're in the hospital?"

"Oh, I'm sorry. Eileen tried to kill me." He pulled down the collar of his hospital smock, revealing a stitched wound four or five inches below the left clavicle. "She stuck a steak knife in me while I was sleeping. We'd been fighting all afternoon and evening and I'd dozed off on the couch. When I woke up she was standing over me with a funny look on her face and her suitcase by her feet. 'Where you going?' Then I noticed the knife handle sticking out of my chest. Wait'll you see the X-rays. The doctor says she missed the heart by millimeters."

Bob sat considering this tale, and the way it existed in contrast to Ethan's apparent amusement, when a nurse entered with a questioning face. "Are you behaving yourself?"

"Hello, Roberta. Yes, I am. Look, look at the flowers."

"Oh, my goodness." She saw Bob and asked, "Did your friend bring you flowers?"

"He sure did. What do you think about that?"

"I think that's just nice. Let's get them in some fresh water." Roberta located a vase and filled it with water. She unwrapped the flowers and arranged them in the vase and set this down on the table at the foot of the bed. "I'll leave them here so you can enjoy them."

"Thank you, Roberta. Enjoying the flowers is important to me."

Roberta was patting the flowers this and that way. "I'll put some sugar in the water," she said to Bob. "That makes the flowers stand up and say hello." She left the room to seek the sugar out.

"Where was I in the story?" Ethan asked.

"You were lying there stabbed."

"I was lying there, stabbed," said Ethan. "And Eileen was gone and I just figured, okay, this is the end. But then time passed and I felt fine. A little bit tingly in the feet and hands, but otherwise all was as usual. I wasn't about to take the knife out myself though, and I did crave the advice of a medical professional, so I put on my pants and slippers, no shirt, and went down to the pay phone on the corner. I made myself understood to the operator, then sat down in the booth and went to sleep, or maybe fainted, then I woke up here and the knife was gone and they won't give it back to me and I think they lost it, actually. My one nice knife."

"How are you feeling now?"

"I'm sore as hell and it's uncomfortable to breathe but I didn't die and I don't have to get married. So, all things considered, I'm fine."

"And where is Eileen?"

"I don't know."

"Has she been arrested?"

"Oh, no. I'm not going to press charges or anything like that."

"Why not?"

"I don't think that would be very gentlemanly, do you?"

"I'm not sure there's a precedent for such a thing."

"What do you mean?"

"I mean, I don't know that a gentleman would have found himself in the position in the first place."

"Okay, touché. But that only leads to my next point. I've been lying in this bed thinking about my habits and behaviors, Bob. And it seems to me that I've been spoiling for a stabbing for a good little minute, here."

Bob didn't disagree, or he didn't disagree strongly, and he let the statement alone. He asked Ethan, "So is this to be your new-leaf moment, and now you'll become chaste and worthy?"

"I don't really know. Maybe this is just my lot in life. But I can't claim that the violence against me was unearned, and I've decided to take my medicine without any gripes." In a summing-up tone of voice, he said, "I'm not malicious, but I am careless. I don't know that I know how to change, or if I even want to, but I'm thinking about the kind of man I want to be for the first time in my life, so there's your silver lining."

Roberta returned with the sugar for the flowers and news that it was time for Bob to leave Ethan to his rest. Ethan said he didn't need rest but Roberta disagreed. She told Bob, "You can come back tomorrow."

"I'll come back tomorrow," Bob told Ethan.

"Bring Connie," Ethan told Bob.

"Who's Connie?" Roberta asked Ethan, but he didn't answer and neither did Bob. He waved and was away down the corridor. The next day he returned with Connie. When they entered the room, Ethan was sitting up in bed and reading from a stack of papers. "Well," he said. Connie had been alarmed by Bob's explanation of what had landed Ethan in the hospital; and though she was soothed by Ethan's healthful demeanor, when she saw his knife wound, then did her alarm return, alarm that soon gave way to upset, and finally anger directed at Ethan and Bob both for treating a potentially fatal event as though it were only a lark or trifle. She asked what in the world was the matter with them, and they said they didn't know what. She wanted to have Eileen arrested and said that if Ethan wouldn't call the police then she would. Here Ethan held up the papers and said, "Even if I wanted to press charges, and I don't, I couldn't."

"Why not?" Connie demanded.

"I'll explain," Ethan said, "but only if you'll stop yelling at Bob and me."

She crossed her arms and was silent. Ethan said that just before Bob and Connie arrived, Eileen's father had come to visit, along with an associate of his, a funereal little man holding a briefcase. Eileen's father's attitude toward Ethan was cool at first; he was behaving as if he had just happened to be passing by and had paused to offer an impartial salutation. But soon enough he named the purpose of the visit, which was that he wanted to know what to expect in terms of legal repercussions so far as his daughter was concerned. Why hadn't Ethan contacted the police yet? Ethan explained, almost reluctantly, as he didn't like the idea of giving Eileen's father what he wanted, his disinclination to bring Eileen to justice.

"Would you sign an agreement to that effect?" Eileen's father asked.

"I don't see why I should," Ethan told him.

Eileen's father looked to his comrade, who took an envelope from his briefcase and passed this to Eileen's father, who passed it to Ethan. It held a cashier's check for ten thousand dollars, made out in Ethan's name. Ethan stared at the numerals. Eileen's father said that he understood his daughter had misbehaved. Ethan told him, "There's misbehavior and there's misbehavior."

"You signed?" asked Connie.

"Yes."

"So you're rich," said Bob.

"I'm a little bit rich."

"And now what?"

"I don't know. I mean, this happened fifteen minutes ago. I guess I'll make plans? Heal? They're discharging me tomorrow morning. Can you come get me and drop me at my apartment, Bob? You'll get your weekly cardiovascular exercise helping me up the stairs."

"Sure," said Bob.

Connie was shaking her head, her face descriptive of both amusement and contempt. "I'm asking again: What, in the world, is the matter with you two?" Ethan and Bob looked on, not understanding. Connie explained, "You're coming to stay with us until you're well again, Ethan."

THE HOUSE ACHIEVED A NEW ASPECT BY ETHAN'S PRESENCE, WHICH for Bob took some getting used to. Each weekday morning while Connie and Ethan slept, Bob rose and began his preparations for the workday; only now he no longer lit his fire, or fixed himself a full breakfast, actions that Connie said would cause a disturbance and work at cross-purposes with Ethan's rehabilitation. One evening Bob reached for his alarm clock and discovered its bells had been wrapped in cotton batting.

"What did you do to my clock?" he asked Connie.

"It wakes up Ethan."

"It wakes up me. That's its job."

"It'll still wake you up, maniac." And it did, but Bob missed the instant of piercing terror the naked bells drilled into him.

He found he disliked leaving the house for work, leaving Connie and Ethan alone for so many hours, and would shudder in crossing the threshold of the front door, as though revolted by a magnetic field. The days at the library were longer than usual, and when he came home Connie was distracted, either tending to Ethan or cooking for him or else tiptoeing around because he was having his nap. Bob recognized that Ethan had truly needed a place to recuperate and was glad to give shelter to his friend; but he also felt that his household had become infected by an imbalance that was, at the very least, an imposition. He was approaching the tipping point toward a true unhappiness when Ethan began his return to health, and Connie became less distracted by her caring for him, and so she came back to Bob. By the end of the first week of Ethan's three-week stay, Bob was relieved of his petty fears and jealousies by simply witnessing the way Ethan and Connie behaved around each other. The truth was that they liked each other. The truth was also that they loved and adored Bob, always so enthusiastic at his return in the evening, wanting to know all the gossip of his workday. They laughed together at the dinner table—Ethan could only gently laugh—and Bob understood that nothing of his relationship with Connie had been compromised.

Ethan improved further, and with his awakening he was visited by a desire to spend some of the money his wound had yielded him. He began making purchases by telephone and mail so that each day when Bob came home there was something new to show off, a wristwatch, or robe, silk pajamas, a shaving kit, all the little male niceties he had until that time gone without. He gave Bob any number of gifts in this same line; Bob suggested Ethan might buy Connie something as well, and Ethan became shy and said that he knew he should but that when he'd brought it up to Connie she had refused him in a way that he took to be heartfelt.

By the end of the second week Ethan was ambulatory and spent the days climbing up and down the stairs, circulating through the bathroom and kitchen and living room, making small messes at each location he visited. Bob had seen Ethan's apartment and knew he was a sloppy man, but to experience such disarray in his own orderly home was something else. Ethan was a great one for picking a book off the shelf and taking it to some far corner of the house, leaving it open-faced on the floor, where it would remain until Bob dusted it off and returned it to its home. When Bob found a book left out overnight on the grass in the backyard, he went to get Ethan from the kitchen and walked him, in his pajamas, to the back door. He pointed at the book. "No," he said. "I'm sorry," Ethan told him.

One evening Bob came home to find Ethan and Connie bickering in the living room. "Ethan is trying to give us money," Connie said. Bob had had a bad day at work and was climbing up the stairs to seek out a bottle of aspirin in the bathroom. "So he wants to give us money," Bob said. "Let him." Connie and Ethan both raised their eyebrows at that. Ethan never did give them any money.

At the end of the third week, Bob and Connie were married, with Ethan standing as best man. The newlyweds didn't ask Ethan to leave, but he was left to his own devices while they were hidden away in their room all through the weekend. On Monday Bob came home from work to find Connie sitting alone in the nook, reading a magazine, but angrily. "Good news, Bob. You can take the cotton off your alarm clock."

"He's gone home?" Bob asked.

"He has."

He sat down opposite her. "That's not so bad a thing, is it?"

She said, "Of course he's well enough now, and if he wants to go, then go. But no, I don't understand why he did it the way he did it."

"How did he do it?"

"He came downstairs after you left for work and he was dressed and packed and said he was going home and thanks, a lot. Those were the words he used, comma after the thanks. Walked right out the door."

She was confused by the suddenness of his departure, and she was unhappy by the way it was achieved. When Ethan came to visit Bob at the library the next day, Bob took him to task for his rudeness. Ethan bowed his head; in his defense he claimed that he'd had a sudden case of ants in the pants, and Bob surely knew what that was like. Bob said that, actually, he'd never had ants in his pants, at least not that he could remember. "Well," said Ethan, "trust me when I say it makes it so you've got to move." Bob encouraged Ethan to apologize to Connie, and Ethan said that he would, but he didn't. Connie merely shrugged when Bob recounted the interaction; she said it was a shame, but people would often let you down, and that was all there was to it. Bob felt, for the first time, unimpressed with Ethan; he wondered if he hadn't finally achieved the full-scope portrait of the man. Later, after the household went to pieces, after the thing with the string, Bob supposed that what had actually happened was Ethan had fallen in love with Connie during his convalescence. This was why he had left in such a rush, and this was why he began to hide himself away from her; to pretend, really, that she didn't exist in relation to Bob's life. Perhaps he thought if he ran away fast enough and stayed gone long enough then he might get clean away from the cursed, blessed feeling.

CONNIE DECIDED THAT SHE AND BOB WERE NOT TAKING ADVANTAGE OF their proximity to Oregon's natural surroundings, and that they should go on hikes, and become hikers, and she bought a book on the subject of hikes and also a pair of hiking boots. Bob didn't want to give away a Saturday's worth of couch reading to what he believed was a fleeting desire of Connie's, but in the name of peace-in-the-home he agreed that they would and should attack a five-mile loop at the base of Mount Hood that coming weekend. The afternoon before the hike, Bob met Ethan for lunch at the Finer Diner. Since Ethan had left Bob's house he'd taken on a paleness or apartness from the world that on this day was mounting in the direction of the acute. Bob asked Ethan what was the matter, and Ethan made a long inhalation through his nostrils. The impression he had, he said, exhaling, was that the current was directly, unmistakably, and for the first time in his life, against him. Every step he took was wrong; every natural decision and inclination resulted in some manner of snubbing or rejection. Bob still had no true comprehension of the reason for Ethan's crisis; he told Ethan that slumps were a part of life and that his would soon pass him by. "You don't get it," said Ethan simply. "Something is wrong. Even my good news is bad news these days."

"What's your good news?"

Ethan hesitated. "Never mind." He began busily stirring his black coffee.

"Then what's the bad news?"

"Nothing, Bob." He put his hand on Bob's arm, and he looked contrite. "I'm sorry I said anything. I'm fine. Let's skip it."

Bob invited Ethan to come on the hike and Ethan demurred, but when Bob pressed him he agreed that it might be helpful to get out of town, out of his apartment, away from the fumes of himself. "Though, Connie probably won't want me along," he said.

"Sure she would."

"You think she would?"

"Why wouldn't she?" He told Ethan they'd pick him up at nine o'clock the next morning. At eight o'clock, Bob stood lurking at Connie's elbow while she cooked their breakfast. "You're emitting that wants-something ozone, Bob," she said, and he admitted it was true, and explained about his idea that they should bring Ethan along with them to Mount Hood. Connie's face expressed nothing; finally she said, "Can we not?"

"We don't have to. But I think it could be good for him."

"Why, what's the matter with him?"

"I don't know what, and he doesn't know. But he's very low, lately."

Connie still wore a blank face, her arm stirring a pot of porridge. "I wanted it to be just us."

"Just us is not new," Bob told her. He didn't mean it as a complaint, didn't intend it to be anything other than true, but Connie did harden up after he'd said it, and now came the concession: yes, Ethan could tag along, if that was what Bob wanted and thought was best. When the Chevy pulled up outside Ethan's apartment he was waiting on the curb, standing hatless in the drizzle and staring into the air, ruffled and damp and confused-looking. "Jesus, he's like a hobo," Connie said. Ethan climbed into the Chevy as though he were getting into a taxi. He sat in the back, looking out the window, not speaking, not responding to Bob's good-morning greeting. Connie turned around in her seat and began to tease Ethan, pinching his nose and poking his middle, as if he were a baby. "Stop," Ethan said in a flat, croaking voice.

"Maybe," Connie said to Bob, "maybe his heart was nicked by that steak knife after all, and now it's all flat and rubbery like a popped balloon." She took Ethan's face in her hand and crushed it slightly. "Does that not look like the face of a man with a popped balloon heart?"

Bob couldn't understand where Connie's meanness was coming from, and it made him uneasy as they moved away from Portland and in the direction of the mountain. They drove for forty-five minutes along a winding, two-lane highway. The cloud cover lifted and the sun came down over the road, steam rising off the pavement. Connie put on a pair of sunglasses and rolled the dial on the radio, landing on an antic jazz number. She snapped her fingers and popped her mouth; when the station dropped away she changed over to the news station. They came to an isolated diner and Connie volunteered that Bob should go and get them a thermosful of coffee. It had been Bob's job that morning to fetch the thermos from the Chevy, but he'd forgotten to fill it before they left. "Now," Connie told him, "you can turn back the clock and set your mistake to rights, Bob. Isn't that lucky?" Bob pulled over and walked across the parking lot with the empty thermos. He entered the diner and the waitress said it would be five minutes until the pot was brewed and so he sat in a booth to wait. Looking out across the parking lot he saw that Ethan was sitting up high in the backseat of the Chevy, and speaking to Connie as if he were scolding her. Connie had shifted to the driver's position, hands on the steering wheel, looking forward, sunglasses still on, expressionless. Bob watched as Ethan reached up and touched Connie's shoulder. Connie pulled away and turned to face Ethan, addressing him sharply, fiercely. After she had finished, and resumed her forward-facing driver's position, Ethan dropped back in his seat, his posture sullen and low. Neither of them was speaking anymore. Minutes later, as Bob crossed the parking lot with the full thermos, they still were silent, ignoring each other. When Bob got in the car, and before he could ask what was the matter, Connie said, "Ethan's trying to ruin the day, Bob. But we're not going to let him, are we?"

Bob asked Ethan, "Why are you trying to ruin the day?"

"I don't know why," he said.

"Notice that he doesn't deny he's trying to ruin it," Connie said.

"I did notice that," Bob said. He asked Ethan, "Won't you deny it?"

"I won't, no. Because I am trying to ruin it." He reached for the thermos and, unscrewing the lid, poured himself a cupful.

Connie was adjusting the rearview mirror. "Well," she said, "if he's going to try to ruin the day then he should just get out of our car and walk home, or walk into traffic, either one."

Bob turned to Ethan and made a face of mock shock. He wished to defuse the situation, to undo whatever was the matter, but Ethan was distracted by his own bitter mysteries and wouldn't go along with this. He took a sip of the coffee, winced at the heat of it, fanned his tongue, and put his tongue away. "You know what, though, Bob? She's right. And I'm sorry. I'll stop. I'm stopping." And then he did stop; by the time they arrived at the trailhead he was sitting up and behaving normally, or more normally than he had been.

It had turned into such a pretty day: brisk but not cold,

damp but not raining, with bright, dazzling sunlight coming through the breaks in the branches of the trees as the trio
moved along a footpath toward the rounded static-sound of
the running river. Ethan was leading the way and moving at a
skipping half-jog, with Connie behind Ethan, and Bob behind
Connie. From time to time Ethan would look back, his face
reflecting a high and uncomplicated happiness. Bob wondered
what it was that had made him so sickly before, and also how
he could simply turn that sickliness off. Connie rolled her eyes
at Ethan, but she was amused, back to liking him again.

The river was high and roiling and they had to raise their
voices to hear one another. Connie consulted the map in her
hiking guidebook and pointed north, upriver. There was a
footbridge, she said, that would connect them to a trail on
the far side of the water. But, when they arrived at the place
where the bridge was said to be they saw it had been damaged and almost entirely washed away, timber gone, and
the rope handrailing hanging down in a tangle, frayed ends
bouncing and dragging across the surface of the swollen,
glassy river. It was impassable, and they continued walking
north in search of some other way across.

Farther on and they came to a fir that had fallen fully
across the river. It was wide enough to carry their weight but
rested at a sharp incline and was covered with a coating of
slick moss. They spoke among themselves and decided that in
the spirit of resourcefulness this would pass for their bridge—
but who would be first to cross? Ethan volunteered that Bob
should do the honors; Bob countered that the honors clearly
belonged to Ethan; Connie said she would go, at which point
Ethan and Bob both pushed forward, each in a hurry to be
the foremost conqueror. Bob arrived ahead of Ethan and
clambered up to stand atop the broad base of the uprooted
tree, looking down at his wife and friend as they looked up at

him, Ethan encouraging Bob onward, Connie half-covering her face, scared of what might come.

Bob endeavored to ground himself. He considered the way across, the best and safest route he could follow; he breathed and made himself calm and now moved forward, step by step, arms out like a tightrope walker. It was not so bad when there was solid earth on either side of the tree but once he cleared land, and with only water underneath him, then did he become less sure of himself, his vision distracted by the fast-moving river. He was bending to achieve a crouch when he lost his footing on a slimy patch of moss and his feet went out from underneath him; he landed hard on his backside, sliding down the length of the fir and at such a sickening speed he hadn't the time even to curse or exclaim in his mind. Happily, half-miraculously, he didn't fall into the river, but was shot out onto the farther shore, rolling over fully twice before coming to rest in a tangle of branches. When he stood and turned, Connie and Ethan were jumping up and down and shouting and clapping, but he couldn't hear them at all. He waved and noticed his hand was bleeding; also his backside ached. But nothing was broken, and he wasn't seriously injured. In the wake of cheating disaster, he was experiencing something like euphoria.

Obviously, however, and in light of Bob's crossing, it was established to be too dangerous for either Connie or Ethan to follow after; and neither could Bob return the way he'd come. And so, what came next? Across the river, Connie and Ethan were talking about the same thing. Ethan explained to Bob by hand gestures that they should all continue on in a northerly direction to seek out some other, safer passage over the water. Bob didn't like this plan, but could think of no alternative, for there was none, and so the bisected group struck out upriver.

At the same time Bob's euphoria was receding, his pain

was growing more pronounced. His backside stung, and his hand was throbbing, though no longer freely bleeding. He trudged along, watching Ethan and Connie, who were enjoying a lively conversation. Connie was in the lead; whenever she called to Ethan he would rush up closer to hear, then shout out his response, and she would nod and he would nod and they went happily back and forth like this, without care or concern, certainly without concern for Bob, that he could see. He noticed that their path was leading them away from the water and into the woods. They still were blithely chatting as they disappeared behind a line of trees, unbothered to be out of sight. Bob was walking more quickly now, hurrying to reconnect with them; but long minutes were passing where he couldn't see Connie and Ethan and though it wasn't anyone's fault, he felt he was being treated cruelly—that fate was behaving cruelly toward him.

A mile, and there was a sharp eastward bend in the river; once Bob walked clear of this he saw a little footbridge in the distance, and that Connie and Ethan were waiting on the far side, still immersed in their conversation. He crossed the bridge and came upon them; they looked up at Bob, untroubled, as though nothing was wrong. They welcomed him as an explorer back from the edge of the world, teasingly, not unpleasantly; but Bob was stung by a sense of exclusion, so that he wasn't sure how he should behave just then. Connie inspected his hand but he took his hand back and said that it was fine; she asked if he was limping and he said that he wasn't. Here was the very beginning of his realization that there was something dangerous moving in his direction, and that he wouldn't be allowed to escape it, no matter what clever maneuver he might invent or employ.

Connie and Ethan told Bob they'd had enough of hiking and wanted to head back to the car. Bob said that was fine, and it was, but as they made to leave, Connie took Bob by his shoulders and set him at the front of the group. Why had she done this? He walked on, carrying his worries, and he told himself he wouldn't look back, not even once, but then he did, and he saw Connie was herself looking back at Ethan. They weren't speaking; she just was looking at him, and Ethan at her, and he was smiling behind his eyes so Bob knew that Connie must also have been smiling. Bob turned around to face the path. "You *are* limping, Bob," Connie told him. They came away from the river and the sound of it became quieter, while the highway sound grew louder. They arrived at the car and settled into their seats; there was a silence among the three of them that for Bob had the texture of a nightmare. He had a bad moment where he thought he might shriek or come away at the seams of himself, but then he turned the key in the ignition and the news came on the radio and saved him: a bland male voice imparting sensible human world knowledges at a patient rate of speed.

IN THE DAYS AFTER THE HIKE BOB WOULD ENTER A ROOM TO FIND Connie standing at a window, lost to some dream or reverie. When he would ask her what she was doing, she would kiss his cheek and breeze away to stand at another window. This phase lasted a week. Then there came another phase, also a week, of peevishness. Bob felt she was not angry at him, but at the world. Actually, she doted on Bob during these days; she cooked all of his favorite meals and instigated bullying intercourse during which she demanded to know what pleased him—was it this or was it that or what was it? Bob wasn't sure what was happening but wondered if he hadn't stumbled onto a chapter of the marital experience undiscussed by the masses.

Ethan stayed away from Bob and Connie's house, but his visits to the library carried on as was usual, and he and Bob had their weekday lunches at the Finer Diner. His apartness had returned, deepened; he still claimed not to know what was bothering him. He never ate; he only drank cup after cup of black coffee.

"You don't eat anymore," Bob said.

"No," said Ethan.

"You should eat something. You should eat food."

"Okay." But, when Sally came to take their order, Ethan

wanted only coffee. He told Bob, "I'm not sleeping, I can't sleep."

"You should sleep," Bob counseled.

Ethan groaned, and began rubbing his face with his palms. He seemed agitated, even angry; after a long silence, he told Bob, "Say something." There was an accusatory slant to these words which surprised and confused Bob; it was as though Ethan believed Bob was keeping some crucial truth from him. And Bob wasn't sure what Ethan actually needed, but decided to tell him about the two children whose conversation he'd overheard at the library that morning: a boy and a girl, seven or eight years old, were sitting side by side in the children's nook. As Bob was passing by, the boy was proclaiming that something, some event he'd just described, had really and truly occurred—the girl having apparently doubted the tale. The boy's face was solemn, his voice sincere. "But I swear that's what happened," he was saying. "I swear to God it did." And the girl, without looking up from her book, without raising her voice, told the boy, "Don't bring God into this."

Ethan's laughter in response to the anecdote was loud, true, and weird; their fellow diners all were startled, and Sally came by and said, "Goddamn, Patty, can you spare us a laugh or are you gonna hog it all for yourself?"

"I'm going to hog it," Ethan said. He walked Bob back to the library; when Bob waved goodbye, Ethan only stared. He looked so hungry, Bob thought. "Eat," he said, and Ethan waved a hand that he would.

Meanwhile, back at home, Connie was entering into a third phase, another phase of happiness, but this was different from the looking-out-the-window happiness. It was something richer, more like a baseline satisfaction, a thorough confidence. She no longer was cooking for or seducing Bob; she only performed a caretakerish doting over his person, as though he were suffering under some nonfatal yet unenviable impairment.

These days and phases amounted to clues for Bob. The clues came together to form a sense of error in him, and there was a return of the revulsion in crossing the threshold of his front door when he left for work each morning, as though the house itself was telling him, *stay*.

One day, a Wednesday, and after Ethan stood Bob up for lunch, Bob came home early from the library. He didn't tell Connie he was coming home early, he just did it. When he pulled into the driveway he saw that the front door was half open, and he wondered what this could mean, and why it made him feel afraid. He walked up the path and into the house, moving from room to room, slowly, stepping softly. He was listening, but there was nothing to listen to. He walked to the living room and saw the back door was open and that Connie was sitting on the bench in the yard, sitting up very straight and staring upward, as one in the grips of a beatitude. She wasn't smiling but her carriage and expression presented a higher joy, like a religious fanatic filled up by the Spirit. Bob walked over and sat next to her on the bench. He saw that she had a length of fat red string double bow-tied around her wrist, and that she was pinching and petting it. She still was looking away when she said, "Hello." She was wearing makeup, perfume. She turned to look at Bob.

"Are you all right?" he asked.

"Yes."

"You seem strange."

"I'm not." She rested her face against Bob's chest. "Your heart's beating so fast." She leaned back to make a study of Bob, and for a time she was herself again, in her eyes, in the way she looked at him, worried but also amused—Connie.

"What's the matter?" she asked.

Bob said that it was nothing, just that he'd missed her, and then he kissed her, and she kissed him back but quickly pulled away. She stood up from the bench and asked if Bob was hungry and he said that he wasn't. She said she was going to make soup for dinner and he said soup was fine. She pulled him up to stand and walked him to the living room. She sat him down on the couch and pressed a book into his hand and brought him a beer in a chubby brown bottle. She returned to the kitchen and Bob was not reading the book or drinking the beer but visualizing Connie's sounds as he heard them: the clap of the cutting board laid out on the countertop; the knife unsheathed from its block. She began chopping up an onion. Bob could see her movements so clearly in his mind, as if he were standing just beside her.

"What's that string on your wrist?" he called.

She stopped chopping the onion. "Some string."

"But who tied it on you?"

"I tied it on myself," she told him—just like that. Bob didn't say anything more about it. They hardly spoke through the afternoon or at the dinner table. After they ate, they cleaned the kitchen together, but it felt as if each person was pretending the other wasn't there. They moved upstairs and Bob undressed and redressed and got into bed while Connie shut herself up in the bathroom and ran a bath. When she came out after, she was wearing her pajamas, and the string wasn't on her wrist. She got into bed with Bob and they lay there in the dark. After a while, he could hear the sound of Connie sleeping. Bob lay awake for a long time, but eventually he also fell asleep, without meaning to or knowing that he was. He woke up just before five, slipped out of bed and into the bathroom, closed the door, and turned on the light.

He looked in the trash but the string wasn't there. He'd

wanted it to be there; it was important to him that it was and he felt disappointed to learn that it wasn't. But where was it? Connie kept an abalone shell in the medicine chest, which was where she put her rings and earrings; the string had been carefully looped and was resting in the shell atop the jewelry. Bob picked out the string and lowered the toilet seat and sat. He lay the string out on the countertop, then set his left hand, knuckles down, over the top of the string, breaking at the line of the wrist. Using his right hand, then, he tried to tie a double bow; but the string wasn't uniform, its fibers were kinky and sticking out every which way, and he only made a mess. He untangled the string and tried again but found he couldn't tie even a single bow. He made a third and fourth attempt, a fifth attempt, but he soon understood he could try a hundred times and would never be able to tie a tidy double bow with fat hanging loops the way the string had been on Connie's wrist. He could never do it and she could never either, and he stood away from the string, watching it, sensing his person in the mirror on the periphery of his vision but feeling unable to look up and meet his reflection. He took the string and left the bathroom and sat on the edge of the mattress. Connie stirred and blinked and looked at him through half-shut eyes. When she saw the string in his hand she began to rise in the bed, as if some force was evenly elevating her, and her eyes were opening wider, and she was watching the string with a sick look on her face. Bob told her, "I don't see how you could've tied that double bow all by yourself. Will you show me how you did it?" He was speaking quietly and not unkindly, and she was nodding agreeably, yes, all right, of course, and took the string away from Bob and set about attempting to tie it to her wrist. When the bow fell apart in her hands, then she tried again, and a third time. When the bow fell apart a fourth time she tilted her face upward, looking at Bob with a puzzlement, as though she didn't know quite what they were doing, how they had come to find themselves at this obscure intersection. The very beginnings of the new morning were evident in the curtain covering the bedroom window; the room was growing by the first traces of daylight. Connie snapped the string to its full length and draped it across her wrist as if to try again, but now she'd begun to cry, and Bob watched this, watched as she balled the string in her fist and brought her fist up to cover her face, shuddering, crying harder, but silently.

Bob still didn't fully understand, he was not allowing himself to completely understand what had happened to his life when his alarm clock sounded and the noise filled the room and terrified him, so that he lunged and snatched the clock from the bedside table to silence it. He began stepping backward and away from Connie, backward until he was clear of the room, pausing at the top of the stairs, the ticking of the clock in the flesh of his palms and now, yes, now he understood what had happened, the sound of the alarm had hopped into the center of him and told him what, and this was the way it had all gone so badly for Bob Comet; this was the thing with the string.

3

1945

AT ELEVEN AND A HALF YEARS OF AGE BOB COMET RAN AWAY FROM home. The actual decampment was not purely accidental; he had been playing at running away for months. But it's unlikely he would have actually gone through with it had it not been for the incident with Mr. Baker-Bailey, which had repulsed him in his soul and furnished him with a specific something rather than a general anything to run away from.

His desire to leave was brought on by all the traditional things. In answer to the narratives of the adventure novels he'd been reading he had fabricated a narrative of his own, which was that he was unhappy, and that his mother didn't love him, and that he hadn't a friend in the world. This was what he told himself, and it was true, but only partly true. His mother did love him; it was just that she didn't understand him. He could have had friends if he wished it but he knew a separation from his peers that made comradeship feel impossible. That he was unhappy, however, was a fact. The story of his wanting to run away was built in homage to what he then considered his tragical fate.

Bob never missed a day of school, and he did the work required of him, but he had no belief that the work was important. Occasionally it was that funny or interesting things happened at school, as children are often both funny and interesting, but just as often, or more often, Bob thought, they were neither. Throughout the week, he thought of and looked forward to the weekend: Saturdays he rose early, made himself breakfast, took up his running-away knapsack (clean socks and underwear, pajamas, a novel, a toothbrush, a comb, and the entirety of his savings, twenty-one dollars), walked down the hill, and crossed the Broadway bridge for Union Station. GO BY TRAIN the neon sign said, and Bob thought that sounded like an intelligent idea. He liked to sit on the long wooden benches in the main hall, to watch the bustle of it, the travelers' stories playing out all around him, the soldiers' comings and goings, their weepy familial separations, the romantic reunions. He liked the way the trains eased into the station, hissing and stuttering like someone easing into a hot bath. He liked the flipping and clacking of the letters on the arrivals and departures board. There was no one city he wished to run away to, not Bakersfield, California, or Greenville, Mississippi; Abilene, Texas; or Gallup, New Mexico; but he liked the names of the places and it was exciting to think of the destinations as real, that the people climbing onto the trains soon would be breathing the air there.

After some weekends spent lurking in the main hall, Bob became emboldened and began inspecting the interior of the trains as they sat in the station. It was good to be one among the many in motion, to step down the aisle, squeezing past men and women while they stowed their luggage in the over-head racks or settled into their seats. "Excuse me," he liked to say. "Excuse me, please." When he got to the caboose, or whenever he heard the call of *all aboard* from the plat-form, he would exit the train and return to the long wooden benches, or wander back across the bridge, and home, only to wake up the next morning and relive the experience all over again.

One Friday afternoon in May, Bob returned home from school to find his mother pacing about the living room, smoking and drinking a cocktail, and her face was heavily made up, her hair in curlers, and a crisply new dress was laid out over the long shoulder of the sofa. She explained to Bob that she was hosting what she named a *social function* that same evening, and that Bob would be sleeping over at a coworker's house across town. "She's got a boy about your age. Rory's his name, and he sounds like a great kid and I'm sure you'll get along great and have a very good time." Bob had never slept over before, and felt strongly he did not want to do this, and so began to plead and bargain with his mother: he'd stay hidden in his room that night; he wouldn't make a sound, and no one taking part in the *social function* would know he was there at all. But his mother refused, the finality in her voice total. She ordered him to pack a bag and Bob fetched his running-away knapsack from his room, then went out and sat in the car to wait. When his mother came out of the house, her curlers were wrapped up in a sheer pink scarf and she was talking to herself and wagging the car keys from her red-nailed pointer finger. On the drive across town she tried to cheer Bob by reminiscing of the sleepovers of her youth: the games she and her girlfriends played, the fits-of-insanity giggles, the way they would attempt to stay awake all through the night, and the way they always failed. "Maybe you and Rory'll go the distance, though, huh? Maybe you two'll make it clear to sunrise." His mother was rushed, distracted, looking at her watch every few minutes, chain-smoking and ashing nervously out the window. Bob sat in silence, the prisoner on his way to the gallows. "Don't make me feel bad about this," his mother said.

"I'm not."

"You are."

"Not on purpose I'm not."

Her voice was tight with annoyance: "I want you. To have fun. For once in your life. Do you understand me?" Soon she pulled up at the curb out front of a small house with an overgrown lawn and a pile of warped scrap lumber in the driveway. "I don't have time to come in," she said, "but they're expecting you, so just go on up and knock, okay?" Bob took his knapsack and walked toward the house. His mother honked as she pulled away, which summoned her co-worker, who opened her door and stood staring after the car as it drove quickly away. "Wow," she said. "I guess your ma's in a hurry, huh?"

"I guess."

"And you must be Bob?"

"Yes."

"Nice to meet you, Bob. I'm Rory's mom and hey, look at this, here comes Rory." Rory moved to stand beside his mother. He was two or three years older than Bob, his face meaty, disinterested. He held a basketball under his arm, and when his mother said, "Say hello to Bob, Rory," Rory did not say it.

"Hello," Bob said.

"Maybe Bob would like to play basketball with you?" Rory's mother suggested.

Rory asked Bob, "You want to?"

"Yes," Bob lied. He left his knapsack on the porch and followed Rory around to the side of the house, to stand beneath the netless hoop attached to the face of the garage. The boys weren't speaking very much, but both were trying to make a go of the forced interaction; unfortunately, Bob had almost no athletic experience or ability, and couldn't get the ball to go through the hoop even once. Bob thought his own performance comical, Rory less so—he began groaning at Bob's ineptitude, shaking his head and muttering little outraged complaints to himself. Soon he announced he'd had enough, and he took the ball and walked into the house without inviting Bob to come with him. Bob wasn't sure what to do, now. He loitered by the garage awhile, then made an inspection of the pile of wood in the driveway, then sat on the lawn and watched the cars go by. The sun was setting and the soil was damp and soaked through the backside of Bob's pants. He heard the front door open; Rory's mother said, "Bob? What are you doing?" "Sitting," Bob answered, not turning around. "Why don't you come in and eat some dinner?" Rory's mother asked. "I've got you and Rory set up in the den. Rory's listening to *Fibber McGee and Molly.*" Bob stood and followed Rory's mother. Rory was sitting on a green couch in the wood-paneled den eating from a plate on his lap, and a plate had been set out on a tray for Bob. Rory's mother asked Bob what he wanted to drink. "Milk, please," Bob said, and Rory's mother touched his head and said she'd be right back. Bob sat and examined his plate and began eating the mashed potatoes. *Fibber McGee and Molly* went to commercial, a boisterous encouragement to purchase war bonds; Rory turned to look at Bob and told him, "My dad's too old to fight in the war." He said this as if it were something that had been bothering him, something he needed to get off his chest.

"Okay," Bob said.

"He'd have gone if he was younger. He wanted to go."

Bob ate a forkful of potatoes.

Rory said, "I guess your dad went over there, huh?"

"No. I don't know. I don't think so."

"What do you mean you don't know? Did he or didn't he?"

"I don't know," said Bob.

Rory's mother had reappeared, glass of milk in her hand. She set this down on Bob's tray and said, in a calm voice, "Rory, would you come away with me for a minute, please?"

"We're listening to the radio, Ma."

"Just a minute, Rory."

Rory went away with his mother and came back alone. Now he was behaving differently toward Bob; not friendlier, but curiouser, stealing sneaking glances at him whenever he looked away. Bob understood that Rory's mother had explained about Bob's not having a father. It wasn't Rory's knowing that bothered Bob, it was Rory's gruesome awe, and that he didn't have the tact to know he should hide his awe away. Rory knew, at least, that he shouldn't verbalize the thoughts occurring in his mind; from this point on he said hardly a word to Bob.

After *Fibber McGee and Molly* they listened to Bob Hope's strained entertainment of the troops, and then to the news: *German forces in Denmark have surrendered to the Allies.* Rory's mother came in holding Bob's knapsack and said chirpily, "Time for you boys to get ready for bed, all right?" As Bob passed her by she again set her hand on his head and he inwardly winced at the contact, which he now knew was inspired by pity. The boys made for Rory's room, taking turns in the bathroom, brushing their teeth and putting on their pajamas. Bob lay in a sleeping bag on the floor in the dark; he wasn't tired, and in a little while, when he heard Rory's even breathing, he pulled his street clothes on over his pajamas, took up his knapsack, and left the room. He came down the stairs, stepping quietly along the hall toward the front door; in passing the kitchen he turned to find Rory's father bent at the waist, squinting into the fridge. He wore a white undershirt tucked into a pair of high-worn pajama bottoms, and he was lumpy and pale. When he noticed Bob, he stood up straight and said, "You must be the sleeping-over kid I've been hearing about." Bob said that he was and Rory's father asked, "Well, what are you up to?"

"I'm going to go home now."

The man looked at his watch and back at Bob.

Bob said, "It's okay. I'm okay. Goodbye. Thank you."

"Don't thank me," said Rory's father, returning to bow and squint before the refrigerator. "I didn't do anything."

It was a miles-long walk through a balmy, windless night, and Bob was relieved to be free of the feelings the sleepover had provoked in him. He walked slowly through various suburban and urban areas. He'd never been out so late before and found the nighttime not at all frightening, but easy and safe in its emptiness. He was neither lost nor not-lost; he understood the general direction home and he used the bridges as guides. Crossing the river at Morrison, he made his way up the long hill and toward the mint-colored house.

It was after midnight when Bob entered his neighborhood. His house was the only one on the block with the lights on, and there was a black Packard in the driveway, gleaming and new beneath the reach of the streetlamp. Bob could hear the stereo playing; he crept up the front lawn to the kitchen window, standing on his toes to look in. Down the hall from the kitchen he could see a piece of the living room, and in the living room was the broad back of a man, coat off, the sleeves of his shirt rolled up, and Bob's mother's disembodied hands hung over the man's shoulders, her red nails clinging to him as they slowly danced. When the music ceased, their bodies compressed in a clench of passion, and Bob turned and walked away from his home and to the park down the street. The park was empty and Bob sat, then lay down on a bench, to look at the sky, because he didn't know what else to do. What he felt was something deeper and richer than nausea: nausea of the heart. But the clouds were a mysterious show of patient, moonlit shapes and moods; they lulled and distracted Bob, they tricked him into falling asleep. When he woke up it was after seven o'clock, and he stood and stretched and walked back to the house. There was a puddle of oil on the driveway but the Packard was gone. Bob let himself in and found his mother standing in the kitchen and staring at the sink, overfilled with dirty dishes and greasy pots. The house smelt of burned oil and cigarette butts and Bob's mother was ill-looking and she was clutching her kimono shut at her neck. When she heard his approach she turned, like a mannequin on a dais, to look at him. Her eyes betrayed nothing; in a croaking voice, she said, "Here's Mr. Popularity." She didn't think it odd he was back so early, or that he'd seen himself home. She explained she wasn't well and that she needed rest and silence and she went away and up the stairs in search of those things. Bob sat awhile in the kitchen nook, looking out the window he'd been looking into the night before. He decided he would run away, and truly, that same day, that same moment, and he left the house and walked back down the hill and across the river to Union Station, his pajamas peeking out past the folded cuffs of his blue jeans.

BOB WAS SURPRISED AT HOW EASY RUNNING AWAY WAS. HE SAT IN a moderately populated third-class compartment, and fifteen minutes later the train came unstuck from its track and they were off. Five minutes after the train left the station and already Bob didn't recognize the landscape: drab, flat, rocky fields with power lines overhead and forested hills rising up in the distance. The train was traveling toward those hills, traveling west to Astoria, where the Columbia River meets the Pacific Ocean. When Bob saw a conductor taking tickets at the bottom of the car he stood and walked in the opposite direction, up through the second-class cars, the dining and observation cars, and into the first-class car. He came to a compartment with a RESERVED sign hanging on the doorknob; but he could see through a slit in the curtain the compartment was empty, and so he entered, closed the curtain, sat, and waited. When he heard the conductor pass, calling out for "Tickets, tickets, please," then he relaxed a little, glad to be alone in his ritzy, superior quarters. He studied the passing landscape, which grew ever prettier: soft-rolling green hills, whitewashed churches set away in meadows, dairy farms, silos, and sentry box bus shelters standing at the intersections of country roads. When the train pulled into the station at the town of Vernonia, Bob peered down to see what he could see of the platform. As it happened there was a story taking place, and just beneath his window.

At the center of the story were two middle-aged women in tweed coats and skirts, and both wore hats with long, bowed feathers sprouting from their hatbands. Large of breast but modest of chin, the women had something paired with the city-living pigeon. They were accompanied by two diminutive and bright-eyed dogs, both black with white socks and who looked to be siblings. Each was nestled in the nook of the arm of its respective master and their entire beings were devoted to watching the movements of and sounds made by the women. The women were speaking with a porter apiece, making gestures with their free hands, naming their instruction or desire, and there was nothing faltering or coy in their body language.

The issue at hand and the focal point of this meeting was the women's baggage, which was imposing in scope and confusing to consider. The pieces were uniformly fashioned from a heavy, dark blue canvas, but there was not a single piece of the lot which was not unique in its dimensions. One was as long and narrow as a stretcher; another tall and upright, like a postal box. Some were collapsible, while others were solidly constructed, canvas wrapped over board with leather corners fixed by brass rivets. The collective contents obviously spoke to some specific function, but what this was Bob couldn't guess.

The porters were older men whose attitudes spoke of the hard truth of any working life. They were listening; they were not smiling. At one point a bag sitting uppermost on the island of luggage leaned, then dropped to the bottom of the pile; when it hit the platform it exploded and now there were wigs, of all things, strewn across the pavement. They were powdered wigs of the Victorian age, tall and white with long, trailing curls, and the women were agitated by this occurrence of spillage. They set the dogs on the ground and hurried to retrieve the wigs, to investigate their every curl and part for smudges, damages. The dogs followed behind, stepping from one paw to the other, the pavement being too cold to suit them.

When the women were satisfied the wigs had not been significantly damaged, they repacked them into the bag and took the dogs back up in their arms, returning to their original positions beside the porters, who had elected to take no action in the wig business, preferring only to observe. The women resumed with their pointings and speakings, the thorough description of their expectations per their luggage. By now the porters looked to be situated at an emotional outpost beyond amusement or disappointment, a sort of desert state, where one might do little else other than count the minutes as they rolled by. The women tipped the porters before stepping down the platform and out of sight; once they were gone the porters each produced a silver whistle, turned back to back, and together blew a sharp, shrill note into the air. Soon two junior porters, only just older than Bob by their looks, hurried up to meet their betters, who pointed to the tower of luggage, then the train, then walked away, in the direction of the canteen attached to the train station. The young porters looked at each other, and the luggage, and back at each other, and began the workaday labor of shifting the bags onto the train.

THE WOMEN AND THEIR DOGS ENTERED THE CABIN AND BOB PUSHED himself into a corner in hopes of achieving a smallness. They did not notice him at once, busy as they were making themselves comfortable, pulling off their leather gloves, loosing their neckerchiefs, removing their hats. Their faces were without any makeup or powder; they were well made, they were vigorous, and they cut a legitimate swath.

As they attended to their settling in, then did the dogs begin an investigation of Bob, approaching him where he sat, the both of them together, shoulder to shoulder as if in harness, to sniff and retreat, to look up and into Bob's eyes and make their critical deductions. They sensed his passivity or goodness, and, concluding he could never be an enemy, they lay themselves down beside him, each upon the other, to take their rest. The woman nearer to Bob saw by the attentions of the dogs that he was there among them. She gave a hard squint and said, "June."

"Yes, Ida, what is it?" asked the second woman.

"What is it, yes, that's what I'd like to know." The woman named Ida was pointing at Bob with one hand and patting her pockets with the other.

The second woman, June, looked to Bob and said, "Oh my goodness, it's a boy."

Ida had located her eyeglasses and donned these. Her squint melted away and she confirmed, "It *is* a boy. I'd thought for a moment it was a cushion, or a scrap of fabric." She turned to June and asked, "Well, what is it doing here?"

"Much the same as the rest of us I should think, dear Ida."

"But why here, when we have reserved, at some unreasonable cost and at a point in our lives where luxury is out of the question, this compartment for our own exclusive use?"

"Why must you ask me questions I cannot know the answer to?"

"It's that I want to know things," said Ida.

"We all want to, and we are every one of us disappointed, and we shall die not knowing." June sighed. "I do wish it had announced itself. I feel rather nude, frankly. I hope we haven't named any old scandals, or created any new ones."

Ida looked up, through time, rearward. "No," she said.

"Well, then, let us accept that we shan't be alone, as was our hope. In brighter news, however, it does appear the boy is a mute, perhaps deaf into the bargain, and so we can easily pretend to be alone if not actually live out the reality of aloneness."

With this, the women resumed situating themselves, and time passed in silence. The train now was traveling at a downward angle through a dense wood. Bob took out a book from his knapsack and began to read. In a little while he saw by the side of his eye that June was tapping Ida on the arm and pointing a chin at him. Quietly, but not so quietly that Bob wasn't meant to hear, she said, "It's at its studies."

"What?"

"It reads, Ida." June said to Bob, "Boy," and Bob looked up from the book. She made a beckoning gesture, and he passed the book across to her. She inspected the spine and flipped through some of its pages. She told Ida, "It's one of these stories where a lone man suffers considerably in an unforgiving wilderness, and if a vicious wolf or two has to perish in the meantime, so much the better." June handed the book back to Bob, who received it but did not resume his reading, being hopeful June would speak with him further, and then she did this. "I'm waiting," she said in a confiding voice, "for some guardian of yours to arrive, but it seems that shall not happen."

"No, ma'am."

"But surely you're not traveling alone?"

"Yes."

"How old are you?"

"Eleven and a half."

"Where is your family?"

"There's my mother."

"Where is she?"

"Working."

"And what does she do?"

"She's a secretary, in Portland."

"And here you are, not at all in Portland, and without her."

"Yes."

June sat thinking. She asked, "Are you running away from home, boy?"

"Yes."

A smile broke out on June's face. It was a surprising thing, this smile; for her face, in expressing a natural joy, became dented and smashed, and her teeth were stained and crooked. It looked, really, that she was in pain; but no, she was elated by the news, and she said, "Oh, I had *thought* you might be. Ida, didn't you think he might be? Running away from home?"

"I didn't think he was," Ida said. "But then, I didn't think he *wasn't*, either."

"Well, I find it very romantic," said June. The smile had passed but her face still wore the folds the smile had occasioned. "And to where will you run?" she asked Bob, and he shrugged, having no destination in mind.

"Perhaps he'll simply run until his legs give out," Ida answered. "Motion being the thing. If I were you, boy, I'd run away to Florida. It's a nice climate for living out of doors."

"We mustn't assume so much," said June. "He may well luck into a more comfortable situation. Perhaps he moves toward some peaceful pastime, a loving benefactor eager to set him up in healthful endeavor. Perhaps he moves toward a position in the clergy."

"He could become a bell ringer."

"He might very well achieve prosperousness as a bell ringer, that's true. Do you know," June said, "I always wanted to run away when I was a girl, but I never had the pluck. Didn't you ever want to, Ida? To run away? To teach the world its bitter lesson?"

Ida said, "What I wanted was to jump in the river with a pocket full of stones."

"Oh, yes, that," said June, as if recalling a first love. She told Bob, "I notice that you are alone in your adventure. But why? I should think you'd have wanted some of your school chums to come along with you, no?"

Bob didn't answer, but looked away and at the ceiling, as if something interesting was happening or might soon happen there.

"Yes, I understand," said June.

Ida said, "I used to wonder what it would feel like to smash one of those great plate glass windows with gold leaf lettering bowed across the face of it. A butcher's, bookkeeper's, a pool hall—I didn't care what, the smashing was the thing."

"And with what would you smash it?" asked June.

"A brick, naturally." Ida displayed her hand in the holding-a-brick shape. "It would arc through the air, landing at the center of the broad pane of glass, which would drop into itself, and the shimmering noise would satisfy my deepest, most destructive urge, and forever, I should think."

June, speaking from the side of her mouth, told Bob, "Ida had no friends in school, either."

Ida said, "June, however, always had a good many friends and companions. But they were every one a betrayer in the end, isn't that right?"

"Truth, yes. And then, after the final savage treason, I thought, I won't be falling for that wicked business again. And I vowed that I should walk alone."

"But then, do you see, and she met a certain someone," Ida said.

"Yes, yes, and now look at me. Up to my neck, boy. Dragged into a life of uncertainty and vagabondery and I don't know what all else." June wagged a finger at her friend as she told Bob, "One must be careful about whom she meets. But then, how careful can one be? Each time we leave our home we're witness to fate's temptation. People fall into unexpected communion every day of the week, whether or not they want to. Like an illness delivered on the wind." June paused. Soberly, she said, "It can be upsetting to one's plans, I'll say that much."

Ida sat breathing awhile. "I'm sorry, which plans were upset?"

"You aren't familiar with them," June answered, and she winked at Bob.

"Obviously and I'm not," said Ida. "Will you name them now?"

"Oh, Ida," said June tiredly.

"Name the plans which I've upset. I should like to know.

And perhaps I could make some reparation to you for all the damage I've done your life."

June told Bob, "I think we've gone down the wrong path."

"Oh, is that what you think?" said Ida. "Is that what you think has happened?" Her cheek was flushed and her breathing had become a little ragged.

June apologized in the sincereish tone of the repeat offender, and Bob had the impression it was not uncommon for Ida to feel insulted or slighted by June; also that June was less sympathetic to Ida's feelings than she once perhaps had been. But Ida was now succumbing to a proper funk, and June, hoping to avoid any emotional calamities, invented an idea in response to this hope, and she touched Bob's hand to alert him of its arrival: "I believe we should ask the boys, then, what they think the solution might be." She turned to the dogs, still curled up on the bench to the side of Bob. "Boys," she said, and the dogs both opened their eyes. "I come to you for counsel; may I borrow a portion of your time?" The dogs raised up their heads. "Dear Ida and I have come once again to an impasse. We are the both of us very tired, and there is the unreliability of our comforts both current and to come; weariness has taken hold and I do feel it has made the both of us into—peeves. What, do you think, is the best way forward and out of this? What might we do to turn Ida's mood around, and before it's too late and we lose a day to it?" As she spoke, June pulled a small hand instrument from the pocket of her coat. It had a chunky wooden base with metal tines attached; she held it steady upon her knee and began to play a plunking, buzzing little waltz. Once June's song achieved recognizability, the dogs stood up, first on all fours, then rising to their hind legs. Resting their forelegs on one another's shoulders, they began the approximation of a dance in the ballroom fashion. June played with facility, her fingers nimbly picking out the melody while she hummed a countertune; Ida was ameliorated by the performance, and watched the dogs with a forgiving, or anyway a forgetting, face. For Bob's part, he could think of no words to say in reply to the occurrence of the waltzing dogs. The train plunged deeper into the still and ancient forest. Bob could not yet see the ocean but there was the sense of an ocean pending.

THE TRAIN TERMINATED IN ASTORIA AND THE WOMEN STOOD TO COLLECT their effects. In watching their departure, Bob discovered a desire in himself, which was to follow them and make an investigation of their movements and behaviors, and he decided he would do this but without alerting them to the fact, if the fact could be avoided. He stood and took up his knapsack, altering his facial expression and physical carriage to represent one not-following. As the women turned to go, June looked back at him with what he took for a question of concern on her face, but there was no question, or else she chose not to give voice to it. "Well, good luck young man" was what she said, and Bob bowed his head, and they all left the compartment, traveling in single file down the narrow passageway and toward the exit, the dogs both looking at Bob from over the shoulders of their masters.

The five of them descended onto the busy platform and Bob hid himself in the crowd, loitering at a distance while the women oversaw the transfer of their baggage from the train to the hold of a Trailways bus idling in the roundabout out front of the depot. After the women boarded the bus, and while the driver was distracted by the closing up and securing of the luggage compartment, Bob snuck onboard and made to find his seat. There were none available except at the rear of the bus, which was where the women and dogs were situated. It was Ida who noticed Bob's approach, June being distracted by the view out the window. "It's back," she said.

"What's back?"

"Your train project. The foundling."

June turned to look at Bob, and there again was the face-breaking smile. "Bold life-liver," she said.

"Hi," Bob told her.

"Never mind the chitchat," said Ida. "Where do you think you're going?"

Bob didn't answer; Ida asked, "Perhaps you're thinking to go wherever we go."

Bob said, "Well."

"Well, nothing." Ida turned to June. "I'm going to alert the driver to the particulars of this child's situation and have him call ahead for a policeman to meet us in Mansfield."

June said, "Ida, you thorough maniac. The boy can go wher-ever he wishes to go. He isn't bothering anyone, my goodness."

"He's bothering me."

"You bother yourself. That's your Lifetime Problem. Just leave this to me, thank you." June pointed at the seat to the side of theirs and told Bob, "Become comfortable, please."

Bob did as June instructed while Ida sat quietly fuming and complaining. This went on for some length of time, so that June finally reached up and covered Ida's mouth, at which point Ida's eyes became wide with high emotion; but, when June removed her hand, Ida no longer spoke. She curled up against the window and shut her eyes. The bus was rattling and hissing and now was away.

They were traveling in a southerly direction on a strip of winding two-lane highway with the ocean on their right and the sun angling toward the horizon. June crossed the aisle and shooed Bob over that she might sit beside him. She pulled a Baby Ruth from her coat pocket, opening its wrapper with care so to produce as little noise as was possible. Holding out the exposed candy bar, she made a questioning face at Bob; he broke off a piece and slowly ate it while June consumed the remainder, nodding that she agreed with the taste of it. After, she dropped the wrapper on the floor of the bus and swept it beneath her seat with the toe of her leather boot.

"Well, now," she said, "what's your name?"

"Bob."

"And your surname?"

"Comet."

She watched Bob as one not understanding a joke. "Spell it," she said, and Bob did, and she glanced at Ida, but Ida was sleeping, as were the dogs. Speaking at half-volume, June said to Bob, "Tell the truth, Bob. You are following us, aren't you?"

Bob shrugged.

"But why are you?"

Bob shrugged again.

"Well," she said, "I truly don't mind it. Actually I find it somewhat flattering. But I hope you're not under the impression we'll look after you?"

Bob shrugged a third time, and here June set her hand upon his shoulder. "Bob, the shrug is a useful tool, and seductive in its way; but it is only one arrow in the quiver and we mustn't overuse it lest we give the false impression of vacancy of the mind, do you see my point?"

Ida mumbled something unintelligible from her slumber. June said, "I do hope you'll forgive my friend. It's nothing personal, just that she suffers from an incurable affliction, and its name is grumpiness. She finds strength in hostility, and joy in strength. But at any rate, and as I was saying, it would be foolish to assume we might be in a position to help you. If you want to know God's truth, Ida and I can just barely keep ourselves clothed and sheltered." June's face went blank with waiting. "Perhaps you'd like to ask *me* some questions," she ventured.

"What questions?"

"Oh, you know. Who we are, where we're going, why we're going there, why we have twenty-three unique pieces of luggage, why my pockets are filled with musical instruments, how it is that our dogs can waltz."

"Yes," said Bob, because he did want to know these things.

"Well," she said, "I'll tell you, since you feel so strong-burning a curiosity." Her voice dropped further, and she gave a look around, as if to be certain none of their neighbors were listening in. "Ida and I are *thespians*, Bob."

Bob wasn't certain just what the word meant, but the way June had said it alluded to something shameful, so that he blushed to hear it. "Yes," she said, pointing at the red of Bob's cheek. "It shocks, I know. But let's not pretty it up: we're a pair of desperate thespians seeking out any small venue where we might engage the cursed inclination without causing overmuch unpleasantness. Certainly we hope to avoid imprisonment. Sometimes it has happened we are given monetary reward for services rendered; but it's a hard life, and that's mildly put. Both our families have disowned us, naturally. And it has been a long while since we were barred from polite society. But it's not as if we had a choice in the matter; one is born a thespian or one isn't, and one cannot deny the needs of her own mind, her flesh, after all, can one?" She looked away, over the top of Bob's head. "I won't take offense if you wish to change your seat, Bob. I'd hate to bring shame upon the house of Comet." But Bob did not leave, and June squeezed his arm and told him, "I knew you'd stay. You wear your heart in your face, your eyes."

"You're actors," Bob said.

June said, "We are dramatic stage performers. We are also playwrights and producers and directors and designers and stagehands and prop masters and dog trainers and dogs. We are not all these things at the same time owing to ambition, but because we are alone in our work. Yes, my little running-away friend, that is truly and finally what we are." Bob asked if they were traveling to perform somewhere, and June brightened. She reached across the aisle and poked a finger in Ida's stomach. Ida's right eye opened very slightly. "Bob Comet *interrogates*," June told her.

"Who's Bob Comet?"

"The foundling, Ida. His name is Bob Comet, and it's all I can do to keep up with his queries."

"Leave me my rest," Ida said, then shut up her eye again.

June turned back to Bob. "My not-pleasant companion and I are traveling to a town called Mansfield to premiere our latest work, which consists of a series of somewhat-connected vignettes. Do you know what a vignette is?"

"No."

"It's a story that's too small to be called a story, so you call it a vignette. By pretending you've made it small on purpose, you avoid the shame that accompanies culpability. Do you know what culpability is?"

"No."

"It's the bill coming due. This work is not our strongest. It is not bad work, but it doesn't have the power of our past labors. That power, which was once effortless, and which we wielded as if it were the most natural thing in the world, is now dimming, and there isn't any vitamin or medicine I can find to remedy the lack. The watch winds down, Bob Comet, the pebbles of sand slip through the trim waist of the hourglass, and don't let anyone tell you otherwise." She snapped her fingers. "There is a hotel in Mansfield that, in the years before the war, showcased a number of our efforts, and we enjoyed some unlikely-yet-not-insignificant regional success. This was during the timber boom of the late 1930s, when the barons and their foremen and their mistresses wished for some semblance of culture of a Friday or Saturday night. I felt at the time they didn't understand what we were showing them, but we have always created a certain spectacle, and with musical accompaniment, which is enough for some. Anyway, they were a game audience. They knew when to clap, and they spent money on wine, which pleased the hotelier. But then the barons and foremen and mistresses moved on, and the hotelier's invitations dried up. Now, years later, and he contacts us from out of the blue, making claims of a revitalization. That's fine, and I can't say I wasn't happy to hear from the man, but I do believe we're headed for Flopsville. You know Flopsville?"

"I think so."

"Yes, well, we're almost there." The sun had fallen farther and the bus was making wide, swooping curves in mimicry of the shape of the coastline. "You're too young to know the melancholy of returning to a place where once you had thrived. I can say it is not as bad as it sounds. But then, Bob, I'm making a distinction between melancholy and sorrow. Do you understand the difference?"

"No."

"Melancholy is the wistful identification of time as thief, and it is rooted in memories of past love and success. Sorrow is a more hopeless proposition. Sorrow is the understanding you shall not get that which you crave and, perhaps, deserve, and it is rooted in, or encouraged by, excuse me, the death impulse."

Ida shivered and stirred. "How could anyone ever sleep with all this chatter buzzing in her ears?" she asked.

"It lives and breathes," June told Bob. "It walks among us."

Ida suddenly was awake and upright in her seat. She looked

all around her, as if she had forgotten where she'd been sleeping. She said, "Where is my Baby Ruth? I want it." And June, wincing, took a breath and told her friend, "As I was just explaining to young Bob, here: we are prepared for melancholy, but we must also and at the same time steel ourselves against the likelihood of sorrow."

THE BUS PULLED OFF THE HIGHWAY AND ONTO A PATCH OF DIRT SEPARATING the pavement from the ocean. The driver cut the engine and Bob could hear the wind coming off the water, buffeting the bus's exterior; he could hear the even sound of the receding waves raking pebbles down the shore. June was looking to her left, away from the sea. "There it is," she said.

The Hotel Elba was built up in the Victorian style, rounded shingles, a covered wooden walk along its facade, a conical tower rising from its southernmost aspect. The tower held itself at a slant, its weathervane bowing in what looked a gesture of deference or bashful welcome; actually the tower, along with the rest of the hotel, was sinking into the ground. Bob thought the hotel was handsome but hungry-looking. It must have been very grand once.

"Mansfield," the driver called out.

From the vantage point of the bus Bob could take in the town in its entirety, two roads sitting in the shape of a T, the highway, and a road running east and into a darkening forest. The sun had not set but the storefronts along the highway were closed for the day, or forever. Up the road, Bob saw a movie theater and a diner, both apparently open for business, but not a soul about to take part in either experience. June stared at this somber portrait, saying nothing. A light came on above the bus driver's head and he made a notation on a clipboard hanging off his dash.

"Mansfield," he said again.

He opened the swinging doors and a stiff wind poured in, traveling the length of the bus, disturbing each passenger in his or her turn and annoying the dogs, who growled at the unseen force. Ida's and June's hat feathers were bobbing as they stood to gather their things.

The driver exited and stepped to the rear of the bus, opening the hold to attend to the baggage. There came a thump from outside and Ida, craning her neck to look out the window, said, "He'll break the guillotine, the fool!" Taken by a panic, Ida and June hurried down the aisle, with the dogs at their heels, and Bob following after the dogs. There had been no discussion about his presence among them but he thought to keep on until he was told in clear language to stay away. He slunk from the bus and stood at a distance, watching the driver unload the baggage while the women pointed out this and that bag's fragility while also explaining the man's many mistakes to him. The baggage was stacked in a tall pile and Bob took refuge behind it.

The driver lingered, dabbing at his face with a hanky and looking up at the women expectantly. Perhaps he thought them wealthy eccentrics, and that they might bestow some outsize gratuity upon him. But time passed in silence and the women did not offer the driver any cash bonus or even a kind word, and so he tucked the hanky away and returned to the bus, flopping into his seat in a gesture of petulant defeat. In a moment he sat up straighter, as if inspired; turning the key in the ignition, he started revving the engine and dropping it in and out of first gear while standing on the brake, actions that prompted a backfire, a voluminous black cloud of burned soot that surrounded both women, who coughed and sputtered and waved their hands to chase the smoke away. The bus driver tooted his horn and eased the bus back onto the highway; June, cleaning the grime from her face with her handkerchief, said, "Credit where it's due, Ida. The man knows his instrument." Ida stood motionless, seething in place, and she couldn't speak, or didn't. Meanwhile, a joyful-looking man with one arm stepped out of the Hotel Elba and crossed the highway to stand before June and Ida. "Good evening, good women!" he said.

"Mr. More," said June, inspecting her handkerchief. "What is your news?"

"Just that I was minding my business at the front desk when I happened to look up in time to see the pair of you engulfed in a plume of exhaust. Can you imagine my surprise?"

"I *can* imagine it," said June. "I should think it was probably quite a lot like our own surprise, only not nearly so unpleasant."

"Indeed," said Mr. More. He pointed his chin at the place where the bus had been. "It looked as though he meant for it to happen, was that your impression as well?"

"That's right."

"And what transpired, to bring the driver to such a vengeful place? I do hope that your talent for friendshipmaking has not left you?"

"Not totally, no. It has become, I will admit, less reliable. Or perhaps it is that there are fewer we wish to be friends with in the first place. Your own talent for observational clevernesses is still evident."

"Yes, I've hung on to it. I keep thinking it might become suddenly useful someday. It is a weapon against the rest, is it not?" He brandished an invisible sword and made his face warlike, slashing on the air. Now the sword vanished, and his face resumed its kinder attitude, and he asked, "What would you say to a nice bowl of soup?"

"Perhaps not on the highway," June said.

Mr. More turned to face Ida. "Hello, Ida." When Ida did not reply, Mr. More observed, "Ida isn't speaking at all, is she?"

June said, "She has had a long day."

"We all have had one."

"Ours was uncommonly long, Mr. More."

Mr. More said, "Take comfort, strong Ida, the day is near to passed." But Ida was voiceless still. "Do you think she'll resume speaking in time for rehearsals?" Mr. More asked.

"She will speak sooner than that or I miss my guess." June began cleaning Ida's face with her handkerchief.

"I can't recall what Ida's feelings about soup are?"

"Our feelings about soup are that we enjoy it, Mr. More, but not to the degree that we wish to discuss it quite so much. And, that you have brought up the soup twice before we have even entered the hotel does not fill me with optimism at the prospects for our success here."

"Why ever not?"

"Because I know you, Mr. More. If you are so aggressively pushing an appetizer, then there is likely not so very much behind the appetizer." She pointed at the hotel. "Why is there no playbill in the front window announcing the coming performances?"

Mr. More began shuffling his feet, and a look of alarm came over his face. "Well, now, I have something to say about that actually, June."

"Will you admit to us that you have not had the playbills printed?"

"I repeat: I have something to say. Why not let me say it?"

Ida made a clearing-the-throat noise and spit onto the highway. This was a gesture made to command the attention of the group, and the gesture was a success. Said Ida: "You obviously have not had the playbills printed, Mr. More. As such, there must be very little public interest in the performances scheduled to commence four nights hence. In this way you have broken our contract, of which I have a copy on my person. Shall I show it to you? Shall I bring your attention to the clause regarding a kill fee? Perhaps you're telling us our run will be canceled. Well, what a disappointment that would be to us. We four living beings, we four creatures, who have been toiling in our rented rooms for several months now, months that we've been tinkering, preparing, inventing, destroying, and building up again, in spite of illness and irregular heating and an unspeakable communal toilet situation, and with no per diem offered by you, our own private savings hurrying away, Mr. More. *The show must go on*, they say, and a fine saying it is—a fine theoretical sentiment. And we *are* troupers is that not so, June?"

"We are troupers."

"Let us recall our grisly beginnings, when we trod the boards by the seat of our patchwork bloomers, when we ran and jumped and sang for small denomination coins pitched through the air and which did at times bounce off our faces, because that was where the audiences wished for their *pennies* to connect, Mr. More, *pennies* which we did then chase after, midsong, lest they roll off the stage and back into the hands of the animals, the imbecile men in the pit before us, braying at us, their mouths foul holes funneling rot-scent into the air which we were made to breathe, these same men offering up abusive encouragements at our persons. Am I inventing, June?"

"Not a word of it."

"Do I invent?"

"You speak only truths."

"We were young girls, Mr. More. We were not yet women, even, and this debasement was our way into the world of the arts, and it was years of it, years before we demanded the opportunity for betterment, demanded it of the world and of our audiences and of ourselves, and we broke off and settled into our true work, our lasting work, the self-authored work that has brought us our modest but deserved renown and that continues on in spite of man's war and man's anguish and man's societal and cultural coarsening, the cinematic influence, dear God I beg you not to get me started. And here, now, we have done our work and we arrive after a long journey with a new show, cut from new cloth, with new costumes and sets designed and fabricated by ourselves, and I speak for all four of us and with the muses in choral agreement when I say that this is a worthy work. And now what, Mr. More? What do you offer us for our labors? Do you offer us soup? Is that what I'm hearing?"

Throughout Ida's soliloquy, Mr. More had stood in a wincing half-crouch; but now, and with Ida silent, he elongated and breathed, attractive in his way, with his empty sleeve folded crisply, pegged in place with a gleaming silver bib pin. "Hello, Ida," he said. "I do offer you soup, yes, and the offer for soup stands. I made the soup myself in anticipation of your arrival, thinking it might hearten you. It goes without saying, though I am saying it, that making soup with one arm is not easy. I tell you this not to complain but to unveil the full picture. Beyond the soup, about which I agree too much has been said, I can also offer you room and board for the duration of your stay. If you wish not to perform, you may consider it a complimentary seaside vacation. If you do wish to perform, and my sincere hope is that you do wish it, and that you will, you can have any and all monies the performances generate, and I myself shall not take one solitary penny. I can't guarantee these monies will be robust, and in truth there may be none. This town has been dying for some years now, and recently succumbed to death. Yes, the town is dead. As I say these words I believe I see a question forming in your eyes, and it is: If the town has died, then why has he invited us to come here at all?" The women both were nodding, and Ida was nodding emphatically. "I will explain," Mr. More continued. "My invitation to you came on the heels of a town council meeting wherein it was announced the timber companies were returning. The companies themselves were in attendance and made a good showing; they had maps which they pointed to with retracting pointer-outers and they were passing out embossed business cards and pencils with little tassels sprouting off the ends, so that I believed their fictions. Here is an error of judgment I admit to; I was told a whopper which I took for truth. Well, I wanted it to be true; there's a powerful pull in that. I still think it was true at the time, actually—I believe the companies themselves believed they were coming back to us. But something has happened, or has not happened, and while the timber companies continue to ply their trade both upcoast and down, Mansfield is missed and missed again. Their secretaries have ceased engaging with me telephonically and through the mails, and I don't understand the why of it and I likely never shall."

A girl of sixteen exited the hotel pushing a rusted old hand truck. Her face was pale, her hair greasy, and she looked unhappy, perhaps angry, as she awkwardly navigated the hand truck down the blue-painted stairs. There was much clattering and crashing and wheel screeching, which alerted Mr. More of her approach; he brightened when he saw her, pointed as she wheeled past him. "My grand-niece, Alice. She was not with us when last we met. Alice also is excited about the show. Alice, aren't you excited about the show?"

"Oh, I'm excited," said Alice, in a bland tone that embodied the opposite of excitement. She arrived at the edge of the hill of baggage and began loading up the cart. Soon she would discover Bob's obscured person, and the waiting for this created an agony in him. Electing to hurry the discovery along, he stood, and Alice shrieked, and the rest all turned to see him. Mr. More said, "Would you look at that, a hidden-away boy, whatever in the world."

"It's Bob!" said June.

"You know him?"

"Yes, he's Bob. Hello, Bob. I was thinking of you during Ida's—rant."

Bob waved hello to June.

"I was thinking," said June to Mr. More, "'Oh no, where's Bob?'"

"And now you've found him, and isn't that nice?" Mr. More replied. "But, what is he doing all bent down like that?"

"He's a desperate figure on the run, Mr. More, and so we can only guess at his motives."

"He looks like a normal boy to me," said Mr. More. "Hello, hello."

"Hello," Bob said.

"Do you like soup, Bob?"

"What kind of soup?" Bob asked, and Mr. More and June and even Ida, though not Alice, all laughed at his innocent query, and Bob didn't understand why but was happy to have connected them with a pleasing amusement.

MR. MORE WANTED TO SHOW EVERYONE THE FRESHLY LAID, SPECIALLY ordered white pea gravel surrounding the hotel, and so the group moved in a lazy cloud formation to circle the property. Mr. More spoke as they walked. "I had the perimeter graveled around the time I sent you my optimistic missive encouraging your return. Now I lament the cost, but I do like the crunching sound it makes underfoot. Does it not create the impression of approaching drama? Is it not somewhat like a moat?" Picking up his thread from before, he turned to June and said, "Regarding the playbills. Let me get it over with and say it: yes, there are none. But I was the passive victim in that caper, and here is what happened: the printer hanged himself the day after I put in my order. What do you think of that? Thomas Conroy was his name; and I'd known him since 1905. We were in the one-room grade school together, in Astoria. Once we were caned for making cow sounds in Mass, and here he goes and does something like this. He tacked a note to the front door of his shop, which I read with my own eyes. It was a very sober and, I felt, fair summation of the why of it all."

"He named his reasons for hanging himself?" said Ida.

"He did."

"And what were they?"

"Tiredness."

"Just that?"

"Pronounced tiredness, let's say."

"He should have taken a little vacation," June said.

"Yes, and I do wish he would have, if only that he'd have completed my order. He was a talented printer, and there are none in the area to replace him." Mr. More paused. "Do you know, now that I think of it, he was not a joyful child, either."

"A woe-is-me type?" Ida said.

"I don't know that he cultivated it, exactly. But the bitter crop came in all the same, and this year's was apparently overwhelming in its fullness."

"Was he distraught when you placed the order?"

"He was his usual not-so-glad self. But distraught? No, not particularly. He asked for five dollars down payment, which he'd not done before, and which I did give him, in cash, and who can say why he required this, but now I can't help but wonder: Did he know what he would do some eighteen hours later? And if so, why did he take my order at all, to say nothing of my money, which I can only barely spare and shall never get back? In his letter's postscript he stated a wish that the note would be printed verbatim in our local paper, and I myself brought this to the attention of the paper's editor, but he wouldn't allow it, suffering as he does from a grievous Catholicism."

Having lapped the hotel's exterior, and with the nighttime coming down and chill onshore winds growing stronger all the while, June proposed the time had come that they should remove themselves from the elements. Mr. More agreed; climbing spryly up the blue steps, he turned to face the group, taking advantage of his temporary elevation to give a little speech before granting them admission: "Friends," he said, "I see you're disappointed by the state of things, and I understand the disappointment, accustomed as I am with that mode of being; but in the meantime I am revitalized by your presence, and will do all I can to ensure your successes. I've wrapped the stage in three-quarter-inch red oak and rewired the footlights with a dimmer feature and the curtain has been cleaned and mended and dyed. Beyond this, I am simply beside myself with happiness at the thought of learning more about this new work. I put myself at your disposal, then, utterly and thoroughly; and while my abilities are finite, please know that my devotion to your practice is boundless." June was pleased by this, but she was not quite ready to bury the whole hatchet, and so she repressed her pleasure as much as she was able. The truth was that she liked Mr. More to a degree that was uncommon in her life and experience. "Thank you, that's fine," she told him. "We can speak of the show after this much-heralded soup. Will you be asking for a role in the production right away, or later on?"

"Oh, right away," said Mr. More assuredly, propping open the front door of the hotel with his foot and waving in his guests one by one. When Bob passed, Mr. More explained, "I always make an attempt to take part in their performances, and they always turn me down. It's one of our small traditions. But in my two-armed youth, I was not unfamiliar with the life of the stage."

He followed behind Bob, and now the group was standing together in a conservatory which preceded the lobby proper, and which was filled with the largest and wildest jungle plants imaginable. The temperature and humidity were adjusted to meet the needs and preferences of the plants, and so they were thriving in the environment, more than thriving. Actually, they had engulfed the enclosed space; certain of the plants were monsters over seven feet tall, with creeping vines crawling clear across the ceiling. Bob was impressed by the atmosphere; Ida and June, less so. They stood close by one another, quietly taking in the visual while Mr. More studied their physical behaviors in hopes of decoding their opinions.

"What has happened to the conservatory?" Ida finally asked.

"It's all down to Mr. Whitsell."

"And who is Mr. Whitsell?"

"He is Mr. Whitsell. Our lone long-term resident. He was an insurance man in North Dakota all his working life, from the age of eighteen and through to retirement at sixty-five, at which point he came west by bus, making his tour of the Pacific Ocean. But bus travel did not agree with him, and one morning he showed up with a look in his eye that read to me as an SOS. I took pity on the road-worn soul and gave him one of our finer suites at a fair rate. That was some years ago, and here he remains. My understanding is that he did not dislike the insurance game, and I do believe he had the knack, but there was always at the rear of his mind the belief that he had a second calling that he'd not addressed, namely hothouse botany. He spoke of it in the spring of last year and I, having an affection for the man, endeavored to enable him by furnishing him a space with which to achieve his ambition. The conservatory has always represented a lag or lack, for me. It's its own separate locale, but what is it *for*?"

June said, "I quite disagree, Mr. More. I found the space perfectly charming." She told Bob, "It used to be that this room was lined with deck chairs. And at dusk, Ida and the boys and I would lay our weary bodies out and witness the death of the day."

"We sometimes did encourage the death of it," Ida admitted.

"The sunsets were very striking, and were a balm against the collection of insults one gathers across the length of an afternoon," June said. "Now you can hardly make out even a sliver of a horizon." Mr. More was unhappy at the critical nature of the discussion and had begun opening and closing his mouth in the style of a fish freed from water. June set a hand upon his shoulder. "Soothe yourself. I'm not unimpressed by the room's transformation; but it is a radical departure, and it is ungodly hot in here, don't you think?"

Mr. More wouldn't say whether or not he agreed with this; he would only allow that the time had come to exit the conservatory, and he led the group through to the hotel lobby by way of a rattling steam-wet six-pane French door. Bob did not follow along but lingered, as something in the far corner of the conservatory had caught his eye and he felt compelled to remain.

It appeared that a man was hiding himself away amid the greenery—hiding but looking back at Bob. Yes, a man surely was there and surely was hiding, and Bob said, "Hello?" and the man stepped out and presented himself: a small figure, a senior gentleman with white, neatly combed hair, and in an outfit of pressed pants, starched shirt rolled up at the sleeve, a knitted tie of a bright green coloring, and an immaculate white bib. He held in one hand a dainty tin watering can and in the other a gleaming silver spade, and altogether he was the cleanest gardener one could ever hope to see. Bob deduced that this was Mr. Whitsell, and, thinking the man may've been offended by Ida's and June's careless descriptions of the room, said, "I like the plants." The man held the flat of the spade against his heart and bowed before returning to hide himself away amid the prehistoric leaves. Not knowing what else he might say or do in response to this person's behavior, Bob left the conservatory and shut the door behind him.

The lobby was outfitted in dark-stained wood and was dimly lit by shaded lamps. There was no sign of Mr. More or

Ida or June or the dogs but behind the front desk was a half-size door, which was ajar, and beyond which Bob believed he could hear voices. He ducked underneath the counter and stepped closer; when he heard June's voice he felt emboldened, and he passed through the little door, following a worn carpeted runner down a thin hallway and toward the growing noise of the ongoing discussion. He stepped into Mr. More's dining room to find the man and June and Ida seated at a table with bowls of steaming soup set out before them. Ida was eating determinedly while June was listening or pretending to listen to a story Mr. More was sharing or performing for her. When she saw Bob she brightened and pointed at the empty seat beside hers, then at the bowl of soup that had been set out for him. Bob could smell that it was a beef stew, and he was very hungry, and he moved to sit and eat and listen to these talking, talking people.

THE SOUP WAS CONSUMED AND THERE CAME THE TIME OF CONTEMPLATIVE
quiet that often occurs at the end of a satisfying meal, and which
Mr. More eventually interrupted by asking June, of Bob, "Well,
now, what of the fugitive?"

"What of him?" said June.

"What shall we do with him? I suppose you think we
should harbor him."

"My suggestion would be that we do harbor him, yes."

"You're vouching for him."

"I vouch."

"And what of the sheriff? I should think he'd take an interest."

"The sheriff can go be ten-gallons sick in his ten-gallon
hat."

"Easy to say without the sheriff here."

"I'll say it at high noon on the steps of town hall."

"Easy to say when there is no town hall."

"Well," said June. "You asked what I thought and now you
know. I believe Bob is a fine young fellow and I vote we take
him on."

Mr. More thought awhile, then said, "I am on the verge of
agreeing to harbor him, but I've one condition, which is this:

if the boy is caught, and my harboring comes back to haunt me in the form of the sheriff darkening my door, I must be able to say to him I was under the impression he was seventeen years old, and had no knowledge of his being to the side of the law."

June said, "You may say whatever you wish, Mr. More."

"Yes, but you and Ida must both back me up as witnesses to my being misled."

"Fair and fair enough," said June. "Does that suit you, Bob?"

"Yes," said Bob.

"Tell Mr. More you're seventeen, please."

Bob told Mr. More, "I'm seventeen."

"See there?" June said to Mr. More. "Now you won't even have to lie."

Mr. More said, "And Ida? You are on board with all this?"

Ida did not say yes, but neither did she say no, which for her was much the same as a yes. Mr. More asked June, "Who will pay the cost of the fugitive's room?"

June asked Bob, "Do you have any money, Bob?"

"Yes."

"It's four dollars a night," Mr. More said warningly.

Bob pulled his roll from deep in his sock and counted out four limp ones. He made to pass them to Mr. More, who asked Bob to leave the money on the table. "Give the bills some time to catch their breath," Mr. More explained to June. He stood and left the room and returned with two keys. "Bob, you will be on the second floor, across the hall from Mr. Whitsell, who I suspect will be ecstatic for the company and who will likely introduce himself just as soon as he might. My good and durable women, you will be in the tower, in keeping with bygone preference."

"Yes, thank you Mr. More." June took the key in her hand,

turning it over and scrutinizing it with a wondering look. "May I ask a question about the tower? Or, may I make an observation about it?"

"Yes, what?"

"It's true that in the past we spent our pleasurable times there. But, and in the years we've been away, well—the tower looks as though it might collapse at any moment, Mr. More. And while I know that death comes for all, and that it is the fact of this great equalizer that gives our days such a tragic poetry, I don't know that I'm ready to pass over just yet, to say nothing of my not wanting to perish in a state of terror."

Mr. More sat listening with a sympathetic look on his face, but he said nothing to bring comfort to June.

"Will the tower hold us, Mr. More," she said.

"I believe so, yes."

"Do you believe it strongly?"

"I would be quite surprised if the tower should collapse this week."

"Oh, would you be."

"I would."

"To be clear, though, you admit that it will at some point collapse."

"Oh yes, it surely must, as must the entire building. But even still, and with this in mind, I do feel that the tower is best suited to your needs as it is the largest and most elegantly appointed room we have. You are welcome to any space in the hotel not already occupied, but I suspect you could investigate every corner of the property and that you would come to the same conclusion."

"You think we should push on and cross our fingers, then."

"I don't believe you need cross them, June, but if it brings you solace then please do do it, and just as tightly as you wish."

The group broke up and made their way to their respective quarters. Bob climbed the steps to the second floor; as he passed down the length of the hallway the tilt in the building became pronounced, so that he felt his speed increasing with each step. His room was the last on the right, unremarkable, unwarm, dark, a little dingy, even; but Bob was very much impressed by it, for it was a room and it was his, at least temporarily. He stood awhile in honor of his having a location of his own before making an investigation of the area, opening and closing each drawer and dresser, searching for something but finding nothing, not even a Bible. Next and he lay his remaining dollar bills in a marching line across the bedspread, counting out seventeen singles, which meant he had three to four days before any true crisis came into focus. Altogether he was feeling very much a distinguished young man of the world when the girl named Alice knocked once and walked into the room. She halted, backlit by the light from the hallway. Squinting, she said, "What are you doing in the dark, Mr. Sneaky? You're not going to jump out and terrify me again, I hope." She clicked on the light and crossed over to stand with Bob. Glancing at the money, she folded up her arms and said, "Christ, it's freezing in here. Why don't you turn the heat on?" She knelt to turn on the radiator, then moved to sit on the bed, dollar bills sticking up at kinked angles from under her backside. She commenced rolling a cigarette and said, "So, let me get this straight. You're standing around in the dark and cold, counting out your five dollars?"

"It's seventeen dollars," said Bob.

"Ho ho," Alice said. She lit her bumpy cigarette and waved the smoke away. Bob saw that she'd put on lipstick, and that her greasy hair was pulled back by a bejeweled barrette. As if in response to Bob's noticing this, she said, "I don't have a lot of time to talk to you because me and Tommy are going to the movies."

"Who's Tommy?" Bob asked.

"Tommy's the guy who says we can go steady if I sit up in the balcony with him. I think it's probably a trick, but I also think I might do it anyway. Sound like a plan?"

"Okay," Bob said.

Alice took a drag from her cigarette, head tilted to catch the stark light of the naked bulb on the ceiling. She looked Bob up and down and said, "My uncle told me I should be nice to you?"

Bob said, "Okay."

Alice shook her head. "I'm asking, why'd he say that? Is there something wrong with you?"

"I don't know," Bob said.

"You don't know if there's something wrong with you?"

"There's nothing."

"Well, I'll tell you what, Mr. Sneaky. I'll be nice to you if you want me to be nice to you. But you have to say it so I know, okay?"

"Okay," said Bob.

"Say it."

"Be nice to me."

Alice stood and kissed Bob softly on the cheek, then left the room. Bob stood touching the place where she'd kissed him, then checked his reflection in the mirror, gratified and impressed to find a faint smudge of lipstick on his face.

Bob stacked up his money and hid it away in his shoe. He still wore his pajamas under his street clothes; he took his street clothes off, turned out the light, and climbed into bed. There was a portable radio on the bedside table and he listened to the war news for some minutes; when this grew tiresome he shut the radio off and tried to sleep, but the moon was near to full, its light bright as a streetlamp in the window, and Bob got out of bed to lower the shade. Looking out, he could see Alice standing in front of the movie theater across the road from the hotel. She was alone, and looked small under the glow of the marquee. She peered down the road, once, and again. She turned and bought herself a ticket to the movie and went in by herself.

IN THE MORNING BOB WAS AWAKENED BY A KNOCK ON HIS DOOR, AND there again was Alice. She was not the playful youngster of the night previous but the sullen hotel laborer who had found him hiding behind the mountain of baggage. "You want breakfast? It's fifty cents if you do." She held out her hand beneath her chin, as if to catch her own spit. "It's porridge and coffee. We're out of cream."

Bob disliked porridge, and had no use for coffee. "Can I have eggs?"

"No, because there are none. If you want eggs, you should go to the diner. That's where your *interesting friends* went."

"When?"

"Just now."

Bob said he would go to the diner and Alice went away. He quickly dressed and left his room. Mr. Whitsell was sitting in the chair at the end of the hall, hands on his knees, his shoes set to the side of his stockinged feet. He was distracted by the light coming in the window but came alive when he saw Bob. "Good morning! You're going forth? To what end?" Bob said he was going to the diner and Mr. Whitsell asked, "Are you not a fan of porridge? Well, between us second-floorers, I don't like it much myself. The food here is fair but for the lack of variety. Actually, I've never once visited the diner, in all my time at the hotel. Do you know why? I'll tell you why: because I'm afraid. Afraid of people! Can you top it?" He rolled his eyes at himself, then pulled a ten-cent coin from his vest pocket and said, "Will you be a chum and get me today's newspaper and a five-cent cigar? They'll both be available at the diner." Bob agreed that he would do this and received the coin, turning and dashing down the hall and to the stairs, past the front desk, through the conservatory and into the brightness of the morning, still and cloudless. He was startled by the sight of the ocean, which in daylight took up the bulk of the vista and which seemed friendly and lazy and endless. He stared awhile, then came away from the sea and walked along the road and to the diner. June and Ida were sitting in a window booth, each with a dog on her lap, and June waved Bob over that he should join them. "I was wondering whether we should rouse you or not," she said. "Ida thought not. Did you sleep well? Is your room satisfactory? Mr. More is not the most efficient hotelier in the land, but he has a high-quality spirit, and that's worth something, after all."

Ida said, "Tell him about your dream, June."

"Should I?" asked June. "No, I shouldn't."

Ida told Bob, "She dreamed you were set upon by tramps."

June scowled at Ida. "You know, Bob," she said, "I support your project in every way. But I'm uneasy at the thought of one so young as yourself being alone in the world. Because the world sometimes is a complicated place."

Ida said, "You always hear about tramps buggering children."

"Ida, Ida," said June.

"What? You do hear about it. Forewarned is forearmed."

June patted Bob's arm. "You'll not be buggered, Bob."

"But if you are," said Ida, "don't say we didn't warn you."

"Anyway, it *was* an unsettling dream, and I couldn't sleep

for quite a long while after, and now Ida is cross with me because I kept her up speaking of you."

"On and on and on," said Ida.

"We were wondering if there mightn't be some place for you among us. You know. A job, Bob."

"It would be temporary," Ida added.

"But it is a quite important position, in its way," said June.

"But there is no pay," said Ida.

"But there must be *some* pay."

"I had thought his pay would be room and board."

"How will the boy buy his cat's-eyes and aggies and what have you? Here is what I propose: we vouchsafe his shelter and nourishment and offer the young go-getter a full dollar at the start of every day."

"That's just fine, June, but who will pay us to pay him?"

"One hundred pennies, Ida. I do believe we can manage. Well, Bob, what do you make of it?"

"Yes," said Bob.

"Yes you will work with us?"

"Yes."

"And Ida?"

"What?"

"Are you comfortable with the arrangements and do you agree with my heart's instinct that Bob is not some passing idler but one among us?"

Ida gave Bob a long and unwavering look. "Actually, I do agree," she said. "You are hired if you wish it, young man, and may God have mercy on your soul."

At this, June and Bob shook hands, and Ida began rapping an empty coffee cup on the table to commemorate or celebrate Bob's inclusion. The waitress, a young woman with a sanguine face, came by and said, "Yes?"

"Yes what, dear?" said June.

"Weren't you banging for me?"

"Not for you, no. Just banging."

"Oh," said the waitress.

"Emphasizing a point in time," Ida said.

"I guess that's all right, then," said the waitress, and she went away.

Ida said to Bob, "This scenario brings another question to mind, and it is: Can you play a snare drum?"

"No."

"Have you had any experience with any musical instrument?"

Bob shook his head.

June said, "Perhaps the question should not be, can you do this or that, but rather, would you be amenable to taking instruction that you might become competent in this or that."

Ida asked, "Would you be amenable to taking instruction that you might become competent at putting lipstick on a dog, when the dog doesn't want to wear lipstick?"

"Yes," Bob said.

Ida began rapping her cup on the table again. This time it was intended to bring the waitress tableside, but the waitress, having so recently been taught the rapping was not for her, was slow to come. With the rapping ongoing, though, eventually she arrived, and Ida explained that, yes, the noise now was meant as a summons.

"This banging on the table is a new one for me," the waitress said.

June said, "Communicative percussion predates the written word by thousands of years."

"Well, there you go." The waitress held her pencil to her pad and became poised to take the order. June was squinting at a menu; she asked, "What is frizzled beef?"

"It's hard to describe," said the waitress.

"Mightn't you try?" wondered June.

The waitress said, "Okay, well, it's beef, you know. The meat of a cow."

June joined her hands together to form a temple.

"And it's boiled," the waitress continued, "then it's shredded, then it's fried in oil, then it's salted, and then they put something that's like ketchup on it, then set it under a lamp to warm it up and sort of soften it. And there you are."

"It's frizzled."

"Right," said the waitress. "Is that what you'd like to have?"

"It's not, no." Addressing the table, June said, "The word *frizzled*, to my mind, evokes the visual of a dish of meat with hair still attached."

The waitress said, "There's no hair on our meats."

"There's a confidence-inspiring phrase," said Ida. "You should put it on a matchbook."

June still was squinting at the menu. "I shall have—the Lumberjacker."

"The Lumberjacker or the Little Lumberjacker?" asked the waitress.

"The Lumberjacker."

Bob likewise ordered the Lumberjacker. Ida quietly asked for cottage cheese and a cup of coffee; June raised her hand and said, "No, Ida. That is not your order. You will order more. Yes, you must." She turned to Bob: "She cheats herself at breakfast and thinks she's getting one over on someone, God in heaven, for all I know. But then at about eleven o'clock she becomes monstrous because she's so miserable at the emptiness of her stomach." She collected the menus into a stack and handed them up to the waitress. "My friend will also have a Lumberjacker, thank you."

"The Little Lumberjacker," said Ida, and the waitress went

away. In a short while they were served, and they all ate well, and happily. June asked Bob if he didn't want a nap after all the syrup, and Bob said he didn't.

"You wish to begin your labors now, then?"

"Yes."

"All right, here's my thought. Ida and myself will retire to the hotel to plot out our day of rehearsals. Certain of the scenes do not feature the boys as players, and we have learned that the boys can disrupt when they are idle, especially when we're setting up a stage. And so, while we are setting up, you will show the boys the town, all right? Yes?"

The bill came and June lay down money for the group, then passed Bob a dollar. When the waitress returned to make change, Bob set his dime on the tabletop and asked for a newspaper and a cigar, and the waitress looked to June, who looked to Ida, who, looking at Bob, said, "Cat's-eyes and aggies, indeed."

Later, out front of the diner, June and Ida and Bob stood by with the dogs, now leashed. June told Bob that their names were Buddy and Pal and said, "I hope you understand Ida's and my need of these animals. They are not pets. They are the entirety of our lives, beyond our relationships to one another and ourselves and our work."

"Well, it's all one thing," Ida explained. "But the thing cannot be without their input."

"Yes," June agreed. She asked Bob, "Will you be careful and good?" And Bob said that he would be, and June told Ida, "Bob understands."

Bob took the leashes into his grip and the women walked toward the ocean, the hotel. Once they rounded the corner, the dogs looked up at Bob. They were not distressed; perhaps they were curious about what should come next. Bob giddy-upped the leashes and he and the dogs crossed the road to stand before the dead printer's storefront. The suicide note still was taped up, an eerie document that Bob did read fully through. It struck him as levelheaded when he considered its proximity to the author's act of self-murder by hanging. *Friends of my community*, it began. There followed a sort of curriculum vitae: where he was born, schooled, which church he attended, and how he came to work in his field. He wrote, *I found many answers and comforts in my profession, but not every answer and not every comfort. In particular I could never find the answer to the question of why; and if a man cannot answer this question, there shall be no lasting comfort available to him.*

Next to the printer's was the movie theater, dark now, the ticket booth standing empty beside the entrance. After this came the post office. It was a very small post office with a single employee sitting behind the counter wearing the somber look of a man wondering where the magic had gone. A customer was leaving just as Bob passed so that they collided with one another, and the man set his hand on Bob's shoulder and told him, "Watch yourself, son." This person's stature was such that he blocked out the sun; Bob, peering upward, saw he wore a gun belt and badge and realized that this was the sheriff. Bob lowered his face to obscure his guilt-ridden runaway's eyes, pulling the dogs along and ducking into the corner market, which sat beside the post office. Bob was afraid the sheriff would somehow intuit his status as lawbreaker, follow him into the market, and apprehend him; but the black-and-white patrol car rolled slowly past and pulled onto the highway, heading south. Bob relaxed, then, and began a perusal of the contents of the market. It was the sort of place that endeavored to answer every possible need for the local citizens: fresh venison, jumper cables, fabric by the yard, and bait worms all were available for purchase. The aisles were cramped, the merchandise stacked in listing bales.

Behind the counter sat a brooding young man of twenty years. His hair was slicked back and he wore a white T-shirt with the sleeves rolled near to the shoulder that he might display the sculpted musculature of his arms. He was reading a magazine laid flat on the counter, his eyes scanning left to right. One of the dogs growled at him and the young man looked up. "Get those mutts out of here." He pointed to the door and resumed his magazine reading.

Bob left and sat down on the bench out front of the market, to bask in the sun's warmth and to listen to the ocean and feel the wind coming in off the surface of the water. The dogs became infected by Bob's restful demeanor and curled up on the pavement. Bob was looking up at the southern face of the hotel across the road and noticed Alice pacing slowly in his room. She moved in and out of view, talking to herself and trailing smoke from her cigarette and making little gestures of explaining with her hands. She didn't look unhappy; but what was she doing? Bob stood and crossed the road with the dogs. He picked up a piece of the white pea gravel and tossed it against the window. Alice opened the window and leaned out on her elbows. She took a drag off her cigarette and said, "Well?"

"What are you doing in my room?"

"My job."

"But you're just walking around in there."

She flicked her cigarette away; it soared over Bob's head and landed in the road behind him. "Look, Mr. Sneaky," she said. "You can't just jump into scrubbing a floor. You've got to sort of ease into it, okay?"

The window beside Bob's opened up and there was Mr. Whitsell. He was squinting hard in the sunlight and waving or wagging his pale hand. "Have you forgotten me, young man?" he asked. "Have you forgotten my needs?" Bob said he hadn't, and patted his coat pocket to show he had the newspaper and cigar on his person. Mr. Whitsell asked, "Do you have a thought for when you'll deliver these things? The news will not be fresh by the time it arrives, is my fear." He leaned out the window to look at Alice, who was leaning out the window to look at him. "I like a womb-warm, just-born newspaper," he said, then turned back to Bob. "Shall we rendezvous in the conservatory?"

"Okay," Bob said.

"Now?"

"Yes."

When Bob didn't move, Mr. Whitsell paused. "Now now?"

"Yes."

Mr. Whitsell ducked his head back into his room and shut the window and drew the curtains. Bob returned his attentions to Alice, who was standing straighter than she'd been, and she wore a stricken expression, her gaze aimed above and behind the place where Bob stood. Bob turned and saw the young man in the T-shirt leaning coolly against the brick exterior of the market, smoking and looking up at her. They both were breathing through their mouths and staring at each other with what appeared to be hostility, but which Bob later understood was likely more on the order of simple lust. Whatever was happening between these two, Bob knew there was no place for him in the equation, and he led the dogs away, following the gravel moat around and to the front of the hotel and climbing the five blue steps. Mr. Whitsell was waiting for him in the conservatory, eyes shining, panting from his second-floor descent. He took the paper and cigar up in his arms and stepped to the rear of the room, vanishing wholly into the overgrown foliage. Bob soon heard a rhythmic creaking over the floorboards and thought it must have been that Mr. Whitsell had a rocking chair hidden away back there.

THE REHEARSALS TOOK PLACE IN THE AUDITORIUM, SO-CALLED, WHICH was actually just the dining hall with the tables removed and the chairs set up in rows before a stage built up against the farthermost wall. Bob quietly ushered the dogs into the room and took a seat in the back row, that he might spy on June and Ida and learn something about their coming performances.

The stage was lit by footlights, a warm, yellow-gold glow against the painted backdrop, a realistic rendering of a public square in the eighteenth century. A full-size guillotine was set up center stage, and Ida fixed in its stockade, her face and hair made up to resemble a filthy and dejected man, a prisoner on the verge of execution. June was the executioner in pointed black leather hood, leather vest, and elbow-length leather gloves. Bob paid close attention to their words and behaviors; eventually he realized they were not rehearsing anything, but had interrupted their rehearsal to have a disagreement. Ida, the angrier, said, "How can I be meant to represent a criminal's emotional reality if I don't even know what crime I have committed?"

"I say again that you're thinking too much about it," June said, reaching under her leather hood to scratch her chin. "It doesn't matter what the crime was. Actually, Ida, and in a way, that's the point. I don't think of your character as a hardened criminal, but rather, one due to have his head lopped off in reply to an infraction."

"But what was the infraction?"

"It is irrelevant."

"It isn't."

"It is in that an infraction must never result in the lopping off of one's head, for it is merely an infraction. The function of the scene is the description of a man's costly error in a savage era."

"It is just as savage now."

"Yes, but in a newer way."

"It is no less savage, June."

"Fine, yes, I didn't say I disagreed with you. But that's to the side of the point, just as the man's crime is."

Ida said, "You don't know the crime in the first place, do you?"

"As a matter of fact I don't. I have not authored the crime because it is superfluous."

"May I author a crime?"

"You may not."

"Perhaps I'll author one in my mind and keep it hidden from you."

"Ida, it is far too late in the day for you to succumb to your lunatic nature."

Ida wagged her finger in a style that said she would not be deterred from her principal point: "By inhibiting this process you are intentionally demeaning the quality of our work."

"All right!" said June, and she punched the air with her black gloves. "I'll name the crime. But you must promise me now that you won't succumb. You are already dipping a toe in, you know that you are, and I demand that you promise me you'll not fully indulge."

Ida said chastely, "I do promise it."

"Because I can see the lunatic rising up in you and I must insist that you halt her from taking shape."

"Yes, yes," said Ida. "What is my crime?"

"Let me think." June paced in her creaking leather garb. "You are many seasons in arrears with your land tax."

Ida made the face of thinking. "No, not that."

June said, "You slapped an officer of the court in a tavern."

"Well," Ida said. "Was I drunken?"

"Quite drunken, yes."

"But," said Ida, "I'm not a common drunk."

"No, you had some bad news, someone has died, and so you went to the tavern to drink away your sorrow."

"My own son had died."

"Died by drowning," said June.

"He drowned in the quay and he was my one and only boy."

At this last word, Buddy commenced making a needful growling noise, and then Pal also did, and June and Ida ceased their discussion to look out into the darkness. June held her gloved hand over her eyes. "Is that Bob out there, and does he have the babies?"

"Yes," Bob called.

"How did it go, Bob? Are our comrades alive, and unafraid, and did they behave, and did everyone enjoy everyone's company?"

"Yes," Bob called.

The dogs both were whining and pulling against their leashes, and June said, "You may set them loose, Bob." Bob did as instructed, and the dogs were off. Pal had the lead; he beelined for the stage, taking its lip in one leap, then soaring up and through the air and into June's arms, while Buddy bounded up the steps to the side of the stage, hurrying to Ida and licking her all about the face. Ida, powerless to stop this, flapped her manacled hands and cried out bloody murder that her makeup should be ruined.

THE GUILLOTINE WAS WHEELED INTO THE WINGS, AND JUNE AND THE dogs went away to the tower to rehearse in private while Bob and Ida sat in chairs facing one another on the stage, and Ida made to teach Bob how to play a snare drum. She got an almost frighteningly serious look in her eye when she performed the drum roll, what she called a press roll. The drum rested on her lap, the sticks held at odd angles in her hands as she drew them across the drum and toward herself, over and again, evenly, machinelike. Ida had mastered this percussive effect so that it did not sound like many individual raps upon the drum but rather a whole and complete sound: dense, sustained, fraught. She was staring hard at Bob as she made her demonstration, and she continued drumming as she spoke: "The drumsticks are loose are in my hands. I am not banging; I'm not tapping. I am exerting an even pressure as I drag the hopping sticks over the skin of the drum. Press, roll, press, roll." The sticks were blurred smudges in the air. "What is this sound?" she asked, while still making it. "What does the sound say?"

Bob said, "Pay attention."

"What else?"

"Something is coming."

She abruptly ceased drumming. Ida looked pleased, or less

displeased than her usual. "In any language, Bob, in any town on earth, that's what a press roll says, yes. It's an important signal and a critical aspect of the last scene of our coming performance. I'd like for you to take the drum to your room and practice what I've shown you. We have a phonograph recording of a press roll that we could use in a pinch but we always prefer the true human activity. Do you understand what I'm telling you?"

"I don't know."

"I'm telling you that if you can arrive at a place of proficiency with this particular flourish, then we should welcome you to join us."

She passed the drum and sticks to Bob and he set them on his lap, wondering at their shape, materials, weight. June returned with the dogs, and she wore the face of defeat as she told Ida, "It was a fine idea and I hope you know I appreciate it but I just don't believe it's possible to teach a dog to goose-step, and I'm sorry."

Bob was relieved of his duties for the afternoon, and he took the drum to his room and sat with it on his bed. Recalling what Ida had said about holding the sticks loosely, he understood that what he was after was a bouncing effect; it was gravity at work, the player collaborating with natural law. He soon could summon a consistent roll with his right hand, but not his left. An hour passed like nothing when there came a knock on the door and there was Mr. Whitsell, who began with a casual appraisal of the afternoon weather but soon admitted that Bob's drumming was making him nervous. "And a little angry," he said. "The sound is making me nervous and angry both, and I'm happy you're bettering yourself, but please take pity on an old man with a frail and fussy disposition, won't you?" Bob carried the drum and sticks down the stairs and across the highway to the seashore; and here he sat and practiced. It was good to practice beside the even roar of the ocean because he could hear his drumming but the noise didn't travel and so could not disturb anyone. Periodically he would cease drumming and there was a tingling in his hands and up his arms, but when he returned to it then the tingling went away, or was hidden somewhere, subsumed by his activity, just as the sound of the drum was subsumed by the sea.

BOB AND IDA AND JUNE AND THE DOGS WENT TO THE DINER FOR DINNER

but the diner was closed. There was a note taped to the front door: *The diner's shut b/c the cook's run off. We don't know where. Do you? Management.* As there was nowhere else to go, the group returned to the hotel; when Mr. More saw them shuffling in, and when he learned of their not being fed, he became gladly agitated and proposed an impromptu dinner party in his and Alice's quarters. Ida protested that she would prefer to eat in her room but Mr. More, not understanding, or pretending not to understand, said he wouldn't hear of it, and he rang the bell to rouse Alice with instructions to prepare the wine and then to seek out Mr. Whitsell and encourage him to join the festivities. "Friendly but firm," he called to her as she trudged up the stairs.

Now Mr. More moved the group like a drover into the dining room, encouraging Ida and June to drink from the breathing bottles of red wine before he retired to the kitchen, where he clanged pots and ran water and hummed and praised and admonished himself. Alice returned without Mr. Whitsell and began the work of setting the table. Bob looked up at her as she lay out his napkin and cutlery; she knocked him with her hip and tugged at his ear, familiarities which did not escape

Ida and June, who both began whistling casual melodic scales at the newness of the information that he and Alice had established some style of bond. Mr. More called out from the kitchen: "What did Mr. Whitsell say, Alice?"

"He said to say he wasn't sure. He said to say he wants to think it over."

Having apparently done this, Mr. Whitsell did shortly arrive in a cloud of perfume and with a look of delight stamped upon his small, soft, rounded face. He lapped the table, greeting each diner in turn with a bow and a shoulder touch. As he took his seat he said, "Well, I didn't see this coming!"

"We hope we haven't disturbed you?" asked June.

"Disturbed me? My good woman, you could have knocked me out with a feather! There I was, making my nightly bedways trek, when young Alice came rapping. Talk about a bolt from the blue! An invitation to dine? If you insist, then I must accept!" He unfolded his napkin and set it across his lap. "But, what shall we speak of? I never know just where to begin in a conversation—or where to end, for that matter."

"Let us speak of small and easy things," June proposed.

"Or not at all," said Ida.

"Like monks, eh?" said Mr. Whitsell. "Well, it's your party, and so I will follow your lead."

Mr. More soon brought in a steaming bowl of spaghetti and a loaf of bread under his arm. There was no butter to be had, and the bread was days old, but the meal served its purpose, and was devoured. Bob was digesting when he noticed a framed poster on the wall above the table featuring a full-body photograph of Mr. More, and in the place where his arm should have been there was an arm-shaped text that read: LES IS MORE! Across the bottom of the poster, in a soberer font, were the words: GIVE ME A HAND THIS ELECTION DAY! ELECT LESLIE MORE TO THE OFFICE OF CITY COUNCILMAN!

Mr. More, having noticed Bob's interest, was turned about in his chair, pointing at the poster with his fork. "Yes, Bob, I did once dabble in local politics. I don't regret the time and money spent, but it *was* a lesson learned for me, and a bitter one. You talk of corruption? I thought I knew my neighbors. Not by a long shot I didn't."

Alice, in her monotone, said, "He got nine votes."

"That's what they would have us believe," said Mr. More.

"Nine votes," said Alice.

"It was folly, top to bottom, side to side, and clean through to its center. You should have seen the man I lost to, my goodness. He was unburdened by human dignity or even an animal dignity; he was without shame, scruples, and social grace, and he won by a landslide."

June was grinning into the palm of her hand; and neither did Ida look uninterested. "How do you account for the loss, Mr. More?" she asked.

"Welcome to my dark night of the soul, Ida. It's a question I can't ask myself straight out; I need to approach it indirectly, and stepping lightly. It may be that the very notion of public office was a fool's errand but I always felt, I don't know, that I was meant for something larger than hotelier."

"What's wrong with being a hotelier?" asked Mr. Whitsell.

"Nothing in and of itself. But am I not capable of something more demanding and challenging?"

"It's not an uncommon story," June told him. "Just about anyone you pass on the sidewalk is wondering why they've not fulfilled their potential."

"But I'm not talking about garden-variety disappointment, June."

"I think perhaps you are."

Mr. Whitsell told Mr. More, "I voted for you."

Mr. More set his fork down. "I wondered if you had," he

said. "I hoped you had. But tell the truth, now, did you vote for me because you felt duty bound, or because of your admiration for my platform?"

"I did feel duty bound."

This was not the answer Mr. More had hoped for, judging by his expression. "Perhaps," he said, "perhaps it was that you felt duty bound while also admiring my platform."

"I haven't half an idea what your platform was," Mr. Whitsell said.

"Did you not read the literature I left in your room?"

"Shame on me, but no, I didn't. I'm sure it was a thrilling document. I'd have voted for you twice if I could have."

"Then he'd have had ten votes," said Alice.

Ida had been watching Mr. Whitsell for a time, and now she addressed him: "Mr. Whitsell, can I ask you a question?"

"Oh, yes, please, fire away," he said, and he then propped himself up in his seat, preparing to be asked he knew not what.

"I'm just curious as to why you've been living here at the hotel for such a length of time?"

"I don't know, really. Why shouldn't I be?"

"Have you no other plans?"

"No."

"Possibly you had plans when you came here, but then mislaid them?"

He thought about this. "I don't believe I did, no," he said.

"So you just were passing by and washed up here?"

"Well, I'm not enamored of your wordage, but yes, I'll play along and tell the truth, because really, that's exactly what happened. In passing, I paused, and then could not move on, and so was washed up like detritus, and on the seashore to boot. It was a funny thing. I had made my retirement and enacted my plan, which was to leave North Dakota and travel by bus all through the Americas. I experienced a high optimism at the commencement of my voyage, but by the time I arrived in Oregon I had been on the road some five weeks and had long since come to grips with the truth of the matter, which was that I disliked most every single feature of my life aboard that slum on wheels. No matter what the advertisements had promised me, I was not 'accumulating life experience,' nor was I 'seeing the country.' I was trapped in a state of thorough mediocrity, and escape was the only option. But where? I had no friend or relation outside of the Dakotas, and was not at all eager to return home. Days went by and I sat looking out the dirty window, a prisoner studying his cell for some weakness he might exploit to make good his getaway. It was an August afternoon when the bus stopped here, and I got out to stretch my burning back. When I looked up, there was Mr. More, standing on the porch of this hotel, and he waved at me, and I waved back. 'Are there any rooms available?' I asked, and his reply: 'Nothing but rooms, yes and you bet.' I asked the cost and he said it was so close to free that I wouldn't believe it. Now he crossed the highway and we made our introductions. He asked after my mood and I explained in shorthand my dissatisfactions and he asked if he might fetch my satchel from the hold of the bus and I allowed it, and then he did it, and that was how it all was started. It's been, what, three years now? Four? And still no plans to leave except by pine box. I find the hotel perfectly charming. There is a feeling of waiting that at times can be oppressive, but likely that's not inherent to the location but rather is a part of the particular era of my life. The end era, you know." As if speaking to himself, he said, "No, I don't want to leave the hotel, and I hope I shall never have to."

He finished the last of his wine and stood, speaking of a tiredness brought on by the unanticipated but very much appreciated dining diversion. He thanked the assembled for their friendly company and excused himself. After he left, Alice asked if she might also be excused as she had, she explained, plans to see a movie with a friend. Mr. More said that it was important for a young lady to keep her appointments but wondered if she had been getting quite enough rest these last days. Alice countered that young people did not need hardly any rest at all to carry on, and she quoted a doctor she'd heard on the radio who made the claim that sleep deprivation, in moderation, was actually regenerative. Mr. More said he wasn't buying what Alice was selling but that he admired her spryness of mind, and Alice said thank you, and departed. Ida asked Mr. More about the possibility for coffee, as she and June planned to rehearse into the night, and Mr. More raised a finger and went away to the kitchen, soon returning with the coffee and cups on a tray. He poured out one cup, and then another, while June and Ida watched him, liking him.

Ida said, "How *did* you lose your arm, Mr. More?"

"I lost it in the First World War, Ida," he answered, passing her her coffee. "You knew that, didn't you?"

"I must have, and yet I'm surprised to think of it. What a thing that must be, to lose an arm."

"Very much a thing, yes," said Mr. More.

June said, "May I ask if it was your good arm?"

"Anyway it was not a bad one. I think the truth is that once an arm is taken from you, you can't help but recall it as the arm to end all arms."

Ida said, "Where do you think they put it?"

"I don't know. Some pit somewhere. But it's not like I wanted it back later. What am I going to do with it? Swaddle it? Wear it like a stole?" He made the face of amused suspicion. "I do hope that our conversation isn't moving in the pacifistic direction?"

Ida drew back in her seat. "Me, pacifistic? Honestly, Mr. More, how could you say such a thing? Why, when I think of the violence that exists inside my own heart."

Mr. More shook his head, and he said, "I fear you're being clever with me, dear Ida."

"Cleverness I'll admit to," she said.

June asked, "What do you think of this current concern, Mr. More?"

"Which concern do you mean?"

"World War the Second."

Mr. More said, "I think standing under the chill shadow of any nation's flag is a dicey proposition, is what I think." He began stacking dirty plates. "Now, why don't you both take your coffees and get to your rehearsals."

"May we help you with the dishes?" Ida asked.

"You may not."

"Are you sure?" said June. "We really don't mind."

"No, no. You've got your work to do, and to tell the truth I've entered into a period of my life where I actually enjoy doing the dishes, and by myself. Which is odd when I consider to what degree I always loathed the practice before; but recently it feels like time well spent. What does it mean?" Bob was nearly asleep in his chair; Mr. More gently crushed his foot under the table and said, "Someday, Bob, when you're an aged specimen like me, and you find yourself suddenly enamored of folding the laundry or edging your lawn, remember your long-gone friend Leslie More telling you to accept whatever happiness passes your way, and in whatever form."

"Okay," said Bob.

"Because it's a fool who argues with happiness, while the wiser man accepts it as it comes, if it comes at all."

"Okay."

THE NEXT DAY BOB RETURNED TO THE BEACH TO PRACTICE HIS PRESS rolls. The first performance was scheduled to take place thirty-six hours hence; with this in mind, Bob endeavored to arrive at a place where he could achieve the percussive effect without thinking of it. An hour and a half passed, and he paused, looking out to sea and having looking-out-to-sea thoughts. He imagined he heard his name on the wind and turned to find Ida leaning out the window of the tilted tower; her face was green as spinach puree, and she was waving at him that he should come up. Bob held the drum above his head, and she nodded that he should bring it with him.

He crossed the road and climbed the stairs to the tower. Ida answered the door and Bob now saw that she was wearing a full and realistic witch costume, with pointy hat and flowing rags, a prosthetic nose and chin, and her teeth were blackened and she said, "Good morning, Bob. Come inside, please." Bob entered to find a room exploded with clothing and costumes and props and banners. The dogs nosed through the wreckage; they too were dressed as witches. June was sitting on an unmade bed, telephone in hand, and she was dressed as half-a-witch: she wore the same green makeup but no nose or chin, a hat but no flowing rags. "How's life on old planet Earth, Bob?" she asked, but before Bob could answer, she was speaking into the telephone: "Operator? Yes, good morning. May I ask you, what's the name of the newspaper in this area?" She waited. "There's two," she told Ida, who wasn't listening, busy as she was making evil faces in a mirror on the wall. June asked the operator, "Which of the two is the smarter outfit? Oh, you know, larger, better, stronger. Which is more widely read, I guess is the question. All right, that's fine. Will you please connect me with their front office? Bless you." While she waited, she watched Ida, lost in her engagement with her reflection. "Ida has bewitched herself," she told Bob, before resuming the telephone conversation: "Yes, hello, I should like to speak with whichever reporter is responsible for the coverage of arts in your area. Oh, the moving arts. The talking arts. Singing arts, sort of, sometimes. We also possess dogs who can do any number of clever things. That's right, we throw it all into a pot and hope for the best." June was watching Bob standing there with the drum in his hands; covering the phone, she whispered, "Ida, release yourself." Ida looked away from the mirror and asked, "What?" June pointed at Bob, then uncovered the phone and said, "Either man sounds fine to me. May I ask you a favor, though, woman to woman? Will you put me in touch with the lesser bastard?" June held the phone out; the woman on the line was laughing hard enough that it was audible across the room. Ida led Bob into the bathroom and shut the door behind them.

"You've been practicing?"

"Yes."

"Will you show me?"

She lowered the toilet seat and gestured that Bob should sit, and so he did, resting the drum on his lap and readying his sticks. When Ida bowed, Bob leaned over and commenced with his audition. Having spent so many minutes and hours recently banging on the drum, in returning to the act, it felt familiar in some elusive way, as though he were re-creating something that had already occurred. This time-confusion marred Bob's coordination, and the press roll began falling to pieces. "Stop," said Ida. Bob stopped and watched her. "Start again." He started again. He was focusing with all his might; Ida held up her hand and Bob ceased playing. She told him, "I'm aware of your struggle." "Thank you," said Bob, and Ida shook her head. "I'm not complimenting you. What I want is to think only of the sound produced by the drum, but not of the emotional truth of the drummer. Do you understand? Your problems are not my problems. Keep them to yourself, hidden away. Take a breath and try again." Bob tried again and was playing well, but peripherally he could see that Ida was distracted; her head was bent toward the closed door and after a time she held up a hand and said, again, "Stop." Bob stopped. "Did you call out to me?" she asked, through the door.

June answered, "Yes, several times I did."

"All right, and what is it?"

"I just was pointing out how timely your drum practice was."

Ida looked to Bob with a weary face. She said, "Did we ruin your powwow, or what's the problem?"

"I don't believe you helped, I'll say that much." June paused. "Do you wish to know how my media-seeking campaign has gone?"

"All right."

"It went well, in spite of Bob's drumming. Not that it was Bob's fault. Bob? It's not your fault. It's Ida's fault."

"Okay," called Bob.

A silence, then June said, "I believe I'll print off those handbills now."

"Yes, well, thank you for your numerous updates." Ida

shook her head and refocused her attentions on the audition. "What I'm after," she told Bob, "is ten seconds of clean playing in a middle register. Take two breaths, deep ones, and try again." Bob breathed and breathed and gave Ida twenty seconds of straight, solid playing. She raised her hand, and Bob stopped. "That's very good," she said. "Do you think you could do it with an audience present? You will be offstage, in the wings, but an audience is very *there*, you know, and so can cause inhibition. I suspect our numbers will not be high, but often the small audience is the more pronounced, the more there. This tension is the very thing lacking in cinema, you see, and this is the reason I detest the medium with such exuberance, with such, such—"

From the next room there came two unique sounds, one after the other: the first was a clanking and grinding, metal working against metal; next was the noise of the dogs, whom Bob had not heard bark before but who were now both barking loudly and dedicatedly, this in reply to the clanking and grinding. Ida and Bob exited the bathroom to find June working a hand crank on a small printing machine set up atop a dresser, and blue handbills seesawed through the air while the dogs jumped and barked and behaved generally in high emotion while the pages drifted down upon them and their pointy black witch hats. Over the noises of the printing machine's grindings and the barking of the dogs, June called out to Bob, "It's the one thing that makes them passionate beyond reason." He picked up a handbill from the floor:

LIMITED ENGAGEMENT!

The TRIUMPHANT RETURN of BELOVED
VETERANS of the STAGE

JUNE & IDA and their TRAINED CANINES,

PAL & BUDDY

shall ENTERTAIN w/ UNCANNY VERVE and
UNLIKELY ACCURACY A DISSECTION of
our COMPLICATED POSITION

JUNE & IDA TRANSLATE this PRECARIOUS
MOMENT w/ LEVITY, BREVITY, GRAVITY,
and ETCETERA!

Ida took the handbill from Bob and read it. "It has a sly something," she admitted, and June continued working the hand crank and the handbills continued their snowing down and the dogs continued to leap about and shout, and a large faux cauldron was leaking the faux smoke of dry ice which moved in a lateral stream across the room and toward the open window. Along the coastal road, Bob noticed, there was a convoy of National Guard vehicles moving south.

BOB WAS GIVEN HIS DAILY DOLLAR AND THE HANDBILLS; HE WAS instructed to move about the town and pass these to whomever he might and to generally, so much as he was able within what Ida called the limitations of his secluded personality, induce the public to attend the coming performance. He was asked to bring the dogs, and to undress and tidy them before leaving; he proposed that their outfits could not but pique the public's interest, which Ida and June did recognize as true and wise, and so Buddy and Pal remained in costume for the length of their outing. When Bob stepped onto the porch of the hotel he saw a second convoy passing on the highway, and in the same southerly direction as the first; each of the covered trucks was tightly packed with glum-faced National Guardsmen, rifles sticking up between their legs. A group of fifty citizens was gathered along the side of the highway, watching and waving at the caravan.

The sheriff stood beside his patrol car, which was parked out front of the market across the road from the hotel. After the caravan passed, the sheriff blew his horn and spoke into a PA mic run through a speaker atop his vehicle: "I'd like a word, please," he said, and the men and women walked all together to stand before him. Bob shuffled himself into the crowd, following along with the rest. There was a lot of chatter coming up, and the sheriff took off his hat and waved it above his head. When the crowd quieted, the sheriff put his hat back on and spoke into the microphone.

"Ladies and gentlemen, good day, hello. As you've probably figured out for yourselves, we've got a situation on the stovetop in Bay City, and you're going to want to avoid that location for however long it takes for things to cool off down there. I don't know how long that'll be, but tonight's looking iffy, and you'd do well to sit tight and await, as they say, further instruction. I don't believe there's very many among us interested in taking part in any disturbances; what I'm thinking of, what I'm hoping to avoid—what I'm asking of you, neighbors, is that you curtail any impulse to rubberneck or lookie-loo. You think you could do that for me?"

A voice called out: "But what's it all about, Sheriff?"

The sheriff said, "Few different things that've been going on for some time. There's two different lumber camps set up in the hills above Bay City, couple hundred men to a camp, and they're pretty much on top of one another out there, and with no law around to keep them on the right side of mischief. Bay City has very little to offer on the order of nightlife, nowhere for the boys to blow off steam, and they've been getting a little weird out there. Started out they were playing practical jokes, right? One camp against another, but nothing too terrible. Then, over the months, the jokes've become less funny, and as you may've heard there was an incident yesterday in one of the camps involving some heavy machinery that did look more than a little like sabotage, and which did result in one fatality, and another man got his back broken. Both of these fellows have or had wives and children, and the entire affair is sitting poorly with certain of the lumbermen. Also it happens that there's an ongoing scuffle about lumber contracts and title disputes, namely, who gets to chop down all those giant firs behind the Gustafson property. This is more to do with the higher-ups than the men on the ground but the negotiations have been pretty mean I'm told, and that type of venom has a way of trickling down, right? Right. Tonight's the night I figure it's all going to come to a head one way or the other. Any rate. The intelligence we've got says they're planning a showdown in the center of town."

Another voice: "Man on the radio said it was going to be a riot, Sheriff."

The sheriff said, "Yeah, I heard that too. And I wouldn't be surprised if it comes true. I also wouldn't be surprised if it didn't. They got eight or nine truckloads of soldiers polishing up their rifles in Bay City as we speak. If those lumber boys want trouble, it will be made available to them."

"What do you think, Sheriff?"

"What do I think what, Ted?"

"What way you think it'll go?"

"I really don't know, buddy, on account of my crystal ball's on the fritz. My hope is that these lumber boys'll lose interest in killing each other when they see all the soldiers aiming guns at them. But they've been mutating in those camps for long enough I figure anything can happen. Maybe they'll decide to go all in. Time to time, a man likes to set things on fire. Or that's been my experience."

"You're heading to Bay City tonight, Sheriff?"

"Yes, Charlie, I'll be going over just now."

"You need any deputies?"

"All the wives are suddenly shaking their heads," said the sheriff, to modest applause and laughter. "Wise women. No, thank you but I won't be needing your help tonight. How about you mind your place and I'll take care of the rest, all right? Just, let me do the job you pay me to do. There ought to be some good coverage on the radio, and if they riot like they mean it you'll likely be able to see some sign of it from your windows."

The crowd raised up a friendly note of approval for the sheriff and he waved a hand before jumping back on the microphone: "Oh, one more thing: stop calling my house! You're driving Mrs. the Sheriff to drink."

The sheriff was getting into his car to leave but was waylaid by a number of men who wished to further discuss the Bay City situation. All the rest in the crowd stood about dissecting their theories and concerns with one another; Bob took advantage of the throng to pass out his handbills. Pal and Buddy caused a small stir, and Bob couldn't give the handbills away fast enough. After, with the crowd trickling away, he and the dogs looped the little town. He saw that the diner was open for business, the waitress chatting away with a line of men at the bar. When Bob returned to the hotel he found June and Ida in the auditorium, setting up for another rehearsal. Ida was onstage with the cauldron; June was standing at the middle aisle amid the bank of seats. They both were back in their traditional daytime outfits. "Left," June said; and Ida moved the cauldron to her left. "My left," said June, and Ida sighed and corrected the position of the cauldron. "More," said June, and Ida moved the cauldron farther to June's left. "That's good. Mark it." Now Ida knelt down to outline the cauldron in chalk while June turned to face Bob as he made his approach. "Here comes our man on the street. Hey, where are the handbills?"

"I gave them away."

"Not all of them?" she asked, and Bob explained about the crowd, and what the sheriff had said about Bay City. Mr. More came in with his carafe of coffee and triangulated sandwiches on a tray. "Chow bell, chow bell," he said.

"Did you know about this violence downcoast?" asked June.

"Yes."

"Well, what do you think of it?"

"I think that it's a good thing I don't live downcoast."

"My God, what next?" June said.

Ida stepped up to meet the group. "What's the matter?"

"They're set to riot in the neighboring town," Mr. More explained.

"Just now?"

"Tonight."

Ida took up a sandwich. "Look on the bright side," she said. "If they riot tonight then they'll be freed up tomorrow, and likely quite placid to boot, having already satisfied their lust for carnage."

June touched Bob at the elbow. "We've been met with violence on numerous occasions. In a mining camp in Ohio they threw stones at us. Ida still believes they were trying to kill us."

"They *were* trying to kill us," said Ida, biting into the sandwich and chewing slowly, suspiciously.

"Because they hadn't liked the play?" Mr. More ventured.

"That was our impression," said June.

Mr. More moved to set the tray on the edge of the stage. "I'll just leave this here for you to work through at your leisure." After he exited the auditorium, Ida tossed her sandwich over her shoulder and into the darkness. "Meat paste," she told June.

"He shouldn't have."

"Really, he shouldn't."

"The diner's open again," Bob said, and June and Ida looked to one another. "But it's too soon to break," June said.

"But I'm hungry," said Ida.

"But it's too soon."

"But: I'm hungry."

"Well, I am too, if you want to know the truth. What about you, Bob? Where do you sit on the hunger scale?"

"Hungry," Bob answered.

"That tears it," said June. "Get your coat, Ida, and mine, and let us dine."

Soon they entered the diner, greeting their waitress friend.

"Oh, hello," she said.

June said, "I understand you've found the missing cook?"

"Anyway, he's back."

"And where was he?"

"Honestly, I'm so mad I don't think I can talk about it. Better you go ask him yourself." She pointed at the square cutaway cubbyhole where the cook received his orders and set down his plates of food and dinged his silver bell. June approached and called out, "Excuse me?" and the cook's face appeared. He looked puffy and red-eyed but not unhappy; June asked, "Where were you, sir, that everyone was so up in arms?"

"Well, I went off and served myself a couple of beverages, didn't I?"

"You had a high time?"

"Yes, quite high."

"And how did you feel after?"

"Oh, disgusted," he said. "But I had fun too, which counts for something, after all."

"Are you glad to be back?"

The cook made the half-and-half gesture.

"Are you very tired?"

"Lady, I'm as tired as a dead dog." He looked at Pal, resting in June's arms. "No offense, partner. Hey, look at your little hat."

June said, "Perhaps once you begin your daily frizzling, then you'll find some obscure reserve of energy."

The cook shook his head. "No, no one wanted to associate with that particular dish, so we had to retire it." He leaned out the cubbyhole and pointed at an artwork pinned to the wall. It was a pen-and-ink rendering of a graveyard, and on every tombstone was the name of a dish that had been stricken from the menu:

Here Lies Meat Medley
In Loving Remembrance ~ Omelette du Veal
Rest in Peace Chix Stix
Beloved Frizzled Beef

At the bottom of the paper in a tidy script were the words: *Gone but not forgotten.*

The cook still was leaning out of the cubbyhole, peering up at the artwork, and he wore the nameless smile of a day-dreamer. "I thought it was not a bad method, myself," he said.

"Frizzling?" said June. "In what way?"

"In the way that it tasted. But also, you know, the making of it. All told I'd have to say it was my favorite dish on the menu to prepare."

Ida asked, "What's your least favorite dish to prepare?"

The cook paused. "Probably I shouldn't discuss it with a custy, I don't think."

"What's a custy?"

"You're a custy."

"Why shouldn't you discuss it with me?"

"Well, think it through. If you learn what I don't like making, and you want it, then we're in somewhat of a pickle be-cause either you don't get what you want, because you don't order it out of a personal niceness; or, you go ahead and order it anyway, which tells me that you don't rate me as a human being to the point of considering my feelings."

June said, "You're quite an emotional cook, aren't you?"

He spoke in a tone of somber earnestness: "Working in a restaurant, the cook is very vulnerable." In a louder voice, he addressed the clientele: "You think I don't hear what you all say about my food? I hear every word!" He dinged his silver bell fiercely with a spatula, his eyes gleaming with devilment. There were only a few scattered customers present, however, and none of them were paying the cook any mind.

The waitress returned, passing an order up to the cook and encouraging June and company to sit, and the group walked all together toward what they thought of as their booth. Later, as they were finishing up their meal, an army jeep pulled up outside the diner and a military policeman entered. The waitress was nowhere in sight; the MP called out, "How much coffee you got in this place?"

"A whole goddamned urnful," answered the cook from the kitchen.

"I'll take it all, and the urn as well."

The cook's face appeared in the cubby. "Urn's not for sale."

"Uncle Sam needs that coffee," said the MP, and he held up a fold of bills.

"Uncle Sam is welcome to every drop of coffee I've got. But he's going to have to get his own urn, because I need mine, and all the time, too."

The soldier hemmed and hawed but eventually went away with a thermosful of coffee. It was his own thermos, and he was disappointed that his gesture had not been actualized. Ida thought perhaps the man had played out a scenario in his mind of arriving in Bay City ahead of the riot with the urnful of fortifying and piping hot coffee for his comrades, and that they would give three cheers in appreciation of his ingenuity. The cook called over from his cubby, "Ever notice what a uniform does to a young man's self-worth?"

"Yes, we have," said June and Ida simultaneously.

After dinner, the two women and Bob and the dogs returned to the hotel, where they found Mr. More and Mr. Whitsell at the front desk, leaning in to listen to the radio coverage from Bay City. The riot had not yet commenced officially but was slowly coming into its own as dusk evolved to nighttime. An almost bored-sounding newscaster depicted the setting: "There are no sides, that I can see. All the lumbermen look strikingly like one another, no visible sign of which camp, which concern each man represents. They are walking about in clusters, up and down the main drag of Bay City, and engaging in skirmishes and brawls here and there; but these have been quickly put down by the National Guardsmen, working together with area law enforcement who are on the scene to lend a hand." Mr. More pointed at the radio and whispered, "That's our sheriff!"

Mr. Whitsell was shaking his head, and he wore a look of concern so pronounced that Mr. More had to ask him what was the matter. He answered, "I should feel quite a lot safer if the sheriff were here to protect us against encroachment. Why must he range so far from home? Doesn't Bay City have its own sheriff to tend its own flock?"

"They do, of course," said Mr. More. "Probably it's that the sheriff felt drawn in by the professional imperative. He'd no sooner miss a chance to help a neighbor than rob a bank."

"And while he's off playing the helpful hero, where are we? Vulnerable to whichever vicious element who happens past. Why, a bandit could come in here and slay the lot of us in our beds and get away clean, with no figure of authority to hinder his spree."

"Mightn't you take solace in the unlikeliness of that event?" Mr. More asked.

"I might not!" answered Mr. Whitsell, and with a surprising bitterness.

Alice emerged from the small door behind the front desk, pulling on her cardigan and smoothing down her hair. Mr. More asked that she heat up some milk for Mr. Whitsell, but she said no, she was sorry but she couldn't, she was already late.

"You are not going to that movie *again*?" he said.

"I am."

"But how many times can you see the same story unfold?"

"However many times it takes." She ducked under the

front desk and threaded her way through the group, poking Bob in the stomach as she passed.

Mr. More went to heat up some milk for Mr. Whitsell, who stood forlornly to the side of the others. Ida and June and the dogs returned to the auditorium to resume their rehearsals. Bob went away to his room and changed into his pajamas and sat on the edge of his bed, listening to the coverage of the Bay City situation, which in darkness had devolved to riot proper: "The five-and-dime's on fire," said the newscaster. "No one's paying it any mind, it's just—on fire. Across the street, meanwhile, a group of men is working to overturn a jeep. Their faces are very red, and there's much shouting going on among them, determined to get the job done. Now another group is attempting to set the post office alight. Why? And where is the fire department? Okay, hold on, the first group has got the jeep over on its side, and they're pleased with themselves. Yes, congratulations all around, men, my goodness, what a sight." There came a wail of sirens, men shouting in the background. "The National Guard are assembling in a line at the end of Bay Road. It is inevitable that the lumbermen and Guardsman will meet in the street." The newsman began shouting questions to the Guardsmen as they passed him by but was ignored or rebuffed. Bob heard someone say, "The town's burning down and this jerk wants my impression of the scene." The newsman took this in stride. "Emotions are running high tonight," he explained.

The coverage droned on. Bob stepped away from his bed and to the window. Alice was standing out front of the movie theater, wrapped up in her own arms and peering down the road. Above the theater marquee and to the south Bob could just make out the tiny, flickering fires of Bay City. He was looking at an epicenter of violence from his safe distance while hearing the sound from within the violence through the radio. Alice looked miserable, huddled into herself; Bob was opening the window to invite her to listen to the riot in his room when she stood up straight and waved, and now here was the young man from the market, Tommy. As he approached, Alice spun around and rushed to the ticket booth to purchase their tickets. Walking into the theater, Tommy draped a lazy arm over Alice's shoulder, while she clung to his midsection. Bob couldn't see if they climbed the stairs to the balcony or not, but they certainly had the look of the balcony bound.

This sorry little narrative infected Bob, so that a blue mood came over him. For the first time since his departure he found himself thinking of his home in Portland, in particular the cosmos of his bedroom. He turned off the radio and shut off the lights and lay down in bed. It was a long time before he fell asleep and when he woke up it was seven o'clock in the morning and the window still was half open and the curtain was puffing its belly out at him and a great noise of commotion was coming up from the street.

A GREAT NOISE OF COMMOTION WAS COMING UP FROM THE STREET. Voices calling, shouting, automobile horns honking, endlessly; Bob assumed the riot had arrived and lay in bed asking himself how to prepare for and react to such a thing. Then he began to wonder why the voices didn't sound angrier. He stood away from the bed and moved to the window; he caught the puffed-out curtain in his hands and drew it to the side.

The streets were filled with people. Cars were stopped on the highway, the roadside overrun; there was no center or border to the activity, and there was nothing like a violence taking place. It was as if an anthill had had its top kicked off and now there was motion all across the area, a giddy chaos, with every individual following his or her own line, place to place, picking out a friend and moving through the scrabble to meet up with them, to grasp, to rave. Bob dressed and hurried down the stairs and through the hotel to stand at the top of the blue-painted steps and consider the spectacle. Mr. More exited the hotel. "That's it, then, eh?" he asked Bob, before walking down and into the crowd. Bob watched him greeting this and that person, shaking hands and agreeing as the mass ate him up. Now Bob walked down the blue steps; instantly he was tossed about and pushed this and that way and it would have been frightening but for how everyone was behaving. People patted his head and shook him by the shoulders; a red-faced woman with gray teeth and tears running down her cheeks seized him and kissed his forehead. A young man was strutting about and blowing a trumpet in the air; he leveled the horn at Bob's face and blew a comical, trembling note, and Bob could smell his sour, stranger's breath. It was as if everyone knew everyone else but they hadn't seen one another in a long while and were made ecstatic by the grand reunion. Bob passed a group of men standing in a circle around a pickup truck. They were listening to the news report coming from the truck's radio; a man with a British accent was shout-reading a bulletin. Bob understood by what this man was saying that the war had ended. The men surrounding the truck threw their hands up and cheered.

Bob wanted to be with Ida and June, and began jumping up to try to catch sight of them. A passing soldier asked him, "You looking for your people?" and lifted him up to scan the crowd. Bob looked and looked but he couldn't see his friends. After a while the soldier lost interest and set Bob back on the ground and walked off. Now the crowd shifted and spit Bob out to its edges.

The sheriff's patrol car was parked against the south side of the hotel and the sheriff was sitting on the back bumper, massaging his temple, and his flesh had a waxy cast, and he was squinting against the sunlight. When he saw Bob, he pointed. "Hey, kid, come over here a minute, will you?" As Bob stepped closer, the sheriff told him, "You want to know what happened? I figured something out about you." He pulled a piece of paper from his pocket, unfolded it, and showed it to Bob. It was a missing persons report; Bob stood looking at a blurred photostat of his school yearbook picture.

The sheriff said, "This came through yesterday morning. I thought I remembered your face from seeing you the other day outside the P.O. I should have tracked you down sooner but it's been a time here, and I've been distracted." The sheriff removed a bottle of aspirin from his shirt pocket and tossed a handful of tablets into his mouth, chewing them up, his face made bitter by the taste. Pinching the bridge of his nose, he peered out at the crowd and said, "It'd have to happen today." He looked back at Bob. "So, what are we going to do about you?" Bob shrugged and the sheriff said, "Maybe I ought to check in. Hang on a minute, kid, will you?" He leaned into his car and took up his two-way radio. "Come in HQ. HQ, do you read."

"HQ here. How's your head, Sheriff?"

"Well, how do you think it is?"

"Shame they couldn't wait a day to call the war off."

"It surely is. What about all the lumberjack crazies? How's their outlook this morning?"

"About the same as yours, I'd say. They're a lot quieter than last night, I've noticed. But say, we're getting a lot of calls about the crowds downtown?"

"That's where I'm at now, HQ."

"Any problems?"

"No, there's folks on the loose, but it's a cheery occasion and no troubles that I can see."

"That's nice."

"I guess we were due some good news. Which reminds me. The reason I'm calling is. I found the kid from Portland. Comet."

"You did? Where is he?"

"I got him here with me now."

"He all right?"

"He looks all right. You all right, kid?" Bob nodded and the sheriff said, "He's all right."

"What kind of name is Comet?"

"I don't know. Kid, what kind of name's your name?"

Bob shrugged.

"Kid doesn't know what. He's the incurious type. Anyway, you're going to want to call Portland PD, tell them the blessed news."

"I will do, Sheriff. When should I say they can expect him home?"

"Well, I'd like you to frame that as their problem to solve, HQ. Maybe they'll send his folks to fetch him, or maybe Portland PD can spare a man. But, shoot, wait a minute."

"What's the matter?"

"Where're we going to keep him until then?"

"Put him in the tank."

"Squeezed in with the crazies?"

"Not so crazy anymore, like I was saying."

"Still, I don't like it." The sheriff was looking at Bob. He said, "I guess I'll just run the kid back myself, HQ."

"You're going to drive to Portland?"

"Well, why not. I'm overdue a visit to my mother-in-law, anyway. There's two good deeds with the one stone. Can't hurt my luck and maybe it'll bolster my self-esteem."

"When should I say you're coming up?"

"Soon enough. Just, let's wait until after these aspirin cast their spell. You'll want to get our brash young deputy out of bed, give him a shake and send him over here to keep watch in my stead. If he complains, remind him it was his idea to stop for a nightcap."

"Yes, Sheriff."

"Tell him it was my idea to remind him it was his idea."

"Yes, Sheriff."

"It might get noisy tonight but I'll be back by then."

"All right. What else?"

"Nothing I can think of. I'll see you, HQ."

"Good morning, Sheriff."

The sheriff hung up his radio and asked Bob, "You got a bag somewhere, kid? Long stick with a hanky on the end of it?" Bob pointed at the hotel and the sheriff said, "Okay, you go on, then. I'll wait here for you. Only don't dillydally, all right?" Bob said all right and stepped away. "Hey, though," said the sheriff, and Bob turned back. "I just want to say that if you run away again then you'll make me look bad and everyone'll make fun of me and I'll be sore and I don't want to feel that way about you because you seem like a nice kid." Bob said he wouldn't run, and he was telling the truth, and so the sheriff believed him. He told Bob, "You're not in any real trouble, by the way. I mean, I'm not sure what your reception at home'll be like but from the legal standpoint you're not in trouble hardly at all. You're in a very mild and manageable amount of trouble, okay?"

"Okay."

"Okay, go get your things. I'll be here."

Bob walked back in the direction of the hotel. The trumpeter had found a fiddler and guitar player and they were trying to come together to make some moment-appropriate war-is-over music, but they couldn't agree on a song, or there wasn't one that they all three knew how to play. The lobby was empty; Bob rang the bell but no one answered. He went to his room and packed up his pajamas and toothbrush. The snare drum and sticks sat on the floor; Bob took these up, along with his knapsack, and left his room. He knocked on Mr. Whitsell's door but no one answered. The door was unlocked and he opened it but the room was empty. Next he climbed the stairs to the tower and knocked on Ida and June's door. Buddy and Pal whined but no one answered; Bob tried the doorknob but it was locked. He left the drum in the hall and made for the lobby. Again he rang the bell and again there was no response. The auditorium was empty. The conservatory was empty.

Bob stood once more at the top of the blue stairs out front of the hotel. The crowd was growing, and he could see cars parked along the highway for half a mile, with men and women hurrying up and toward the excitement. On the sidewalk across the road, on the far side of the melee and all the way up against the long row of plate glass storefronts, Bob saw Alice and Tommy running off together, running away from the crowd and toward a privacy, and their hands were clasped, and Alice looked so happy, her greasy hair flapping behind her as she and Tommy vanished around a corner. The trio of musicians had landed on an up-tempo number Bob was not familiar with. They played badly but sincerely. Bob could see the sheriff's patrol car still parked in the distance. The sheriff was lying down along the full length of his front seat, the door open, his boots hanging stilly in the air above the white pea gravel.

Bob walked along the side of the hotel and to the patrol car. He let himself in by the backseat; the sheriff sat up and said, "No, kid, come on up here." Bob got out and walked around to the front while the sheriff sat collecting or steeling himself. He turned the car on and gave it a little gas. "Okay, now pay attention," he told Bob, and pointed at a row of switches on the dashboard. "See this one here?" He flipped a switch and the patrol car's siren rang out, loudly enough that it made Bob jump in his seat. The sheriff flipped the switch back and the siren ceased. "When I give the high sign," he said, leveling a finger at Bob, "I want you to hit that same switch just like I did, on and off, but quick. Got it?" Bob nodded. The sheriff paused, then pointed at Bob and Bob flipped the switch on and off. "Okay, good—perfect." The sheriff hit another switch to turn on the PA system, and now he addressed the crowd. "Ladies and gentlemen? Ladies and gentleman." The crowd quieted, heads turned to look at the patrol car. "You're all under arrest," said the sheriff, and the crowd booed. "Okay, you're not. But do me a favor and let us through. Me and my deputy need to turn this rig around and get to the highway." He pointed that Bob should hit the switch and Bob did and the patrol car began its slow crossing through the crowd.

The sheriff was sweating, though it wasn't hot. He looked over at Bob, then nudged him. "Roll down that window, kid, will you?" he said, and Bob rolled down his window and the sheriff breathed the ocean air in and out through his nose. "That's all right. Thank you." He looked at Bob again. "Well," he said, "how many days did you make it? How long since you been gone?"

"Four days."

The sheriff ticktocked his head back and forth. "That's not so long, I guess. But the truth is that most kids don't get through the night, so actually you made a pretty good showing. Also, I'd say you made a very good showing in terms of distance traveled. How'd you get all the way out here, anyway? Did you hitch? Hitchhike?" The sheriff held up a thumb.

"A train and a bus," said Bob.

The sheriff whistled. "Nothing to be ashamed of, there. Very good showing." There was the sound of the patrol car's tires rolling over the gravel. The sheriff said, "Speaking generally, and as far as I'm concerned, it's the kid who doesn't run away that you've got to worry about. I did it when I was your age." He pointed at Bob and Bob hit the switch. The crowd was pressing in, and some were slow to move out of the way of the patrol car and so were nudged by the car's bumper. A man and woman were dancing in tight little circles on the sheriff's side; as the patrol car passed them by the man leaned toward the open window and asked, "How would you rate that riot, Sheriff?"

"Pretty shabby, buddy. No passion of intelligence in those boys. Just drunks on a mean streak, really. They did some fair bit of damage, I'll give them that, but altogether I can say they made a poor overall impression." The dancing man waved and wheeled away with his partner. "One fellow," the sheriff told Bob, "I got him in my car to run him in and he told me he'd give me a hundred dollars to drop him back at the camp. Said he had the cash on him and that I was welcome to it and he wouldn't ever tell a soul anything about it. I said, 'What about all your pals?' And he said, 'Well, what about them?' And I said, 'You're not going to leave them to hold the bag while you skip off to bed, are you?' And this bird said to me, looking out the window he said, 'Everyone goes his own way in this world, no matter what they tell you.' I thought about that a minute, then told him, 'Mister, you know what your problem is? It's that you've got yourself a *morbid point of view*.'" The sheriff shook his head and spit out the window and pointed at Bob and Bob hit the switch. A group of noisy soldiers began slapping on the hood of the patrol car and the sheriff told them over the PA, "Do not slap the sheriff's automobile." Then he said to Bob, "You don't talk much, kid, do you?"

Bob shook his head that he didn't.

The sheriff said, "Well, you want to know how many days I ran away for? However many days it's been from then to now, that's how many days. Because I never did go home. What do you think of that?"

Bob shrugged. He was enjoying the sheriff.

"You think they still set a place for me at the dinner table?"

"Maybe."

"Maybe not," said the sheriff. "But, what about you? Think your folks'll be glad to see you, or mad, or what?"

"Glad, I guess."

"Not mad?"

"Maybe a little mad."

The sheriff glanced at Bob. "Reason I'm asking is. If there's something really wrong going on there, you don't have to go home. Do you understand what I'm saying to you?"

"Yeah."

"I'm saying you can talk to me."

"There's nothing wrong."

"You sure?"

"Yes."

The sheriff said, "Okay. That's okay. That's good. But you let me know if you think of something that's the matter, all right?"

They were almost to the highway and Bob was looking out at the crowd when he saw June and Ida standing off and to the right of the patrol car. He saw them only briefly, but with such close-paid attention that the visual became like a photograph in his memory: they stood facing each other, and Ida's expression was pained, her cheek red and damp from crying, while June was staring at her with a loving look, petting her hair and dabbing her face with a handkerchief and saying kind little things to her. Bob felt himself leaning toward them in his mind, but now the patrol car was pulling onto the highway, past the crowd, and accelerating upcoast. Bob spun around and to his knees to watch out the rear window as the crowd and town became smaller and smaller. The last thing he could see of Mansfield was the weathervane rising crookedly from the tilted tower; after that was gone from view he turned to sit, facing forward now.

Something of the moment had upset his heart. He wished he could have said goodbye to June and Ida, but the idea of an official parting also made him feel shy, and that it might have overwhelmed him. But still and there was this feeling, and Bob didn't know where to put it. He sat staring at the side of the highway, the pavement gone blurry as it slipped past. The sun was high and bright, angling down and through the front windshield and the sheriff, squinting, was making grabby gestures and pointing to the glove box. "Sunglasses, kid, sunglasses, sunglasses."

4

2006

AFTER BOB LEARNED THAT CHIP AND CONNIE WERE THE SAME PERSON he hung up the phone and sat in the nook and looked out the window asking himself what he should do. What could he do? There was nothing to do. He took an antihistamine and slept until noon. The sun was out and the snow was melting and he rang Maria at the center, expecting her to take him to task for calling so late the night before but she either didn't remember or hadn't made the connection it was him. She spoke of the significance of her fatigue, and mentioned without prompting that Chip was back from her stay at the hospital; also that she and Chip's son were working together to relocate Chip to more suitable accommodations. "He's nicer, now that he's calmed down. He brought me a soggy muffin this morning as a peace offering." She asked Bob why he was calling and he improvised a story, which was that he had a piece of personal business to attend to which would keep him from visiting the center for a while. Maria was surprised by this. She said, "*Personal business* is what a volunteer tells me when he wants to quit but doesn't have the guts to say it."

"I'm not quitting."

"What's the matter, then? Are you sick?"

"No."

"Okay, but are you?"

"I'm not sick and I'm not quitting," Bob promised. And he wasn't quitting, but he couldn't face Chip knowing she was Connie, and had made the decision to avoid the center until she had gone. Perhaps it was a failure of mettle, some fundamental human test he was not rugged enough to master; and yet the task was so outsize to what he felt he was capable of that he experienced not a twinge of remorse at his turning away from it. Bob didn't believe that Connie would understand who he was—that his presence would bring her comfort; and so to sit with her now would introduce nothing on her side but a significant pain on his, and he decided he'd had quite enough of it, and that was that. Maria told Bob it was his right as a free citizen to engage in mysteriousnesses but that she hoped he would soon get over whatever it was that was distracting him and return to the fold.

"You'll save me my seat, then?" Bob asked.

"Well, yes, I will. Just be good and let us know when you want it back."

And so came the period where Bob had no access to the Gambell-Reed Senior Center, and his days were dreary and lusterless. He disliked being separated from his friends, and the news of Connie brought on a pervasive sorrow which, while neither acute nor dangerous, slowed the clock by half and drained the world of its sounds and colors. He had for some years been experiencing the slow dimming of his capacities, but it was during this time away from the center that the dimming achieved prominence. He was forgetting things, he was burning things on the stove top, and he did occasionally become unsure about where he was going and why. His body, also, was uncooperative; he felt weaker in his limbs, he was falling asleep without knowing he was tired, then waking up confused and unrefreshed. He had increasingly been relying on the rope to climb the stairs to his room, pulling himself up hand over hand in the style of the mountaineer. One evening he fell asleep on the couch in the living room and didn't wake up until four o'clock in the morning. He lay in the darkness for a time, looking, breathing. He stood and crossed the room and started hauling himself up the steps; when he reached the top step, the brass eyelet came away from the wall. There was a sickening instant where he hung in the air, teetering, rope in hand, then gravity seized him and threw him down the stairs like a stone into a pit. When he came to he was lying flat on his back and the pain in his midbody region made his mind pulse white, and his heart felt brutalized with its thuds and poundings. In a while the pain was lessened and replaced by a numbness and he found he could think of other things besides his discomfort. He thought, *I believe I've broken my hip,* and he had broken it. He thought, *How am I going to be helped?* A gauziness came over him, and now he felt bouncy and glad, and he giggled, but this hurt, so he stopped. He was becoming sleepy, and then very sleepy, and he was afraid of this sleep because he thought it could be sneaky death masquerading as an innocent tiredness. But there was no fighting it, and he dropped into slumber and did not die. He awoke at half-past nine in the morning to the sound of someone knocking on the door. "Come in," he called. A young man wearing a safety vest entered, speaking as he stepped deeper into the house, "Hello? Hello?"

"Here I am."

The young man hurried over and knelt beside Bob. "Sir, are you okay?" he said.

"I'm not, no. How are you?" Bob suggested the young man call him an ambulance and the young man took out his cell phone and did this, explaining the situation to the emergency operator so far as he understood it. "I don't know what happened but I can tell you he's definitely injured."

"I fell down the stairs," Bob said, pointing.

"He fell down the stairs," the young man said. He asked Bob for his name and address and Bob told him these things and the young man relayed them to the operator. Now he was listening; soon he told Bob, "They want to know about your pain, Mr. Comet."

"What about it?"

"How is it?"

"It's coming in and out, but when it's in, it's large."

The young man said, "I think he's in a lot of pain."

Bob still was clutching the rope that had come away from the wall. The young man noticed this and became shy. Lowering his voice, he told the operator, "Yeah, he's holding a rope in his hand?" He left the room for the kitchen, speaking softly into his phone; Bob tried to hear what the young man was saying but couldn't make out the words. He noticed the ceiling above the stairwell was cracking and he told himself to remember to address this later. In a while, the young man returned. "Five minutes, they say."

Bob said, "Thank you. You've been very helpful."

"Glad to be of service."

Bob said, "You don't have to stay, if you've got work to do."

"What's five minutes?"

"I'm not suicidal," Bob told the young man.

"Me neither," the young man replied. He pulled up a chair and they waited together. Bob asked him what the purpose of his visit had been and the young man said, "I sell windows. Or I try to sell them. Actually, I don't sell very many at all. When you sign up with this company, management names past employees, all-stars who've brought in such-and-such an amount through commission. But none of these famous past employees are still with the company, and I'm starting to think they didn't exist in the first place."

"Are the windows nice windows?"

"Between you and me? They're defects. Shipment-damaged, mostly, or else banged-up display models. We buy them cheap and sell them cheap—which is how we get our foot in the door. It's our installation of the windows where we make our profit. Or where the company does."

Bob forgot he was injured and shifted his body. This occasioned a pain like an icicle in his stomach; he squinted hard and produced a low growling noise at the base of his throat and the young man asked, "Are you all right?" Bob shook his head: no. "Pain," he said. When the pain passed, he told the young man, "I'd like to hear your patter."

"You don't want to hear that," said the young man, smiling.

"It could be good for passing time," Bob said.

"Okay, then. Only we don't do patter anymore. Now it's all about engagement."

"What's that mean?"

"In the old days, no offense, to sell was to utilize the monologue. But now, people want an active experience. The updated version is to ask questions that, coincidentally, lead the potential client where we want them."

"Where's that?"

"Where they're talking themselves into buying our product." The young man paused. "You really want me to do my thing for you? It's a little gross. Phony-friendly, you know what I mean?"

Bob said, "I'm ready," and the young man reconfigured himself into the shape of a salesman. He sat up straight, and his face became earnest, his voice jumped an octave: "Mr. Comet, you have a beautiful house. May I ask you how long you've been living here?"

"All my life, actually. It was my mother's house before it was mine."

"Are you kidding me? That's wonderful. What a thing that is!" He was surveying the house interior, nodding, impressed. "And you know what? I can see at a glance that this is a well made house. Well made but also well cared for—which is critical. Because there's a responsibility which comes along with owning a house like this, am I right? With a house like this, you're not just the owner, you're the custodian, would you agree with me on that, Mr. Comet?"

"Yes," said Bob; but he wasn't listening very closely. There was a moving or shifting inside him—something slipping into something else, something about to happen, and he was afraid as the something made its approach.

The young man asked, "Mr. Comet, have you ever heard that the windows are the eyes of a house?"

Bob said, "I've heard that eyes are the window to the soul."

"Yes, and that's a lovely turn of phrase—and true too. But, that's not what I'm here to talk to you about, now." He shook his head. "What I'm here to talk to you about is, I'm here to talk to you about the eyes of your *house*. And Mr. Comet?"

"Ah," said Bob.

"Are you happy . . . with the eyes of your house?"

The something Bob had been waiting for arrived: it was a surging sensation, as if his every globule of blood was suddenly moving not in any one direction, but *away*. He was quite sure he was dying now, and he called out, "Oh! Oh!" and the young man pulled a silver crucifix necklace from under his safety vest, knelt at Bob's side, and began silently, reverently praying. But still and Bob wasn't dying; he'd had a spell and the spell was passing. He apologized to the young man, who, returning to his chair, said, "No apology necessary." The ambulance arrived and a paramedic came in without knocking, a lean man eating a sandwich. He set this delicately on the banister at the bottom of the stairwell and leaned over Bob. Bob looked up at the paramedic's chewing face. He asked, "You're not going to touch me and ask me if it hurts, are you?"

The paramedic swallowed. "I was going to do that."

"Please don't. It hurts. I think my hip's broken."

The paramedic pointed. "Move your toes for me?"

"But that'll hurt."

"Pain is good, though; it means your person is intact. An injury like this, it's the nonfeeling you've got to worry about."

"Well, I'll move my toes some other time."

"Unless you can't," said the paramedic. He stood and picked up his sandwich and left the house. He returned without the sandwich but with another paramedic, a stern man pushing a gurney. The gurney was lowered to the ground just beside Bob. The stern paramedic said, "Okay, sir? We're going to get you to a hospital to be x-rayed and tended to, but first we have to transfer you to the gurney, okay? I need you to bear with us."

"Wait," said Bob.

They did not wait, lifting him by the legs and shoulders onto the gurney. They were gentle in their movements but the shift hurt terrifically, and Bob made a noise he didn't know he was capable of making, a prelanguage, animal-mind noise, and the young man in the safety vest stood by, covering his face.

"Can't you give him something for the pain?" he asked the stern paramedic.

"They'll give him something at the hospital."

"But he needs it now, can't you see that?"

The stern paramedic paused to look the young man up and down. "What is your relation to this person?"

"My relation is that I'm the one who found him lying there."

"But why are you here?"

"I'm here because I sell windows."

"Sell windows to who?"

"To whoever has need of them."

The stern paramedic decided to ignore the young man in the safety vest and occupied himself strapping Bob—panting, now, pain fading—onto the gurney. The gurney was raised up and Bob was wheeled from the house and to the ambulance waiting at the curb. The paramedics readied the rear of the ambulance to receive Bob's person; the young man in the safety vest, meanwhile, had reappeared and was proffering a business card. Bob, arms bound, said, "Put it in my mouth." He was embarrassed by the noise he'd made, and now was trying to reclaim a lighthearted attitude; but the young man didn't understand that Bob was joking. "How about I tuck it into your shirt pocket?" he said, and he did this. Bob was loaded into the ambulance. "Good luck, Mr. Comet," said the young man in the safety vest, and he waved as the ambulance pulled away from the curb.

BOB WAS TAKEN TO THE HOSPITAL AND GIVEN A LARGE INJECTION of Demerol, his first of many. The break in his hip was complete, the bone cleanly halved, and it x-rayed beautifully and doctors and nurses and orderlies came from all around to look at it and whistle and shiver. No one could say it wasn't a nasty injury, and yet there was no damage to his spine, and a full recovery was expected. His middle was set in plaster, like an enormous stone diaper, with one tube coming out the front and another out the back. He was installed in a sunlit room with two remotes, one for his bed, and another for the television. A nurse came in and explained about the drip. "See this button? Whenever you feel pain, or if you're bored, press it."

"And then what?"

"And then blastoff. You want a hot chocolate?"

With the button his constant companion, Bob settled into his temporary hospital existence. After decades of rejecting the television medium he experienced a period of not just watching TV, but watching with enthusiastic interest. All his life he had believed the real world was the world of books; it was here that mankind's finest inclinations were represented. And this must have been true at some point in history, but now he understood the species had devolved and that this shrill, base, banal potpourri of humanity's worst and weakest and laziest desires and behaviors was the document of the time. It was about volume and visual overload and it pinned Bob to his bed like a cat before a strobe light. One woozy morning he found the business card the young man in the safety vest had given him. At the bottom of the card it read: *Questions? Comments? Complaints?* These words were followed by an 800 number, and he had his nurse dial for him. A female voice answered and Bob launched into a muddled speech celebrating the character of the young man who had been so helpful and empathetic. After a while the woman cut him off.

"Sir? What is your complaint?"

"I have no complaint. I'm calling to praise your outfit. Because you hired a winner in this person. I wish I could remember his name. Actually, no, I don't think he ever told me. What if I were to describe him?"

"Are you a customer of ours?"

"Potentially I am."

"Well, I'm not in sales. Do you want me to transfer you?"

"Not really."

"Then I'll wish you a good day, sir."

"Oh, good day to *you*," said Bob, and he handed the phone back to the nurse, flush with the belief he'd done the young man a good turn. Later that same day, Bob woke up from a nap to find Linus Webster pacing at the foot of the bed in his electronic wheelchair. The bed was on its tallest setting and so Bob could only see the beret and the bloodshot eyes. Linus wheeled around to Bob's side. "How do you feel, buddy?"

"How do I look?"

"You look pretty fucked-up, Bob. But then, so do I, and I feel great. So: How do you feel?"

"Sometimes good, sometimes less good. How's the gang?"

"Oh, you know. Old, weird. Maria wrote you a letter." He held this up and set it on the table beside the bed. He spied the drip button and his eyes became wide. "They've got you on a drip? What are they giving you?"

"Demerol."

"Demerol? That's cute." He was unimpressed.

Bob told him, "I have nothing bad to say about Demerol."

"Sure. I mean, you know. It'll do. Want me to hit your button for you?" Before Bob could answer that he didn't want him to, Linus was hitting the button insistently with his huge red thumb. "Every day with an opioid drip is a gift, Bob, and you've got to take full advantage of it. You'll be out in the shitty cold of the shitty world soon enough, trust me, I know."

Bob was pleased to see Linus, and it wasn't just the drugs. They chatted blithely for forty-five minutes, when Linus became agitated at the realization his favorite television show, a soap opera called *The Southern Californians*, was about to start. "Okay if I watch it here, buddy? I'll never make it home in time." Again, Linus did not wait for an answer, but began removing snacks from his canvas satchel and laying these on a small table he'd unfolded from a hollow of his chair's armrest. The show began, as did Linus's commentary: "See that guy, Bob? Bob? That's the Duke. He's actually a bricklayer from the old country of Italy but he concocted this big story about his royal lineage and everyone believed it at first, but now they're starting to wonder a little, and his wife's starting to wonder a lot, and anyway she's—there she is, see her? Squinty eye?— she's falling in love with *another* bricklayer, this real proud bastard who's working on their pocket villa and who, dar- ingly, is played by the same actor as the Duke, only he's got a spray tan and a ponytail wig and a truly bad Italian accent. I can't wait to find out how they tie the two bricklayers together. But yeah, the Duke's luck is about to go south, for sure, for sure."

Bob followed the images but was half-submerged in the narcotics. He dozed awhile; when he woke up, the nurse was standing over Linus with her arms crossed. "You are *not* a patient here, sir. You looked me in the eye and lied right to me."

"That's true, I did."

"Well I'm sorry, but you'll have to go."

"Okay but give me fifteen more minutes. Look, Judge Hartman is finally going to admit he murdered his never-gave-a-damn, blackmail-first-ask-questions-later half-brother."

"Do I need to call security?"

"Lady, look at me. What's a security guard going to do to me I haven't already done to myself? I'm asking you for fifteen merciful minutes."

The nurse relented and allowed Linus to finish out his show. She stood by, watching the final scenes, and each time a new character came on-screen, she asked, "Is that a good guy or a bad guy?" After, Linus folded up his tray and stowed it away and wheeled toward the door. Pinching the brim of his beret, he said, "Read the letter, Bob. Let us know what you think."

"What I think what?" Bob asked. But Linus had gone.

He opened and read the letter. Maria expressed her sadness in hearing of his injury, but also a relief of happiness that his prognosis was a positive one. He was very much missed, she said, and not just by her but by most everyone at the center.

*Actually, Bob, there's been something on my mind
since I heard about your accident. I brought it up to
the residents, and their enthusiasm prompts me to say*

that if you ever wanted to join us here, join us as a full-timer, you'd be most welcome. Will you think on it? I've found another living situation for Chip, but her new room won't be ready for a couple of months, so you've got time to consider my proposal. One way or the other, I'll wait to hear your answer before I let the room get away, okay? I hope this offer can be received in the simple manner in which it's meant.

Love, Maria

BOB CAME HOME FROM THE HOSPITAL AND SPENT THREE MONTHS IN bed waiting for his hip bone to fuse back together. He was visited daily by a nurse, or more accurately was visited daily by one in a long string of nurses. He found the lot of them to be both cheerful and efficient, but none came around frequently enough to occasion a friendship. Bob felt bored, then very bored, then patently broody. One day Maria called on him, and he wished to jump up at the sight of her. She bore flowers and gossip and made unsubtle inquiries about Bob's plans. Had he given any more thought to her proposition? He had, actually; and soon after Maria's visit, once he was freed from his cast, he put his house on the market, sold his car and the bulk of his possessions through an estate liquidation company, and moved into Connie's old room at the Gambell-Reed Senior Center.

It was a poky, drafty space that beheld no leftover element of Connie whatever. Bob lined the walls with the choicest books from his collection, installed a dresser and bedside table, set up his favored reading chair and lamp at the foot of the bed, and christened his quarters furnished and complete. Linus was just across the hall, and Jill beside Linus, and they visited Bob often, possibly too often, to complain, or to ask advice, or tell stories, or to borrow small sums of money that Bob eventually understood would not be paid back. The hospital-television-watching era had long since passed, and Bob had resumed his reading; he found he could read for stretches of three hours, four hours, pausing only to eat, or to fall in and out of a shallow sleep, or to watch the world out the window, people walking past on the sidewalk, unaware of the pale, wondering face perched above them behind the glass. He turned seventy-two and the residents threw a party; they sang to him and doted on him and Maria had a book-shaped cake made, its title centered on its face: *The Book of Bob*. His hip had healed beautifully, the doctors told him; and yet, a tiredness clung to Bob that was new, and impressive in its depth and weight. He continued to dream of the Hotel Elba, that he was living in the tilted tower, or standing out front on the blue steps, scanning a blurred crowd for June and Ida; and still, always the same chemical flooding his brain, the feeling of falling in love, and he would wake up in a state of besotted reverence, but impersonally, with never a face to connect to the feeling. He was alone in his dreams of the Hotel Elba; there was no one there with him, the halls empty but resonant with the sense of someone only just departed.

Less frequent, but no less vivid, were Bob's dreams of the library. There had been whole eras of Bob's working life where he knew a lamentation at the smallness of his existence, but now he understood how lucky he had been to have inhabited his position. Across the span of nearly fifty years he had done a service in his community and also been a part of it; he had seen the people of the neighborhood coming and going, growing up, growing old and dying. He had known some of them too, hadn't he? It was a comfort to him, to dream of the place. His favorite dream was that he was alone and it was early in the morning, and he was setting up for the day, and all was peaceful and still and his shoes made no sound as he walked across the carpeting, an empty bus shushing past on the damp street.

Maria sometimes came to see Bob in his room, sitting in the reclining chair at the foot of the bed while he patted his hands exploratorily across his blanket in search of his reading glasses. Other times, when she felt he was becoming resigned, she sent word by nurse or by Linus that she wanted to speak with Bob in her office, and he liked to pretend such summonings were inconvenient, but soon he would be up and dressed and washing his face, and he'd take the ramshackle two-man elevator down through the spine of the old house and cross the Great Room to knock on Maria's office door. She wished to check in on him, and to hear the upstairs gossip, and to engage in it, even perpetuate it. She once confided to Bob that she liked to plant stories within the center and monitor the effect over a period of days. These tales were not vicious or libelous, just enough to awaken the recipient and provoke some return. Her pet theory was that a portion of indignation was much the same as exercise.

"Jill says she's worried you're depressed."

"I'm not depressed at all."

"You don't seem depressed. I think Jill is depressed."

"I think Jill is depression." When Bob made Maria laugh, he felt proud. Maria couldn't speak to the others like this, and Bob understood and appreciated he was one apart.

All in all, he was happy at the center, except that he still found himself harassed by thoughts of Connie. His desire was to learn where she was, and how she was faring, the hopeful idea being that to flesh out her narrative might bring him solace by way of closure. But none of the residents or nurses knew the first thing about it, and Bob felt it would be conspicuous to ask Maria. Eventually, though, his curiosity bettered his modesty and he requested a formal audience with her, presenting her with the story of his marriage, more or less in full. Maria was floored. By this time her trust and affection for Bob was total; at the completion of the tale, and in answer to Bob's questions, she gave him Connie's transcripts. This was not just against the rules, but illegal; Maria asked that he take it to his room, to uncover its cold informations in private.

These are the things Bob learned:

In the years following Ethan's death she worked as a substitute teacher, and then a full-time elementary school arts teacher, and eventually as a public school administrator. At the age of fifty she quit and took a job at a nursery in the southeast quadrant of town, where she worked for fifteen years, all the way up until her retirement.

Bob learned that her catatonia was not symptomatic of dementia, as he had assumed, but was a result of brain trauma suffered after a slip-and-fall accident on the walk out front of her house. She had been perfectly healthy before the injury, apparently; but the blow to her head had led to clotting, which led to stroke, which led to the diminishment of her capacities. She had been a resident at the Gambell-Reed Center for two years before transferring to a facility on the Washington coast.

Bob learned Connie's Portland home had been less than five miles from his own. This prompted Bob to think of the years after Ethan's death, the years of wondering when he would see her again. There were some mornings, as he was shaving or making his bed, when he would intuit Connie's approach, that that would be the day she would walk through the door of the library to see him, and he recalled how distracted he would be, all through his shift, looking up at each person coming in. After he understood she was not going to visit the library, then came a period of ten or more years where he believed fate would intervene on their behalf. He would see her in the market, in the park, somewhere. He would pick out her set, cold expression in a crowd and she would sense his attentions and turn to meet him, and when she saw him the coldness would come away from her face and she would change back to the way she was before, a sort of lighting up, the way she used to look at him when she came through the doors of the library, and she loved him.

Bob was grateful to have accessed Connie's transcripts, but he also was wounded by the collective information. No matter that the notion of fairness was a child's; what had happened to them wasn't fair, and there was nothing that could make it so. He gave the transcripts back to Maria and thanked her. She could tell by the look on his face that he didn't wish to speak of what he'd learned. Most of her patients had areas of their lives that were too painful to be discussed, and she never pried, respectful of the boundary. Maria understood that part of aging, at least for many of us, was to see how misshapen and imperfect our stories had to be. The passage of time bends us, it folds us up, and eventually, it tucks us right into the ground.

BOB WOKE UP FROM AN AFTERNOON NAP TO FIND MARIA SITTING ON THE edge of his bed, and she had a look on her face as if something was the matter. "What," he said. "Chip's son is downstairs, Bob," she answered. "Connie's son. I hope you don't mind my telling you but I figured you'd want to know."

Bob sat up. "What's he doing here?"

"He came by out of the blue asking for his mother's transcripts. I told him they were in storage off-site and now he's waiting around for them to be brought over." She was proud of this subterfuge, but Bob didn't understand her motivations, and asked her why she would tell him such a thing. "I thought you might want to come down and say hello," she explained.

"Why would I? He doesn't even know who I am."

"You can tell him."

"What if he doesn't want to know?"

"Then he can tell you. He's really a very sweet man, Bob. And I know I'm being a busybody, but there's always the chance your meeting him will be a helpful thing. Look, if you don't come down, I'll know you're not interested. But I'll stall him as long as I can, okay?"

She patted Bob's arm and exited and Bob stood up from his bed and paced and considered the situation. He did not want to go downstairs, but that wasn't the same as deciding it was the wrong thing to do. When it occurred to him that this was almost certainly the only time in what remained of his life that he would know any direct connection with Connie, then did he find himself reaching for his shoes, and he pulled on a suit coat and combed his hair and brushed his teeth. As an afterthought, he sought out the short sheaf of snapshots from the Connie days, slipping the envelope into his coat pocket before striking out for the elevator.

He entered the Great Room to find Connie's son sitting alone at the long table and looking at his phone. He wore the same work-worn canvas coat he'd had on before, a bandage on one of his fingers, and gave the impression of a laborer or tradesman on his lunch break. Bob stood on the opposite side of the table; when Connie's son looked up, Bob gave a small bow and asked if he might sit. Connie's son nodded vaguely and went back to his phone. Bob sat down. "You favor your father," he said. Connie's son had no reaction; he was texting. Bob continued, a little louder: "Your father and I were friends, you see. Ethan. If I may, and in my way, I was responsible for your mother and father coming to know one another."

Connie's son again looked up. "My parents met on a bus."

"Yes, but they were both coming to visit with me at the library. In a way, then, they met under my auspices." At the naming of the word *library*, Connie's son's gaze sharpened. Actually, he looked somewhat frightened, and he set his phone on the table, sat up straight, and said, "Oh my God, you're Bob Comet."

CONNIE'S SON'S NAME WAS SAM, AND HE WAS SURPRISED, IMPRESSED, and a little upset that Bob should suddenly present himself, at this late date and in this particular location. Bob also was surprised, also impressed, but not upset, or only very slightly. Sam wanted to know what Bob was doing there; Bob wanted to know how it was that Sam knew his name and history. They were just beginning to formulate these questions for one another when Maria came by with Connie's transcripts, lingering as long as she might, to bear witness and generally take the temperature of the summit. But her nearness was an inhibitor, and Sam proposed that he and Bob take a walk. Bob made a counter proposal, which was that they should walk to the diner, and they did this, settling into a booth and each of them ordering coffee and pie. The waitress knew Bob on sight, as he and Linus and Jill had taken to visiting the diner two to three times each week.

"What are you all spiffed up for?" she asked. "You going to a cotillion ball?"

"I am. And I thought you might like to come along with me."

"Let's see how you tip first. But I'll say this: you clean

up nicely." Turning to Sam, the waitress stared. "You could use a little help, sweetie," she said, and she reached down to smooth his hair. Bob found this uncanny; but he saw that Sam was less aware of the power of his physicality than his father had been—probably a good thing when one considered the misery Ethan had doled out.

The waitress brought them their coffee and pie and left them alone to discuss—what, exactly? Neither knew where they might begin, or what the ultimate purpose of their conversation should be. After a couple of false starts, Bob offered up the photographs, antique visuals that proved a fruitful point of contact. Sam had never seen the images of the era before and he fell to studying them with a keen fascination, while Bob studied Sam's profile, which was Ethan's profile, and precisely.

Sam spun a picture around on the tabletop and pushed it closer to Bob. The image was of Connie and Bob, and they were standing in front of the mint-colored house. Bob was bland in the face, his body held at a tilt, hands at his sides, while Connie rested her fists on her hips, elbows out, and she was winking exaggeratedly, a comical, cheesecake pose. Sam was tapping his finger on the facade of the house. "Is this the place with the rope hand railing?"

"That's right. That's where your mother and I lived when we were married." Bob cleared his throat. "For some reason I'm surprised you'd know such a thing as that. Or anything about me at all, really."

Sam drew the photo back toward himself and shuffled it to the bottom of the stack. He spoke to Bob while still looking through pictures. "I think that if you knew my mother before her accident, then you knew she had a story hidden away in the background. She told me about my dad's death at whatever suitable age, twelve or thirteen, and that was a piece of the puzzle, but for a long time I'd had the sense of something else, you know, lurking. Then one year at Christmas, I must have been sixteen by then, and Mom'd had some wine and she said, 'Sam, I want you to know I was married to another man before I married your father.'" He looked up from the photographs, made a face of horror, looked back down. "Not the best news for a young person to hear. And at first I didn't want to know anything more about it. But then later, when I grew up a bit and got used to the idea, I started asking questions, and the story came together in dribs and drabs." He pushed over another photograph. It was a picture of Ethan and Bob; they were wearing ornate ladies' hats, but both were making their faces solemn, dignified.

Bob was squinting at the image. "Yes, this. The house was in a cul-de-sac, and once a year the neighbors and I would haul out our castaways for a rummage sale." There was a bent shadow creeping up Bob's leg. "Your mother took that one. See her there?"

"Wow," Sam said, shaking his head. It made him happy to see these images, and Bob was pleased by this happiness. Now Sam held up a picture taken just after Bob and Connie had been married. Ethan stood a step apart from the newlyweds, his face blurred. Bob looked at the picture, nodded, and looked away.

"Did you ever remarry, Bob?" Sam asked.

"I never did, no. Did your mother ever?"

"No, no. That would have been out of character, to my understanding of what she wanted. I know there were a few friendships which must have had romantic bents to them. Men bringing Mom presents she didn't really want, men with mustaches and wide ties, tinted Coke bottle glasses.

The '70s, right? The '80s? But I always got the impression she could take it or leave it."

They drank their coffee and ate their pie and Sam passed Bob this and that picture and Bob looked at each one and passed each one back, but he was distracted by an uneasiness rising up in him, an impatience to get at something. He was curious about Connie's life after she'd left him, and after Ethan had died; but when he composed the question in his mind it sounded unfriendly to him. His intentions weren't unfriendly, and so he wasn't sure how to proceed. Finally he simply said, "You know someone, and then you don't know them, and in their absence you wonder what their life was made up of." Sam shrugged, unsure if it had been a question or statement or what. Bob told him, "I'm trying to get an idea of your and your mother's life in the daily way. What was it like for her?"

"Well, she was busy," said Sam. "She had me to deal with, and she had to go to work and keep the house together. That's a lot for one person, you know? But we had our little universe, our street. We were lucky in that we had nice neighbors, a lot of them with kids, and so there were BBQs and birthday parties and Christmas parties, Easter egg hunts. I knew the insides of every house on the block."

"And these people were her friends."

"They were all crazy about her. But they also felt, I think, protective of her, because of Dad's story, and that she was on her own. But it wasn't some sad situation or anything. I mean, my mother was wonderful. Life was life, up and down, but we had so much fun together, you know?"

"Yes," said Bob.

"She was fun."

"She really was."

Sam pointed a thumb over his shoulder. "Back then she was?"

"Always."

Sam stacked the photographs and set them at Bob's elbow. The top image was of Ethan sitting lowly in his car, mischievous eyes peering over the driver's-side door. Bob said, "A police detective came to my house after your father passed away. He wanted to know where I'd been at the time of his death. I always wondered if your mother was aware of that."

"I'm not sure if she was. She didn't think you had anything to do with it, if that's what you mean. Actually, she had an idea it was some rich woman who'd done it. Some old flame of his or something."

"Eileen," said Bob.

"Yes, right. And she told the police about it, but then the woman wasn't even in the country at the time Dad was killed. She never did find out who'd done it. The detectives just told her, it was an accident. And maybe it was, but I know it always bothered her, not knowing for sure." Sam sat thinking. He said, "You know, she didn't speak so much about my dad. Maybe it was because of the way he died, and she didn't like to be reminded. And I understand that he was a smoothie, and somewhat of a shit disturber, but I could never really get an idea of what sort of man he was." He gave a small shrug and sat watching Bob.

"Are you asking me what your father was like?" asked Bob, and Sam said that he guessed so. Bob held up the picture of Ethan and gave himself time to formulate the true words. He said, "Your father had no guile. He wasn't crass or avaricious. He was never dull. He was physically graceful, and fun to look at. He was funny, and he encouraged and abetted funniness in others. He was a little bit seduced by himself, a little reckless in the wielding of his powers, but maybe that's understandable, and so we forgive him for it. I don't know how I should put it to you, Sam, except to say that some people, when they enter a room, the room changes. And your father was a natural-born room-changer."

Sam was concentrating intently on what Bob was saying, and he sat very still after, as if sculpting the words together to formulate the composite of the man in his mind. He told Bob, "That's good. Thank you."

"Yes," said Bob.

Sam picked at the crust of his pie with his fork. He was smiling the smile of secret knowledge. "A couple times over the years it'd happen where Mom'd say, 'I wonder what old Bob Comet's doing?' Or, I can remember her peering out the window one morning in winter, holding back the curtain and saying, 'You think Monsieur Bob's going to work in this snow? With that old bald-tired car of his? I don't know, I don't think so.'"

Bob sat watching the coffee cup in his hand. In a sense this was just what he had hoped to hear, but he wasn't prepared for it, and for him to learn of these tiny moments was at once the most merciful evidence, but there was also a second sense, which was a quick or flashing outrage. That Connie should invoke an old pet name when they were separated by mere city blocks was outrageous to him, and he sat for a half minute choking against this clash of feelings. Sam didn't notice that his words had had any effect; he was signaling to the waitress that they were ready for the check. Sam paid, and he and Bob headed back in the direction of the center. Bob was quiet for much of the walk, so that Sam wondered if something had been spoiled in their meeting; but then when they arrived at the center Bob was again himself, and he volunteered to copy the snapshots and send them along if Sam wished it, and Sam said he did, and he wrote out his address and gave this to Bob. The two men shook hands and Bob watched as Sam drove away in an old pickup truck. He turned to look up at the center and saw Maria standing in the window of her office. She held her hands out, palms up: How had it gone? Bob made the half-and-half gesture, and then walking fingers, and she nodded, and Bob struck out to lap the block and think and wonder about all the things that had and had not happened.

LIFE AT THE GAMBELL-REED SENIOR CENTER CARRIED ON. THE TREE outside Bob's window grew to fullness, obscuring the view completely. It was hot that summer, often uncomfortably hot, as there was no central air conditioning in the building. Bob added his voice to the chorus of complaints; Maria told him, "We're all suffering here, Bob." Bob pointed out that she was getting paid to suffer, and Maria named the figure of her salary, which effectively ended the conversation. Bob went around in a T-shirt and slept with the window open. In the night, a cool wind rustled the leaves of Bob's tree and poured over him as he slept. In the morning, the heat returned. Linus switched out his big beret for a mesh-back baseball hat with an electric fan built into its bill. Jill was the only one in favor of the heat. "I should have been a lizard on a rock," she said. "In a way, though, you are," Linus told her. The rains arrived, the autumn, and the leaves of Bob's tree turned impossible colors and dropped away, his sidewalk view returned to him.

It was incredible to think that only one year had passed since he'd made his failed attempt to connect the people of the center with Poe's "The Black Cat," but here and it was Halloween again, and there was a Halloween party, and Bob was a subtle vampire. Maria said he would look very dashing if only he would move a little more quickly, that the cape would fly out behind him; but he was moving as fast as he could or cared to, he said. He had a pair of plastic vampire teeth but he wore these only briefly because they hurt his gums. Maria was dressed up as a convict with a plastic ball-and-chain that she twirled above her head to good comic effect. Linus was dressed as a graduate, in a cap and silky black gown, and he had rolled up a piece of paper in his hand with a blue ribbon tied around. Jill sat at her distant table wearing no costume and staring at her slippered feet. She'd not had the money or ingenuity to procure or fabricate a costume for herself and felt bitter about being left out. Maria found some cat ears for her, and Jill put these on, and allowed that Maria could draw whiskers on her face with a mascara pen. Maria was solemn as she held a ruler against Jill's cheek to ensure a straightness of line. Afterward, Jill was shy in her thankfulness. "Can you tell what I am?" she asked Bob. "I'm a cat."

At eleven o'clock a bus pulled up outside the center and a stream of costumed children poured in. Maria had organized the visit through a contact at a nearby elementary school; the day before she had described it to Bob as a meeting between two groups at opposite ends of the life spectrum. "There is the youth, their stories unwritten before them, and you all, with your accumulated wisdom, looking back. Isn't it possible that you'll all meet in the middle and establish a connection?" Her optimism was true, and sincerely felt; and yet, Bob wasn't so sure the experiment would yield favorable results.

The seniors were asked to sit side by side in chairs set up in a long row in the center of the Great Room. Each had been supplied with a bag of candy to dole out to the children, who stood in a line and approached the seated seniors one after another, saying "Trick or treat," and holding out their plastic jack-o'-lanterns. There was very little discourse. The children were frightened by the seniors, the seniors indignant at the fear of the children. Maria stood by anxiously. "Feel free to take time and get to know one another," she instructed. Linus and Bob and Jill sat together in the middle of the pack. A boy in a colorful plastic costume was standing before Linus. There was a shallowness to his gaze which presented him as one unburdened by intelligence.

"What kind of living nightmare are you supposed to be?" Linus asked.

"Pokémon."

"What?"

"Pokémon." He pointed at the rolled-up paper in Linus's hand and asked, "What's that?"

"Yes," Linus said, "you'll probably never see one of these again. It's called a *diploma*. Which is a certificate marking one's graduation. Because I shall soon matriculate right out of this mortal coil."

Another child approached, and he wore no costume, just his street clothes, which were not very clean. He looked tired. In a croaking voice, he said, "Trick or treat."

"Where's your costume?" asked Linus.

"Don't have one."

"Why not?"

"Because my mom ran away with my uncle."

Linus made a face of impressiveness at Bob. He told the costumeless boy, "That's unique, if nothing else. And it's due to that uniqueness that I'm going to give you two candies instead of one." Linus bowed his head to fish out the candies from his sack. The boy, sensing a potential weakness, asked calmly, "Can I get more than two?"

"Don't let's ruin the moment, kid," Linus said. He dropped

the two candies in the jack-o'-lantern and waved the boy on. The boy moved to stand before Bob. "What are you?" he asked.

"Dracula."

"You suck blood?"

"Sometimes."

"You going to suck my blood?"

"It depends," said Bob. "It depends on how I'm feeling."

The boy stepped down the line to meet Jill.

"Trick or treat," he said.

"Can you tell what I am?" she asked. "I'm a cat."

"Trick or treat," said the costumeless boy.

After the candy was distributed, the children went away into a huddle to discuss and trade and ingest their bounty. Only the costumeless boy lingered; he and Linus had made friends. At one point he asked, "Can I touch your mask?" and Linus said that he could. The boy's hand was small and fine in contrast to the broad pitted redness of Linus's immense head. The hand reached up and gently touched Linus's cheek—the boy gasped and yanked his hand back. He looked confused, amused, frightened. "Go on, kid," said Linus, "give it a good pull." The boy again reached up, and now took hold of the flesh of Linus's cheek and twisted it around. "That's your face!" the costumeless boy said. He told the other children, "That's really his face!" Bob winced for Linus, but Linus found it hilarious, and he roared with laughter, and the children all were awestruck. From this point in time and until they left the center, they all watched Linus closely, marveling at his every word and action. He was a potentially magical monster, and they couldn't get enough of him. Linus wore the adulation naturally: he came alive and made everything into a comedic performance. At one point he pretended to swallow a pencil. "Oh no! I swallowed a pencil!" he announced. Stunned silence, then Linus, patting his stomach, said, "Tastes pretty good, actually." Shrieks of laughter from the children. And then, he kept "accidentally" knocking his own graduation cap off, six times, seven times, and each time, he'd pretend to get more and more angry, which made for more shrieks, more laughter.

The children's candy intake had not been monitored or policed, and they now were achieving crisis-level sugar highs. A boy in a cowboy costume was wheezing raggedly and dragging his nails down the front of his face, only the whites of his eyes visible. Some children had collapsed and were rolling around on the linoleum floor. Where were the teachers, the chaperones? When it was announced the time for games had arrived the children cried out in what may have been an expression of joy but which sounded much the same as torment.

Two nurses' aides, large men in pale green scrubs, entered the center from the back door, awkwardly hefting a large metal washtub filled with water. They were facing each other and walking crabways, legs bent but with straight backs, panting under their shared burden. Without meaning to, the men had created a spectacle, and the seniors and children paused their business to witness the completion of the task, or else the failure of its completion. The water was rocking broadly back and forth in the tub, and an expectation of spillage gripped the onlookers. When the tub was finally set in its place on a pallet in the center of the room, and without a drop of water on the floor, there came a round of polite applause. Linus loudly asked, "What's the tub for? Are the children going to wash me?" He raised his hand and "washed" his underarm area and the children wailed out their disgust. He turned to Bob. "I keep forgetting to tell you, buddy. Remember the bricklayers?

From my TV show? They teased the story line out this whole goddamned time but yesterday they finally let us have it, and guess what? They're twin brothers. Arch enemies from birth, bad blood going back to the cradle apparently—back to the womb."

"Was there a showdown?" Bob asked.

"Capital S Showdown, you bet there was."

"And how did they film that with one actor in both roles?"

"Good question, Bob," Linus said earnestly. "I'd be glad to answer that one for you. The effect was achieved by rapid cuts and edits. To their credit they did not use the never-effective dummy double, and neither did they succumb to our newest dishonest computer-generated technologies."

"Was it believable?"

"Not really. But, you know, it's a wonder any committee-run artworks even achieve completion, much less pass muster. I was rapt, and that's that."

Maria came to stand beside the tub, holding up a plastic bag filled with apples and grinning enigmatically. When she dumped the apples into the water, the room grew quiet. She explained about the tradition of bobbing to the children, and said that anyone who could come up with an apple in their mouth would receive a mystery prize from the mystery prize box, which was a shoebox decorated with question marks and sparkles. The children were obviously interested in what Maria was saying but when she asked who would be first, none of them came forward. An edgy paranoia had gripped the group, a sort of herd shyness, and they formed into a cluster, peering warily over their shoulders. Maria had imagined a mad rush to take part but there was nothing, no movement at all, and for the first time that Bob could recall, she was embarrassed. He felt he couldn't stand to see her suffer; cutting through the room's psychic agony he came to a quiet place in himself and understood in a sudden and complete way that he would do it—that he would be the first to play this game, the one who broke the ice, with all his peers and all the children watching. He stood and made for the tub; Maria looked confused. "What's the matter?" she asked. When Bob lowered himself to his knees, then she understood, and she draped a towel over his shoulders and quietly told him, "Thank you, Bob. Whenever you're ready." Bob looked down at the cluster of floating red apples. Plunging his head into the water, the children resumed shrieking. The water, Bob discovered, was shockingly, painfully cold.

Bob was alone with his task, half-submerged, thrashing about, thinking the violence of it would land him with an apple in his mouth. When he recognized he was only pushing the apples away, then did he fine-tune his method, approaching the fruit from a slow-moving sideways angle.

Those who knew Bob were impressed by his behavior, but also worried; was it not late in the game to make a change to one's own personality? To suddenly begin acting in a totally new way? Some among the seniors found Bob's actions off-putting, and were hopeful he wasn't having a final-hour identity crisis, which was not unheard of in the assisted-living landscape.

Linus was not among the naysayers; after his initial bafflement wore off he became swept up in the unusualness of the situation and began to root for his friend, first in his mind, and then aloud, chanting Bob's name with such gusto and fervor that it soon was taken up by Maria, then Jill, then by the more charitable seniors, along with a good many of the children. Finally, most everyone in the room was calling out in one strong and unified voice: *Bob! Bob! Bob!* Bob was distracted by his task and had only just managed to sink his teeth into an apple when the chant landed in his mind. The punning aspect of it instantly made him laugh, and he took in a great gulp of water, which in turn sent him lurching upward in the style of the breaching whale. He drew his head back to cough; water shot from his mouth like confetti and the apple launched clear across the room in a long, lovely arc before bouncing off the linoleum, rolling through the legs of Jill's chair, and disappearing under a table. The costumed children scrambled after the apple as if it were a totem or treasure which to possess even briefly was worthy of enormous personal sacrifice.